P9-DMY-845

A JOURNEY OF ASCENT

A JOURNEY OF ASCENT

A Family Saga

Andy P Weller

Book Guild Publishing
Sussex, England

First published in Great Britain in 2012 by
The Book Guild Ltd
Pavilion View
19 New Road
Brighton, BN1 1UF

The characters are based on real people.

Typesetting in Baskerville by
Nat-Type, Cheshire

Printed in Great Britain by
CPI Group (UK) Ltd, Croydon, CR0 4YY

A catalogue record for this book is available from
The British Library.

ISBN 978 1 84624 649 4

In memory of my father, 'Jim' Albert Victor Weller (1923–2008), one of the sons of Frederick Edgar and Cate, featured in this journey, and the earlier generations that have made it possible to relate this story.

Preface

You are about to undertake a journey through generations of a real family and the times and the places that they lived and worked in. Some of their encounters and experiences are real and some could have happened, or something similar may have taken place. It is up to you to decide which is which. There are two Old Bailey trials to hear about as well.

The journey takes us from various places on the High Weald before, during and after the Civil War and then to outlying communities of London, including Chelsea Common and Richmond. During this part of the journey there is a reference to Warwick and that now corresponds to modern-day Redhill (only named such after the Post Office facility was established). All other places on the Weald and around London can be recognised today.

We depart then for most fashionable Bath and hear of an association between Daniel (Sam) Weller and Charles Dickens, and we conclude the journey with the advent of the railways and a re-acquaintance with London and the lead up to the Great War.

By the way, should you be interested in the link between generations then the timeline that follows will guide you on your way.

Let the story begin.

Timeline

Monarch

Elizabeth I (1533–1603)

William (the Weaver) Weller in Cuckfield
Marries Elizabeth Stammer 1598 – Henry, 'Sam' and Jane

1589 Spanish Armada

James I (1603–1625)

Marries Elizabeth Jenner his second wife 1609 – 'Will' and Anna

1618 Sir Walter Raleigh executed

Charles I (1625–1649)

1620 Pilgrim Fathers set sail

'Will' leaves Cuckfield with Henry for Rusper
With wife Mary – Sarah and **'Billy'**

1649 to 1660 The Commonwealth

Charles II (1660–1685)

'Billy' in Rusper
Marries Ann Gunter 1667 – Sarah, William Ann, John and **James**

1665 Black Death

1666 Great Fire of London

James in Rusper
With Sarah – **George**, James, John (who goes to India), Sarah, William, Mary

James II (1685–1688)

1688 James abdicates and flees to France

Monarchs

William and Mary (1689–1702)

Queen Anne (1702–1714)

George I (1714–1727)

George II (1727–1760)

George III (1760 to 1820)

Family

George in Rusper
Marries Sarah – **James**, George

James in Newdigate
Marries Mary – Sarah, Mary, **Daniel** and William

Daniel travels the Weald, the outskirts of London and Chelsea Common before returning back to the Weald

With Sarah – **'Sam'** but baptised Daniel

With Ann – Michael, William, George, Rebecca and Richard

Events

1689 William Defeats James' army at Battle of the Boyne

1715 First Jacobite Rebellion

1745 Second Jacobite Rebellion and 'Bonnie Prince Charlie'

1757 Clive secures Bengal for Britain

1769/1770 Cook's first Pacific voyage

1776 US Independence

1789 outbreak of French French Revolution

1805 Battle of Trafalgar

'Sam' (Daniel) in Richmond and then in Bath
Marries Sarah in Chelsea – John, Charlotte, **Richard**, Eliza, Mary Ann, William and Edward

George IV (1820–1830)

(John is the John that marries Elizabeth and then raises a family with Ann – The Chronicles of John – A Coachman's Journey)

William IV (1830–1837)

1833 slavery abolished in the British Empire

Daniel marries second wife Ann and third wife Mary and dies in Weston near Bath

Victoria (1837–1901)

Richard in Bath, Turnham Green, Kensington and Knightsbridge
Marries 'Kate' Katherine Moran – **Daniel Frederick**, Jessie, Sidney, John and Lizzie

Daniel Fredrick born Turnham Green but mainly around Paddington
Marries Charlotte Roe – **Frederick Edgar**, Sidney and Alfred

1845, 1849 Irish potato famine

Frederick Edgar in Paddington
Marries Catherine Mary Christie in 1905

Edward VII (1901–1910)

George V (1910–1936)

1914 to 1918 First World War

Part I

The Weald and the Cuckfield People

Introduction

Almost every facet of the life and existence of families and individuals such as the Weller family was affected, one way or another, by the fortunes and influence of the likes of Henry Bowyer. This was representative of the normal state of affairs in many communities across the High Weald: ordinary working people and labourers depended so much, and too much, on the fortunes of the landowners and those in pursuit of their own wealth and increased influence.

The Bowyer family had been at Cuckfield since buying the Manor of Cuckfield from the Earl of Derby in 1593. As an ironmaster on the High Weald, Bowyer was indeed a wealthy man. He employed his own blacksmiths, who would take the blooms from his furnaces and fabricate all sort of things from nails and other generally useful things (known as 'ironmongery' and sold through ironmongers), to ploughshares. Bowyer's activities also involved casting such things as cannons and cannonballs.

It was popular folklore that iron had been produced thereabouts from long before the time of the Romans. There were plentiful supplies of ironstone near the surface and the Weald was abundant with woodland, essential for producing the charcoal to feed the iron furnaces or bloomeries. In fact, from any highpoint on the Weald it seemed that in parts tree cover stretched right down to the horizon towards the sea. It required a great deal of wood to make enough charcoal to produce just one ton of iron, and the availability of ironstone and plentiful resources of woodland made the Weald an important place and a place where ironmasters and landowners could make plenty of money. A plentiful labour pool and poor soil for growing meant that ironmasters did not have to compete when it came to paying wages.

Chapter 1

Young Will normally awoke to the rhythmic clacking sound of his father working the loom as soon as it was light enough for him to see to work. Not this morning though. It was quiet, apart from the sound of birdsong, meaning it must be Sunday. It being summer and warm and dry, the night before Will and his brothers and sister, having pulled out their straw palliasses and woollen blankets woven by their father, had slept outside under the lean-to rather than inside the two-room, modest construction called 'home'. The dwelling's redeeming feature was the hearth, fireplace and surround that Will's father had put together from local stones and mortar. The addition of a stone hearth and surround, although the source of some pride on William's part, gave the illusion that the place was more substantial than really it was.

Will liked Sundays despite not being able to play properly on the Lord's Day. It was a day of rest and, as Will was told, a day of reflection. Will did not go too much on the reflection side of things but he certainly enjoyed the rest on a bright, warm summer's day as today promised to be. The family would all go to the morning Prayer Service. Not only was non-attendance a grave social sin in the minds of others in the village but anyone not going to church at least once a month would be fined.

Breakfast was always a simple affair of black bread and oatmeal with Will's father occasionally having an egg if

4

Henrietta was in a laying mood. She was laying less and less often now and would soon surely be bound for the pot. As for Will's father, he was an unassuming and fairly quiet man. He seldom lost his temper or raised his voice. Thin and pale in complexion compared with others that spent most of their time working outdoors, there was nevertheless something about William that suggested that he was a man of considerable inner strength and determination. It was not just out of the respect that all children had for their parents that William the Weaver's children always took his word as the final say in any matter. They loved him dearly.

The church of Holy Trinity, like most churches constructed after King Henry VIII and the Reformation, lacked ornamentation and paintings. Such things were a distraction from worshipping the Almighty as well as being part of the trappings of Catholicism. Such artefacts and decorations that the church once possessed had been removed some years ago and burnt in public or, if they could not be removed, had either been painted over or smashed.

The church had once been the chapel church of the nunnery that had existed in Cuckfield for as long as anyone could remember. Will's father had told him about his father, describing how one day some fifty or so years ago the King's men had turned up in Cuckfield. The nuns were evicted and then, having set fire to the nunnery, the King's men pulled down as much of the walls and structure as they could with grapple and horse. What happened to the nuns no one knew and did not care, for the nuns had shut themselves behind their doors and had had little contact with the village folk or with worldly affairs.

The walk from Will's home to the church took about a half an hour. In the winter and in wet times the main lane through Cuckfield would become churned up with big puddles and always with lots of mud to go with even more mud. The land thereabouts was typical Wealden clay with poor drainage. Horses and carts made the condition of both the High Street and Church Street even worse as travellers traversed Cuckfield either bound for London or Brighton or some of the more substantial communities and villages either along the way or connected to the London to Brighton routing. Carters carrying products from Bowyer's bloomeries and iron works would tend to use the tracks thereabouts and avoid Cuckfield itself, but even so there was a degree of through traffic. Some travellers would stay over at the Talbot Inn. The Talbot provided modest yet adequate accommodation and stabling for tired travellers or served as a sanctuary from bad weather. Lying outside Cuckfield to the north and to the west was the home and estate of Henry Bowyer.

The Parson was a funny-looking man, although no one would dare admit this to anyone but themselves. His head looked too big for his long thin body. He wore a pointed black hat that contrasted with his pale face and a beard that reminded Will of a billy goat. Parson Meade always walked everywhere at great pace and, if ever his wife accompanied him, she could be seen to be struggling not to be left behind. What was surprising, and what Will appreciated, was that the Parson had a relatively soft but high-pitched voice so that his admonishments and warnings against committing sin and risking hell and damnation were not half as terrifying as they might otherwise have been. In fact, on a hot day like today with everyone packed so closely into the church it was a struggle to keep awake let alone take in Parson Meade's pastoral message of impending hell and damnation.

After what seemed an age, and with Will longing to be out in the freshness of a summer's day high on the Weald, Will and the rest of the Parson's flock were released to contemplate, or otherwise, the Parson's message and to reflect on the Glory of God and their own weakness and mortality.

For the rest of the day Will and his siblings relaxed, although they limited their entertainment out of respect for the Lord's Day. All the same, in the eyes of others their behaviour might be considered to be far from what good Christian observance should be.

Will knew that the following morning, as his father would work away at the loom from first light until late evening, he would be teasing out strands from the fleece for his mother to comb and to prepare for spinning into yarn. By the end of the day Will's fingers would be sore and so they would the next day and the day after that and the day after that. Life was predictable but people were largely resigned or content for it to be so and did not question their lot in life.

Nevertheless, being young, Will and his older half-brother Henry did sometimes yearn for a break in the routine of everyday life.

Chapter 2

Will's home was one of the first signs that you were actually entering Cuckfield from the road that led eventually down to the coast. Henry and Will were sitting on a log. The sun was setting but they could still hear the steady clacking of the loom as their father William eked out the last few minutes of daylight before calling it a day.

Henry was some six years older than Will. He was a strapping adolescent already growing some broad shoulders, and his large hands and feet gave him an awkward, lumbering appearance. How unlike his father he was. He had matted dark brown hair and a somewhat grimy countenance that suggested that he had little regard or time for his personal appearance. Henry also had the tendency to be a bit of a grump.

7

Will was a slight lad, quite the opposite in appearance to Henry, and in build at least was more like his father. He had light-brown curly locks, a freckled complexion and a mischievous grin and, for a boy of his age, a well-kept appearance. Also in contrast to Henry, Will nearly always showed a cheerful disposition.

'Henry, you are sleeping at home tonight aren't you? Or do you prefer the fragrance and company of Old Josiah?' said Will with his mischievous grin that little bit wider.

Henry often stayed during the day and overnight with Old Josiah Pearce the charcoal burner who had a hut in a clearing in the woods. Henry's job was to help hew and coppice the wood that Old Josiah would use to turn into charcoal that in turn would be used in Master Bowyer's iron-making furnaces. After cutting and shaping, the wooden poles would be carefully arranged by Old Josiah into a pyramid shape and then be covered in turf or wet clay leaving holes both at the bottom of the pile and another hole at the very top to aid the burning process. Old Josiah would then light a fire that would burn for up to two days. The smoking pile had to be watched every minute of night and day. It was important that there were no flames, and it was Henry's job, during the night in particular whilst Old Josiah rested, to stay awake and at the first sign to shovel dirt over any smoking hole appearing on the side of the pile. It was, of course, important to make sure that there was nothing that would cause a fire to start other than the one intended for charcoal making. After two days the turf and the dirt would be cleared away to show perfect charcoal that Old Josiah would sell on. Henry would then return home tired and smelling of smoke. Sometimes he would bring home a snared coney for the pot before going back to the clearing the following day to help Old Josiah start the whole thing all over again.

'You know very well that I am home tonight,' grumped

Henry. 'Old Josiah may be smelly and a man of few words but he does no one any harm.'

As Henry and Will sat there chatting about nothing in particular as usual, a group of people, evidently a family, came slowly into view walking, or rather dragging their feet, along the track. In the lead was, presumably, the father pulling a handcart loaded with some unrecognisable bundles and two children. Walking alongside the cart and holding on to the side was another child probably not far short of Will's age. Bringing up the rear was obviously the mother looking very weary with one hand on her swollen belly. The father called out to Henry and Will.

'Good day. My wife is with child and is in need of rest soon before we move on in the morning. We will need to bed down somewhere for the night. What can you suggest? Where can we go and where are the places that we should stay away from?'

Henry pointed up the road.

'There is a stable at the Talbot but the innkeeper will want to charge. You will have to sleep in the open but you must stay away from the big park both to the west and where the road continues beyond, as it belongs to Master Bowyer and he will not stand anyone on his land.'

The father raised his hand in acknowledgement and started to yank the handcart into motion. After just a few steps there was a groan as his wife stumbled and fell to her knees. The boy who had been holding on to the side of the cart rushed to his mother's side and tried to help her to her feet. Her husband was quickly by her side as well. Together they helped her to her feet and she leaned herself against the side of the cart. It was clear that she was about done in and would not be able to go any further without rest.

Elizabeth, Will's mother and Henry's step-mother, moved down the path towards the children and the travellers. She felt no need to rush, as every woman at some time is with child and being of a rather stout disposition this did not lend her to rushing anywhere, no matter what the occasion. Henry turned to Elizabeth and said: 'They asked me if there is somewhere they could stay for the night and where are the places to stay away from. I told them not to go near Master Bowyer's land and then the woman fell as they went to move on.'

Elizabeth looked up to the heavens and sighed. She was not without heart and could see that the woman was distressed and just about all in. She spoke to the woman not softly but firmly.

'I can see that you are with child. You can shelter under the lean-to for tonight only and you can take water from the well, but for food you must provide for yourselves. I expect you to be gone in the morning.'

'I thank you for this,' replied the man. 'As you can see, my wife can hardly go on much further today. We will ask The Lord in our prayers tonight to bless you and to look kindly upon you and your family.'

Chapter 3

William, having supped, was taking in some air before retiring. He worked hard and long hours. The income William received from his wife selling his cloth at the market in Cuckfield every Monday, added to what she was able to sell to passing tradesmen, was adequate. Market was always and had always been on a Monday as this had been set down in a Royal Charter from 1312 in the times of King Edward II. What William earned from his cloth-making was enough both to buy the food the family needed that could not be provided from their own small plot in the rear and, of course, to buy the fleece that he needed to earn his living.

William hoped that not too far in the future he would be able to find somewhere to live better than what he considered to be the wattle and daub 'mud and sticks' dwelling they now lived in. Sam, his eldest son, had moved out and was earning from Master Bowyer's ironworks and that was one less mouth to feed. Henry brought in a little money from assisting Old Josiah Pearce as well as the odd rabbit for the pot. Now and then Will was able to bring in the odd penny either from picking stones out of the field or helping out when any general labouring job for a boy could be found such as gathering the hay cut by men with scythes. Things were not that bad and William knew he was better off than some.

There was not quite a full moon but it was bright enough. The traveller came out from the nearby trees presumably having pursued a purpose of his own. As he approached William, he spoke in a soft voice so as not to disturb his sleeping wife and children.

'I am grateful for the shelter tonight. We will be gone in the morning you need have no fear.'

'How far have you come and for what purpose?' asked William.

'From Rustington way. We have been enclosed down there. The agents for the Catholic Duke of Norfolk arrived one afternoon. He has taken all our common land where we used to forage and grow things and where some even raised sheep. Our homes have been pulled to the ground and we have been dispossessed. With enclosure even if we had somewhere to live there would be no work and no land for us to work and to grow our own things to eat. He has taken it all and not just in Rustington.'

'I have heard of such things,' said William. 'The land here is poor for supporting crops and, whilst a few yeomen and husband men grow what oats and wheat they can and raise sheep or pigs, much of the land is given over to coppicing for charcoal making and iron. Master Bowyer hereabouts has the big house and Cuckfield Park and he needs charcoal for his iron furnaces. Even so he is now taking more and more of the land hereabouts wherever he can to raise sheep for wool. Where will you go?'

'I don't rightly know,' the man replied. 'Last I heard my wife's cousin is but a day's walk from here. I hope we can reach there by tomorrow evening. If there is nothing for me there then I will continue by myself to London if I have to. My wife can stay behind to have the baby and I shall come for her or send for her and the children as soon as I can. We are coming to the summer's end and harvest time, so hopefully there will be some work for me somewhere on the land otherwise I will end up in London.'

The following morning the traveller and his family were gone without feeling the need to bid goodbye. They just quietly gathered themselves and set out again on their journey and whatever fate had in store for them.

Chapter 4

There was a fearful storm raging. The countryside was lit up with flashes of lightning and the claps of thunder were as loud as anyone could remember. Every time the lightning lit up the scene, the weaver's dwelling by the track on the way into Cuckfield was revealed as a very lop-sided affair. There had been a mud and earth slide, one corner of the dwelling had almost completely collapsed and a good part of the roof had also given way. No one was out and about in such foul weather and even if someone had been travelling the road it is unlikely that they would have seen anything out of the ordinary through the driving rain.

Henry has been out in the woods with Old Josiah. The

charcoal fire was not in complete ruins but had been badly affected through the day-long dousing of rain. Henry had turned to Old Josiah earlier.

'Josiah, I'd rather stay here tonight. We were going to take the fire apart in the morning anyway and I don't care to go home through this weather only to come back in the morning.'

'Suit yourself,' was all that Josiah had to say.

William had gone to see his eldest son Sam at the Talbot as he was due to marry his sweetheart Ann Cheale the following Saturday. William was now sharing a last bachelor's ale or two with his firstborn where they had been since the middle of the afternoon, having received a good drenching getting there. Left at home were Elizabeth, Will and his sister Anna.

William and Sam had kept their own company and were in conversation. It was rare indeed for William to be seen having a drink. As for Sam, who looked to be a grown-up image of his younger brother Henry, but did not share his grumpy character, he was not adverse to a pint or two with those he worked with. The question was, and this was the subject of their conversation, would Sam be different when he married?

'Well, Sam, here we are, you are no longer living with us and now the first of my children is getting married. We will all be there next week to see it happen but tonight you are staying with us one last time. With it being Sunday tomorrow you have time enough to get to your own home and to see Ann if you have a mind to. No need to try and get home through this storm so it's one last time before you are married when the whole family sleeps together under the same roof.

'I was still at home with your grandparents when I married your mother. My father made me work the loom right up until the eve of our wedding. No chance of sitting in the Talbot, or anywhere else for that matter, having an ale with

13

him. He was a hard man but in his own way he loved your grandmother and us children.

'My lot was cast to be that of a weaver from when I was young. I was never to have any choice in the matter. He gave me some small allowance for working for him but it was never my money to spend. He made sure of that. He was against taverns and ale drinking and the money he allotted to me was always destined to be for the buying of my own loom. Your mother knew this but we were well matched and she did not mind. The same with your step-mother. So maybe a weaver's life is not so bad after all. Still, Sam, you have broken with this tradition and you are up at the ironworks. I wonder what will happen for Henry and Will. I hope Henry doesn't turn out to be another Josiah Pearce. With Will I see something different. He is an alert lad with a happy disposition but I just cannot see what is to become of him as yet.'

'We'll just have to wait and see just how things turn out for Henry and Will,' said Sam. 'They have a closeness and a bond, those two, despite their different natures and characters. It would not surprise me if, whatever happens to them, those two will do it together. Another ale?'

'All right, but let's make this the last one. I don't know what you men get up to at the ironworks but I can guess. I hardly ever come here and I'm beginning to feel the effects. The rain has eased off and I have not heard thunder or seen lightning for some time now, so we should be making our way home. Look see, even the travellers have had the good sense to retire to their beds. We should do the same.'

After all this rain William and Sam knew that the lane leading down from the church would be a sea of mud. They decided to exit the rear of the Talbot, passing through the stable yard and round the back of the cottages then joining the track further down and missing the quagmire of the lane. They could probably find their way home blindfold so a dark night was not a serious problem for them to negotiate but the clouds were beginning to clear and a half-moon sometimes emerged. They thought they had picked just the right time to leave.

Having rejoined the track after about ten minutes, they had about another fifteen to twenty minutes' walk to home, but something did not feel right and, although they could barely see as the clouds had covered the moon again, they looked at each other and without a word quickened their pace. Then there was a break in the clouds and some moonlight appeared.

The sight of the partly collapsed building before them filled them with alarm and panic. Frantic to find what had happened to their family inside, they raced up the path. The door had twisted in its frame and it took all their strength to prise the door open whilst they slipped and struggled to find a foothold in the mud. At the same time they were shouting and calling out. With the door now partly wrenched open, William squeezed inside and again called out their names. His daughter Anna and Will called back.

Their voices were weak and sounded tired. Perhaps they had been calling out for hours but with no one about their cries went unheard. As William and Sam clawed frantically at the debris, taking care not to bring the remainder of the roof down on top of them, Anna called out: 'I can't get mother to answer. I can feel her next to me and she is breathing but she is so cold to the touch.'

It was pitch black inside the partly collapsed dwelling and with all the debris it was impossible for Sam and William to get to them. After much shouting and swearing William sent Sam back to the village to knock people up to bring light and help.

As folk do in a close community in times of trouble, many turned out with most carrying brands to help with the light needed to see what they were doing. People scrambled all over the scene, shouting, pulling and finally working more carefully together trying to ensure that the rest of the structure did not collapse. They reached Anna and Will first and got them outside where they were given a blanket apiece. Elizabeth must have been hit by something solid, for when they finally cleared a way to her she had started to come round but was very much dazed and was shivering with cold. Whilst Anna and Will were able to walk with assistance, they had to lay Elizabeth in a blanket and carry her to the Talbot, where on hearing of their plight, George Washwood the innkeeper let them stay in the stable.

'You need somewhere to stay the night. I cannot let you have a room as I may yet have guests in need of a bed but at least the stable is dry and I can give you some blankets for to keep warm. I have some broth left over and you can share that for now. The Lord's Day is nearly upon us and I cannot see you turned out given your condition.'

One of them, probably Sam, would go early for Henry in the morning in case he should make his way home and find nobody there. William, Sam and Henry would then tomorrow try and find what they could recover from the wreckage. William was worried sick about the loom. The whole family depended on it for their livelihood.

Chapter 5

Will was almost asleep when he heard the sound of horse's hooves approaching. The effects of the ale had ensured that, eventually, William and Sam were fast asleep. Will got up and turned up the oil lamp that hung near to the stable entrance. Two men slowly dismounted their horses and walked closer towards Will and the light. Will could see from the way that they were dressed that they were gentlemen. The horses were obviously very tired with their heads hung low.

'Good evening, sirs. You are about late on such a night as this. Let me tend your horses and if you can rouse Mr Washwood I am sure he will have room for you,' said Will. 'Are you the stable lad?' enquired one of the gentlemen. 'No, sirs,' replied Will. 'My family is here tonight as our home has been all but destroyed I think as a result of the storm and Mr Washford is kind enough to let us stay here for tonight. I can attend your horses in part thanks to Mr Washford.'

'We are obliged,' said the other gentleman. 'We took what shelter we could earlier under a rock overhang and when the moon came out we decided to press on. We will now rouse the innkeeper. We will want supper as well as accommodation so I hope that he will provide for us.'

Chapter 6

Throughout the night and the following morning Elizabeth could not stop shaking. She was to die within the week from the effects of the drenching and catching a chill. The burial would be the next day as soon as the sexton could dig a hole in the ground to take her. Parson Meade's curate, Mr Bartlett, would conduct the burial rites as the Parson reserved his right to conduct services and affairs for better placed persons.

Will the Weaver's dwelling was too far gone and unsafe to be repaired or made good. They had been able to rescue the loom that had suffered relatively minor damage as it was away from where the greater part of the roof and wall had given way. There was an empty dwelling not that far away from where they were before. The Widow Crawford had lived there until a few months back. If Sir Stephen Bowyer's agent gave permission, the family could occupy the former widow's cottage but it would not be possible for all four of them and the loom to fit inside.

Sir Stephen was now largely responsible for running the family's affairs, although Mr Bowyer senior liked to think that he was capable of keeping an eye on things. It was not in Sir Stephen's interest, not yet anyway, to drive the folk of Cuckfield out or see the local population drift away. Sir Stephen did at least take more interest in the community than did his father. His father paid what was owing under his charge for the poor rate as he had no other option, but he neither had the time nor that inclination to be concerned about how the poor rate was used or whether it worked for the good or otherwise. Sir Stephen would at least read a copy of the Churchwarden's and Overseer's Poor Law account. The little bit of land the widow's old dwelling took up was of no importance to him but then neither was the very modest income from rent. Nevertheless, the collection of rent by Sir Stephen's agent continued to ensure that everyone was more or less in his pocket, so to speak.

Chapter 7

Mr Washford had indeed been grateful to Will for him looking after the gentlemen's horses. Will was now an adolescent and he had really enjoyed tending the gentlemen's horses and the animals in turn appeared to trust him. Will had been taking jobs, mainly labouring, where and when he could. Will had no particular skills. He knew about weaving, but had no loom, and anyway he preferred to be outside rather than doing backbreaking work indoors during the daylight hours. He had thought about the possibility of joining Henry and Old Josiah in helping to make charcoal, but the more he thought about it the less he liked the idea of being stuck out in the woods most of the time and stinking of smoke. He was not very keen on trying to see if he could join Sam at the ironworks either. The more Will thought about it the more he liked the notion of looking after horses.

More and more people it seemed were travelling now through Cuckfield either to or from London and places such as Brighton or to other places such as Horsham. Will decided to approach Mr Washford.

'Mr Washwood sir, it was my pleasure to look after the gentlemen's horses the other evening and I would like to learn more if I could. Would you please consider taking me on? If I could stay here at the stables and you could allow me to take food then I would be happy to work for nothing.'

Washwood liked Will's attitude and he had some sympathy for what had happened to the family. The Talbot's stable-keeper was also the stable-keeper at the Rose and Crown and did not live at the Talbot, having his own place just down the road. This is why it was Will who tended the gentlemen's horses on that terrible night.

Washwood replied: 'I admire your pluck, young Will, and the gentlemen spoke kindly of your courtesy and willingness to help. I will take you on for a trial period and we will see how things go. For now you can bed down in one of the stalls at the back of the stable. I will give you breakfast and supper and we will talk of this again when I have seen what you can do.'

Will was both grateful and happy to be given the opportunity. He would not let Mr Washwood down.

Given the small size of the cottage that his father and Anna now occupied, Henry had no option but, for the time being anyway, to return to stay in the hut with Old Josiah. At that time Henry supposed that he would probably end up taking over the charcoal making from Old Josiah. Will wondered how he found the time, but it seemed that Henry was courting. With Henry, Will thought, looking as he may marry one day soon and with Sam now married and seemingly learning more of the skills of iron making, he was starting to wonder what the future family-wise held for him.

Chapter 8

Sir Stephen had acquired his knighthood on the grounds that he was a man of assumed good character and of some considerable enterprise and commerce, but in reality his name had been put forward in Court circles as a means of settling large debts owed to his father.

With one of the main routes from London to the coast running through Cuckfield, Sir Stephen could imagine a time when it could become an important staging post and that perhaps he could devise some means of charging traffic crossing his land. Maybe he could charge a toll to pay for the costs of improving the way and making a handsome profit at the same time. Sir Stephen had no firm plans as yet but perhaps some day he might do this. He considered himself to be a modern man with new ideas for enterprise.

In the meantime Sir Stephen had more immediate and intriguing things on his mind. King James the First of England and King James the Sixth of Scotland had come to the throne and the King had made great efforts to bring to an end the war with Spain and this was achieved through the signing of a peace treaty. In the years that followed England, and to a lesser extent, Scotland had expanded its influence and international trade through the East India Company. Sir Stephen could see great prospects for wealth-generating international commerce and more exotic enterprises than wool and iron making. The East India Company had been formed under a Royal Charter from Queen Elizabeth and even had its own flag and coat of arms. The Dutch had already expanded their presence and trading influence and The East India Company was the result of a reaction to that. Sir Stephen was going to get in on the act.

Sir Stephen would spend some considerable time in London but would also entertain at Cuckfield Manor. He would invite fellow entrepreneurs and bankers and even Parliamentarians to enjoy his hospitality and he would use these occasions to advance his own interests.

Without knowing the details, the people of Cuckfield were well aware of Sir Stephen's increased standing and in a perverse way were proud to be associated with his success. After all, without the Bowyer ironworks there would be little labour about these parts and, although the Bowyers had acquired a lot of land, there remained for the time being at least still sufficient common land for people to use.

Chapter 9

Will had been working at the Talbot for quite some time now. Henry was not to marry after all as 'that fickle thing', as Henry now called her, had decided on someone else. Someone who did not reek of smoke and who spent most of their time with an old man in a hut in the woods.

Will had learnt well how to tend to and look after horses: he seemed to have that natural rapport with the animals and they trusted him.

One morning Will overheard a conversation between travelling companions. Will later ventured to tell George Washford what he had overheard.

'Mr Washford, may I tell you about something that I overheard in a conversation between two gentlemen that may be something that you could consider to your advantage?'

Washford nodded and then leant his head to one side.

'Well,' he began, 'the gentlemen were talking about how useful it is sometimes to come upon a posting house where travellers, particularly those about urgent business, can hire fresh horses before continuing their journey. Is this something we can do here? Once travellers get to hear of this we may attract more business.'

Washford looked thoughtful.

'I'm far from sure on this, Will. Posting houses have been established for a long time but I am not certain that the possible benefits outweigh the risks. Consider this: I have a good horse and it may not be returned to me and in its place I get a winded or worn-out nag that nobody will take. I am out of pocket and my reputation is compromised. Look Will, let me think on it and I will talk it over with Mrs Washford.'

Later, he was in conversation with his wife Margaret.

'George,' she said, 'I think opening up as a posting house is worth serious consideration. If everyone looked upon this business with the same concerns and caution that you have then the system would never have got going in the first place. I'm not saying that we should not weigh up the risks involved but what if we go into partnership with my father at the Star in Rusper? We can each run a string of horses and each share the risks but, as many others have done before us, unless we are most unfortunate, benefit from new and further business. You must admit that most of the tracks on the Weald run from east to west. There must be people therefore coming off of or joining the main road from London to the south coast.'

'Listen, Margaret,' he replied, 'you know as well as I do that at the moment the Star is not well equipped to run anything more than basic stabling. It will need to be grown if it is to be able to run a string of horses as well.'

Mrs Washwood was quick to come back.

'Why not send Will to my father? There is room above the stable that can be made for him as a place to sleep in and he knows about horses enough to be of use and then we can see if this notion of a posting house would work for both of us. Let's put it to my father George and see what he has to say. I for one do not want to be tied to this place until the day we drop.'

Washford pondered on this and the next morning he offered this to Will, who seized on the opportunity with barely a thought.

Washford then wrote to Margaret's father, Francis Wickham, at the Star and imposed upon one of his regular travelling guests from Horsham to deliver the letter on his behalf. A week later back came the reply and Will was set to go to Rusper.

Chapter 10

As things were to stand in Cuckfield, Sam and Ann would go on to have two children, Jane and John. Sam would retire just short of full term when iron making on the Weald declined and as the supplies of fresh wood were beginning to run down.

Henry Bowyer was never to be a fully contented man. However, he was proud in that he had established a dynasty and had seen his son become a knight of the realm. Bowyer's daughter Louise was to marry well. Whilst not in a love match, she was content with her station as the wife of a baronet. Bowyer had offered a dowry of sufficient size to both wipe out family debts and to ensure that his daughter lived in considerable comfort. Bowyer used Louise's husband, and his title, as a sort of ambassador for his business affairs. Her husband knew that there would be dire consequences if he strayed in any way or acted other than in the interests of the Bowyer family.

Part II

Rusper, Through the Civil War and More Besides

Chapter 1

Henry decided against staying in Cuckfield. That 'fickle woman' had spurned him for someone else. He saw no future being stuck out in a hut in the woods like poor and rather sad Old Josiah. He would go with Will to Rusper.

Moving from one parish to another parish was no easy thing for ordinary people. Each parish was responsible for its own poor, and if someone from outside of the parish was unable to work or to support themselves they would be removed back to the parish nearest to where they were born or had a substantial connection.

Henry's brother Sam had worked hard and had shown a willingness to learn. This had paid off and Sam had gradually taken on more and more responsibilities at Bowyer's bloomerie and iron works and he had become more skilled in the art of iron making.

Henry Bowyer and, later to a greater extent, Sir Stephen had seen advantages in growing connections with other iron-producing families on the Weald rather than considering them to be a threat as competitors to their own business interests. To this end Sam had been able to secure for Henry an introduction to the Pelham bloomerie and foundry just outside Newdigate, this being but a few miles from where Will would be at the Star in Rusper.

One early autumn morning, having said their goodbyes to their father and sister Anna, Will and Henry set off on foot. They had but a couple of bundles of clothing and a blanket and some black bread and cheese to sustain them along the way. They were in good spirits as they left. They were both looking forward to a change, but for different reasons. Will hoped he could make his mark by building up the stable facilities at the Star and Henry saw an escape from spending so much time in the woods with Old Josiah and he still desired the companionship of a good woman that he hoped someday to meet.

27

Will and Henry slept out in the open overnight. They settled down for the night just a few miles short of Colgate having spent much the afternoon walking through St Leonard's Forest. The tracks were quite distinct, as horse and cart were used to convey iron products and wood to where they could be used or sold. Sometimes through the trees they could see small farmsteads in glades where the land had been cleared, but these looked miserable dwellings and life could not have been easy. Will was glad that he had found horses and did not have to work the land.

Once they had emerged from the trees of St Leonard's Forest, where there was much activity as they reached the edge of the forest with trees being felled and wood being prepared and stacked in ordered piles, they could see the tower of a church. They assumed this belonged to Rusper parish church. It looked to be, and indeed it is, the highest point for some miles around. By mid-afternoon Will and Henry found their way into Rusper itself. Rusper was smaller than Cuckfield and they had no trouble finding The Star.

Will presented himself to Francis Wickham.

'Good day, Mr Wickham Sir. I am Will Weller from the Talbot in Cuckfield. I understand that you have arranged with Mr and Mrs Washwood that I should come and work for you in the stables. This here is my brother Henry who will be working for Mr Pelham at his bloomerie.'

'You will have your work cut out for you and I expect you to deliver or you will be out on your ear,' said Wickham. 'For the first month I will provide you with both food and somewhere to stay. There is space above the stable where you can sleep. It is not much, but it is dry and I will provide both a mattress and a blanket for your bedding. After the month is out, if you have done your job as I want, I will then take you on and pay a wage. We normally have no more than one or two gentlemen riders staying with us at any one time. Your job will be to clear the stables and make the accommodation good for at least a dozen horses. After you have cleared things out where we need to build new stalls at the back, I shall engage the carpenter. I will expect you to tend all the horses that we stable and this will then leave my son free to help me more inside.'

Will eagerly agreed and secured Mr Wickham's permission for Henry to stay with him in the stable overnight before moving on to Pelham's works. That night they had a hot meal of vegetable stew with just a few bits of mutton. Although Henry used to bring home the odd snared coney from when he spent time with Old Josiah, it was rare for working folk to have meat. Their diet was mainly coarse bread, cheese and vegetables, whereas the rich always ate lots of meat and looked at anything taken from the ground as peasant's fodder.

Chapter 2

Will worked hard, as hard as he had ever worked before. Wickham was impressed enough to take Will on permanently and on a fully paid basis. The stables had been cleared of all the old clutter and hay and mess. Where feather-boards had been in need of replacement this had been done and new stalls for horses were provided. Business at the Star had improved and the stables were more busy. Will had even obtained a few sticks of furniture and had made what he thought was a nice little nest for himself.

Will was also happy for a different reason. He had taken a shinning to Mary who worked both as a kitchen and chambermaid at the Star. Mary was almost the same height as Will. She had long brown hair, green eyes and the same kind of freckles as he had. Mary also liked Will an awful lot. If Will saw her in the yard he would stop for a while whatever he was doing and follow her movements with his eyes. Everyone could see that when he did so his sometimes-mischievous grin was more of a beaming smile. Mary would sometimes catch him looking at her out of the corner of her eye. She would lower her head somewhat so that her own smile was hidden but then just as she was about to go back inside Mary would look up and Will would see that she was smiling back at him.

They would catch a few moments together during the week, but in the main they would have to wait until Sundays when they could walk to church together and afterwards take a stroll whilst remaining in full view of others. One Sunday when momentarily hidden from villagers' eyes by the trunk of a large tree they stole their first kiss together. Will's heart was on fire.

'Oh Mary, Mary I do love you so. I think I have loved you for a long time now. Looking out from the stables or when I was out in the yard I used to hope that you would come outside just so that I could see you. When you did come out you used to look away, but when you started to turn your head and smile at me just as you were going back inside I knew that you are the one for me. And now we have kissed for the first time. I can still feel my heart pounding.'

Looking deep into Will's eyes, Mary replied, 'And I love you too, Will, and I love your curly mop and your boyish grin. I knew you were watching me and I liked to tease you into thinking that I had not noticed but I could never stop myself from smiling. Now tell me, Will Weller. What are you going to do about it? Are you going to make a married woman of me or not? I will not have you trifling with me otherwise.'

'Marry you?' said Will. 'Of course I want to marry you, and if anyone else dares to look in your direction I'll tie him to the back of a horse with a big burr under its saddle and the horse will keep on running until it gets to the sea and he will never come back.'

'Have no fear on that account dear Will. I have no interest in any man but you.'

That was it. Their bond was sealed. They knew that it might be some time before they could marry. Even if Mr Wickham would allow it Will could hardly expect his bride to live in his nest above the stables. Mary never did see inside the stables beyond what she could see from the yard.

Chapter 3

Henry had settled in at Pelham's works. He would mainly undertake general labouring such as using hammer and chisel to break lumps off the outcrops of ironstone or loading the ironstone into barrows so that it could be taken elsewhere to be broken up into smaller pieces. Once broken into pieces the ironstone would then be washed, usually by boys, and allowed to weather before being washed again before being put into the bloomerie or the bigger furnaces. This washing and weathering made for better iron. Henry shared a lodging with two other unmarried workers. They got on reasonably well, but then they had little choice in the matter.

Henry would come into Rusper when he could and this would mainly be on a Sunday when he would join Will at church and for a talk afterwards, but since Will had so obviously taken up with Mary they spent less and less time in each other's company. Henry was not jealous of Will. He cared too much for Will to feel that way, but it did bring home to him just how lonely he was. He decided that he was going to do something about it. Henry was now twenty-seven or twenty-eight years of age, perhaps a bit too old for the girls of the village or nearby, most of whom it seemed to him to be either already betrothed or married or else totally unappealing. His problem was how to work around this. Henry had noticed a woman somewhat older than himself but still of a comely appearance attending church with, what he assumed, was her son and daughter, both of which were coming up to their adolescence.

Henry had no really close friends. He did not find it easy to make friends and his unintentionally grumpy demeanour did not help matters. However, one Sunday afternoon he did turn to someone with whom he was on speaking terms.

'What do you think, John, you can tell me about that woman there with the two growing-up children? I never see her with a husband. Is she on her own?'

John could see where this conversation was going.

'If you must know, and you obviously do, her name is Fortune West and, yes, she is on her own as she is a widow of some years standing. Her husband Henry West had been working on the construction of a pond to serve Pelham's iron-works. Pelham knew that such ponds were necessary so that streams could be dammed and that there was an ample water supply to drive the waterwheel to operate the large bellows needed to work the new blast furnaces he wanted to replace his bloomeries. What you may not know is that the stream goes from here into the River Mole and down the valley and on to the Thames going through London and out to sea.

'Well, Henry West had been working one morning excavating. The side of the hole that he and others had been digging was already two feet above his own height. Whilst some wood had been used to shore up the banks to what would be the pond, the whole lot gave way, burying both Henry West and another worker in soil and mud. The other men working there managed to pull one of them free but Henry West was under too much soil and mud and it would take more men and some shoring up of the bank that had given way for West's body be retrieved in safety. To his credit, Mr Pelham gave the widow a sum of money and said that she could remain in her cottage rent free until such time as her children were old enough to work. As you can see, that time is soon coming. If you have designs on her you should know that she is a woman of good Christian character. The rest is now up to you if you really are interested, but beware she is a well loved and respected woman hereabouts.'

Henry thanked John and decided to become acquainted with Fortune West. Over several months Henry began to win her confidence as being a genuine, if somewhat serious, person. Even though the area around Rusper supported little in the way of crop growing, in fact even less than in and around Cuckfield, Harvest Festival was still celebrated and it was during that evening's celebration that Henry sat down next to Fortune.

'Fortune, I have a proposition for you. We have come to know each other quite well over the last few months. Through bad luck you find yourself a widow with children and yourself to support and I understand that Mr Pelham will not allow you to live where you are rent-free for much longer. For my part I have never been married. Can we not combine our lot? We can offer each other companionship and I would try and be a good second father to your children. I will not make demands upon you as a wife unless or until you should want things to be that way. What I bring home from the ironworks would be to support my new family for it is a family that I crave for. What would you say Fortune? Can we be wed?

Fortune said that she would give her answer the following Sunday. They married that October, it was the year of 1635.

Chapter 4

Disputes between the Crown and the parliament or affairs and wars on the continent were not matters for the common countryman to be concerned about. Will and Henry were fairly ignorant of such things, but this was soon to change as everyone was to be impacted in some way or another.

Will and Mary were betrothed but had yet to set a date to be married, as Will wanted to be able to provide a home good enough for them to start and raise a family.

One day Francis Wickham called for Will to come and see him.

'Will, I have received some bad news today from my daughter, Mrs Washwood. It concerns your father. He has taken to his bed and it does not look as though it will be long before he is with his Maker. I am greatly pleased for what you have done here. Would you wish to visit him for perhaps one last time? I will let you have one of the posting horses and there is something I would want you to deliver to my daughter at the same time.'

It was not always easy for working people to move around the country and never on horseback. Francis Wickham therefore provided Will with a letter, although Will could not read, addressed 'To Whom it May Concern' saying that Wickham had allowed Will to take a horse on occasion of the need to visit Cuckfield to undertake business on his behalf.

As Will was already aware, Cuckfield was by some considerable way a more sophisticated place than Rusper. The reasons for this were its larger size and wealth, partly because it was on a major route to and from London and the coast, but also because of Sir Stephen Bowyer and the significant figure that he had become. Whilst Sir Stephen spent much time in London, there was much toing and froing on the Cuckfield Estate that had continued to grow and expand under Sir Stephen's stewardship. It was here in Cuckfield that, by listening to what others had to say, Will became far more aware of the discontent surrounding the King and the disputes with and within parliament, although he did not profess to understand everything that it was going on.

Chapter 5

Sir Stephen Bowyer could gauge that there were tensions between the Crown and parliament. Whilst he had sought not to take any course that would be frowned on at the court of King Charles, he had seen it as good sense to cultivate contacts both at court and in parliament, or rather with parliamentarians that were, or had the potential to become, important. Some of the more gregarious parliamentarians would come and stay at Cuckfield. Others, such as John Pym, and his friend the newly returned Member of Parliament, Oliver Cromwell, with them both sharing the puritanical beliefs that Sir Stephen personally found distasteful and uncompromising, were contacts that he cultivated in other ways whilst he was in London. Sir Stephen saw it as to his advantage to be known to all and to do nothing to alienate anyone who might some day either be useful in his personal or business ventures or, on the other hand, might become a hindrance to them.

Sir Stephen had some time ago contemplated the prospects of conflict breaking out between supporters of the King and supporters of parliament. Were this to happen, he knew that there was even more money to be made from supplying both sides with munitions. Bowyer started slowly at first then more aggressively to expand his iron-producing and iron-making interests across the breadth of the Weald. Where he did not buy people out completely, he would take over the greater part of running the business. It was now common knowledge that Sir Stephen had taken over the larger part of Pelham's business near back at what was now Will's home community of Rusper.

Other things had changed since Will and Henry had left Cuckfield. Parson Meade had retired just a couple of months previously and gone to live down near the coast with his wife. They never had children. The Reverend James Marsh had now been appointed as vicar as Meade's successor.

Whilst Will took all of this in, his main concern was for his father. Anna had been a good daughter, helping her father by combing and preparing the wool and then spinning the yarn he needed for the loom. She had cooked and kept house for him, but she was a plump and a somewhat slow-witted girl who was unlikely in Will's mind to attract anyone to marry her. William was to die the day after Will returned to Cuckfield. He was old and worn out and it was a distressing experience to see him in this condition, but Will was glad of the opportunity to see him one last time.

The funeral was a simple affair. Sam, his wife Ann and their children John and Jane were in attendance, as of course were Will and Anna. The burial being on a weekday meant that those that had a position and could were working. Will went to see Mr Washwood at The Talbot which, being on the direct road to London, had built up a reputation as a posting house, and Washwood was attracting new and better-class custom. For The Star back in Rusper, on the other hand, things had been slow to get off the ground. Mr Wickham had acquired two horses, one of which he had let Will use, but although some progress had been made to date a steady flow of horse rentals had yet to build up.

Will saw Mr and Mrs Washwood together.

'I have a package here for you, Mrs Washwood, from your father. I am sorry I did not bring it straight to you but I have much to attend to.'

Mrs Washwood nodded but did not say anything.

Will continued.

'I have no right to ask this of you but I wonder if you could find a situation for my sister Anna? She is a little slow in the head at times but she is not afraid of hard work and is an honest and a good girl. My place is now back in Rusper and it would distress me if she was to fall back on the Poor Law relief.'

Mrs Washwood looked at her husband before responding.

'My father speaks well of you, Will, and what you have

done. We are also pleased with what you did whilst you were with us. I shall take Anna on as a skivvy maid and a general help and as long as she does not let me down she will be safe with us.'

'I am truly most grateful to you both,' said Will.

The day after his father's burial Will was on his way back to Rusper.

Chapter 6

Around a year after Will returned from Cuckfield he and Mary were able to wed. Both Sam and his family were able to travel up from Cuckfield, and Henry and Fortune attended the wedding along with the Wickhams. Mary had no family. Her mother had died in childbirth and her father had also died soon after she started to work at the Star. It was left to Francis Wickham to give the bride away and he seemed rather taken when Will and Mary asked him to do this. The small but happy wedding party enjoyed a wedding supper in Wickham's private room next to the kitchen.

Will was able to rent a cottage close by the Star. Particularly during the longer days of late spring through to early autumn he would work long hours as travellers would make as much use as they could of daylight hours to progress their journey. Within the year Will and Mary had their first child. They called her Sarah.

Chapter 7

News came to Rusper that the King had fled London following his dispute with parliament. It was all very confusing. One

story was that the King was in league with his Catholic queen
to bring Catholicism back to England, whilst another story
claimed that this was not the case and that some in
parliament sought to change the way the English church was
organised and run. Will did not know what to believe. All he
wanted was a peaceful life, to do his job and to care for his
wife and baby daughter. What he did know was that food was
getting more expensive and that more and more frequently
Mr Wickham was complaining about both the increased
taxes and the church tithes he was forced to pay.

When Will next saw Henry, Henry said to him:

'Will, Mr Pelham's ironworks are very busy, so busy in fact
that Pelham and other ironmasters were taking on more
men and boys to gather ironstone or to chop down trees for
charcoal-burning. No more coppicing or pollarding of trees
these days. The whole tree is sometimes being cut down as
more and more charcoal is needed for the furnaces that are
now working night as well as day. The favourite seems to be
the production of cannon and cannon balls. It is as plain as
the nose on your face that the trees and woodland are
disappearing. These things will take years to grow back even
if someone has the time and inclination to make it happen.'

There were a number of new arrivals, attracted by the
opportunity for employment and the now slightly improved
wages compared with a few years back. One of these, recently
come to the village to work at Pelham's ironworks was
another William, William Weller from Horsham way, and he
had not been there long before he took up with and married
the local girl Sarah Chase. In just under a year they had their
first child and they decided to call him William. This was all
soon to lead to some confusion.

As time went on, the normal steady movement of travellers
started to tail off as more and more was seen of what were
obviously parliamentarian soldiers in ones or twos presumably carrying messages. Will and Mary had just had their

second child whom they called William after Will's father. The conflict between the supporters of King Charles and supporters of the parliamentarian cause had broken out into the open. Nothing was the same any more. Even going to church was different.

Will was out in the yard one morning when Wickham called him over. Will came at once.

'Well, Will, here's a queer story. I have just heard that the Vicar at Cuckfield, Marsh I think his name is ... yes, Marsh.' Will nodded in agreement. 'Well, I hear that he has been arrested and put in prison for a second time because he is so outspoken in supporting the King's cause. With him out of the way the troopers used the church as a stable and the terrible thing is that the horses kicked and cracked the baptismal font and did also other damage inside. How can this be allowed to happen in the house of God? I also hear that there has been some big fighting way up north and things have not gone well for the King, not that I favour either the King's side or the other side you understand. All I am interested in is in running the Star.'

Will nodded again.

'I hope it all continues to pass us by as well, Mr Wickham. Things are getting harder as it is what with the increasing price of food and things. We don't need any armies or fighting in these parts.'

As things turned out, both on the inland High Weald and on the Low Weald Will's wishes were met and the area was largely to remain unaffected by fighting. The parliamentarians largely had control over the Weald. However, there was much division between the various groupings and they could not even agree amongst themselves how to run the churches and in what manner to honour God. The Rector at Rusper, Charles Williams, was a traditionalist following the way of the established church with its bishops and hierarchy, yet even as a man of the cloth his life was to be greatly changed by the new religious freedoms and liberties that had come about over the past few years. The disruption brought about by the war had made it more difficult for the church to maintain its authority. Increasingly seen in Rusper were roaming preachers or lecturers who thought that, as they had come to know God and to receive His Spirit, they were convinced that they had the right to preach as much as, if not more than, corrupt priests. This tormented the Rector and he would berate his somewhat smaller congregation for listening to others as he impressed upon his flock that only the church and himself as the church's appointed representative could be in communion with God.

The spring of 1645 had been late coming after a long and cold winter. Food was already expensive what with all the disruption and with increasing numbers of parliamentary troopers passing through the village. This was making a bad situation worse by making increased demands on an already limited and expensive local food supply. Many were struggling to afford enough to eat. Even with the odd left-overs from Mr Wickham's kitchen – and there were not that many of those – Will and the family often went to bed still feeling hungry. Mary was again with child and they were looking forward to the birth of what would be their third child. Will had sent for the midwife as the signs were that Mary was close to her time. Throughout the night Mary could be heard screaming as the midwife urged her to bear down. Mary's calls were getting weaker and did at last come to a stop after one last scream. A short while later the midwife pushed back the curtain that separated Will and Mary's sleeping area from the rest of the cottage. The midwife turned to Will with a sad look.

'I am sorry but you have a stillborn daughter. Your wife is weak and has lost a lot of blood. She is asleep for now and you must let her rest but I fear that you must expect to lose her as well. I have done what I can for her and I do not think that having a physician tending her or, God forbid if he is that stupid to be bleeding her, will help your wife in any way. Let me take this poor mite away and clean her. I will return later. Should she awake try and get her to take something hot and keep her warm. You can settle with me another time.'

Mary never did awake, but passed away the following day. Will was beside himself with grief. He had lost his one and only true love and could never ever be with another woman. As for the children, it fell upon Henry's wife Fortune to look after them. This she did with an open and generous heart. Things between Henry and Fortune had worked out well and they were both content with the company and companionship they could offer each other.

Chapter 8

The Rector of Rusper was a particularly orderly man and was proud in his keeping of the parish records. He was required each year to send to his bishop transcripts of his own records. Even though his bishop had been removed, Reverend Williams continued to fulfil this duty, on the assumption that the church would at some time return to its primacy.

He was also entitled to charge for baptisms and it was an offence for a child not to be baptised. The Reverend Williams therefore decided that he needed to make a distinction between the recently widowed William Weller who had a son called William and the William Weller that had come to Rusper and married Sarah by whom he had a son also called William. He decided that as far as the records for the church were concerned, and for the sake of supplementing his income, that William Weller the stableman at the Star, being some years older than the other William, would be called 'William Weller Senior'. The other

William married to Sarah had come to Rusper from elsewhere so he and his family should be called there-after 'William Weller from Horsham' or 'William Weller Junior'.

Chapter 9

The parliamentary army were becoming more and more of a problem. When a couple of years earlier troopers could be seen on the road in ones or twos, now there was an almost a permanent presence in the Weald communities. The roads leading down to the coast were patrolled regularly to ensure that no arms from France or elsewhere could be supplied to the royalist supporters and also to ensure that arms pro-duced by Wealden ironmasters went only to support the parliamentary army and its cause.

Wickham's string of now three horses, intended to enable him to run a posting house and business, had been commandeered by the army. Wickham had been given a note saying that he would be paid, but as the months dragged on there was no sign of the money. If there was any com-pensation for Wickham it was that he did not have to pay for feed for the horses when fewer and fewer independent travellers enquired about hiring a fresh horse.

Will had spoken to Mr Wickham immediately after his wife was buried.

'Mr Wickham, may I ask your permission to move back into my old lodgings in the stable? Fortune and my brother Henry are taking care of my children and with Mary gone I do not want to keep the cottage. As for my job, I know that the posting house business has disappeared but I will do whatever else it is that you need of me.'

Wickham was an honourable and a fair man. He was

responsible for bringing William to Rusper and he had liked Mary.

'Yes, Will, you can and I shall be glad of it. With you moving back there is less chance that I will be forced to billet even more troopers. You know all too well that both the Star and the Plough have lost rooms to billeted officers and men. I want no more of it.'

Chapter 10

News came to Rusper about events going on elsewhere. It was nearly a year since the King and his supporters, led by the King's nephew Prince Rupert of Bavaria, had been defeated at Naseby. Will had to ask Wickham where Bavaria and Naseby were located. Wickham was only able to tell him what he in turn had heard from the officer still billeted in one of his rooms. It was also coming up to a year now since Will had lost his dear wife. Sarah was now six years of age and a bonny looking child. William, who had by now picked up the name Billy, was three and looked more and more like his father as he got bigger.

Even though the King had lost heavily at Naseby, there still seemed that no peace or settlement was in sight. There were problems with the parliamentary forces as well with troopers not being paid. Stories were circulating that in some parts of the country soldiers were being hanged for stealing horses and food. George Wright, innkeeper of the Plough, had suffered the same indignities as Wickham. Although not established as a posting house, Wright also had a horse commandeered by the army and men billeted both in the inn and in his stables. There was no sign of the promissory notes that they had both been given in exchange for the horses or for the loss of income from billeting being honoured. Wickham and Wright decided that they had nothing to lose in approaching and petitioning Charles Pelham as the magistrate, and therefore the law, in these parts. Pelham could see that at some time soon there must be a solution to the years of conflict. The Star and the Plough inns were vital parts of the village community and important in that respect to Pelham's own interests. As there had been little or no fighting on the Weald, the parliamentarian forces throughout the most part of the Weald were under the command of more or less local commanders rather than by officers belonging to the far more fractious New Model Army. Pelham was able to use these relatively local connections and his position as justice of the peace to press for Wright and Wickham to be compensated. Wright's own horse was returned to him forthwith. Wickham did not come out of it quite so well. He received two horses of similar age to the those he had lost but they were not in good fettle. Nevertheless, with proper feeding and care they would regain their strength. For the loss of the third horse he received some monetary compensation but less than he had hoped for and less than he had actually paid for the horse he had lost. Wickham accepted this without further complaint. Now at least William had more work to do in the stable.

Chapter 11

From Will's own family perspective, things continued in a fairly normal and routine way. He could see his children growing up and thriving under Fortune's tender care. He was also glad to see Henry and Fortune grow closer and closer together as they learnt to care for and trust each other more and more.

There were fewer troops around now that the parliamentary army was being disbanded following the King's surrender at Oxford, and the word was that the King had fled north to Scotland. Although elements of the parliamentary army had dissolved, the so-called 'standing army' remained the most potent force in the land. Little evidence of this was, though, seen on the Weald and this greatly suited the local population.

The situation remained confused and confusing. The King had tried to invade England and regain his crown with the help of a Scots-raised army but had been defeated yet again. Even so, it seemed that parliament was undecided about what to do about the King. Then the shocking news came through and all of Rusper was in disbelief. The King, their King, the King appointed by God to rule them was to be put on trial in the name of the people and tried for treason. Will and Harry and Fortune were part of the people and no one had asked them about the possibility of putting the King on trial and probably for his life.

It was a cold winter up on the Weald when news at last came through about the outcome of the King's trial. It was the last day in January in the year of Our Lord 1649. The news spread like wildfire that the King had been executed the previous day in Whitehall in public and whilst it was snowing. For the first time in centuries that constant certainty of Kings or Queen to guide and rule the country was no longer there. The church too had lost its authority some time ago with the removal of bishops. Who now would be there to guide them? There were, of course, the likes of Sir Stephen Bowyer and Mr Pelham who were the glue that held the respective communities together, whilst of course protecting or promoting their own, not necessarily common, interests.

Chapter 12

Mary Thomas had come to the village a few years previously on the promise of finding work as a domestic maid at Faygate Farm where her cousin Jane Wright worked as a cook. Jane Wright must have had exceptional powers of persuasion for Mary Thomas to secure a trial placement at Faygate. That said, two or three of the village girls had been employed briefly at Faygate but had failed to secure a permanent position as they did not meet their employer's high expectations.

After just over a year Mary Thomas left Faygate for employment as a domestic at the Plough Inn. This was far more in keeping with her temperament and nature.

Mary Thomas did not live in at the Plough but shared a small cottage with her cousin Jane. She had a naturally rounded figure and had seemed to have put on some additional weight of late. Each morning she would walk the two miles or so from the cottage to the Plough and back again in the evenings.

One morning, during the time of confusion and turmoil after the King had lost his head, the village was awash with commotion. Henry together with William Weller – that is the William Weller from Horsham – were on their way to the woodland lying to the south of the village at the very edge of St Leonard's Forest. Their job that day was to hew and stockpile more wood for charcoal burning to keep the furnaces going. Others also worked in the wood as 'sawyer men' where they prepared rough wood into sawn planks or veneers for cabinet makers.

Henry and William from Horsham were cutting across the fields when they came upon Mary Thomas bending over an overgrown drainage ditch in what appeared, even from behind, to be a dishevelled and agitated state. Upon approaching her she turned and Henry could see her face was a deathly white and that she was trembling. William Weller tried to look past her into the ditch to see what it was that had been preoccupying her. She tried to block his view but he pushed her aside and found a small shovel, the start of a hole and a bundle of rags. He opened one end of the bundle of rags to find, to his horror, an infant, obviously newborn.

'What have we here? What have you done? Have you murdered this poor child, you wicked woman?' shouted Henry.

'It is the gallows for you. You will pay for this dreadful deed with your life,' William joined in.

In between her blubbering and wailing Mary Thomas kept on repeating:

'I didn't kill it. I didn't kill it.'

The laws against mothers of bastards, or base-born children as they were sometimes described, were strict. Bastards threatened to be a burden on the poor law rates and the mothers upon conviction of fornication could be sent to the House of Correction for punishment. Midwives attending base-born births were expected during labour to extract the name of the father so that he could be brought to book and carry the financial burden of the child. It was not unknown for mothers to hide stillborn infants or, even worse, to do away with them.

With William carrying the sad bundle and Henry keeping a firm hold on Mary Thomas, they turned back in the direction of Rusper to seek out the magistrate.

In such a small community, with roughly 70 families living in or around Rusper, news travelled fast, particularly when something as serious as infanticide was concerned. A message was sent to Mr Pelham, the magistrate, up at Ghyll House. In the meantime Mary Thomas was locked in an outbuilding at the Plough.

With the church locked up because Reverend Williams was away, the Plough Inn, being a slightly better appointed establishment compared with the Star, was the only building in the village large enough to hear the proceedings against Mary Thomas and to accommodate as many as possible of the villagers.

To his credit, Magistrate Pelham was not prepared to oversee a circus. Upon arrival in Rusper he enquired as to why the physician was not on hand to examine the infant. Doctor Greenfield was evidently on his way to London and was not expected back for at least a week. The magistrate then sent for the midwife should she be able to tell him something about the dead infant. Mr Pelham set the trial for noon that day.

First to be called were Henry and William Weller. Henry was questioned first.

'Tell me how, where and when you came into this matter,' enquired Pelham.

'Well, sir, William Weller and myself were set today to cut and pile wood down to the south of the village. Wood to be turned into charcoal to feed your furnaces, sir. We were going alongside the edge of the field when we saw Mary Thomas acting in a peculiar way. She had her back to us but was bent low and seemed to be doing something in the ground. This did not look right to us and we went over to find out what she was up to. She tried to hide what she was doing from us and she looked as she looks to us now a woman who has been up to no good and who has murdered her child.'

Mary Thomas screamed out: 'I did not kill it! I did not kill it! Before God I swear it came early and was stillborn!'

Pelham demanded her silence. Mary Thomas stood there gripping the edge of the table sobbing and shaking. She feared for her life and the hangman's noose if they did not believe her.

Henry was dismissed and William Weller was questioned.

'Tell me now your part in this matter.'

'Sir, it is like he has said. We were on our way to cut wood when we saw this woman up to no good. When she tried to stop us seeing what she was doing I pushed her aside. I could see that she had been digging and next to this there was a bundle of rags. I bent to have a closer look and when I undid part of the rags I found this infant that she must have killed. We brought her back here and news was sent to you, sir, so that you can deal with this wicked woman.'

Then someone shouted: 'Murderer! She should hang and spend the rest of eternity in hell for what she has done.'

Pelham again demanded silence. He then turned to the midwife.

'You have examined the dead child woman. Tell me what you know.'

The midwife, a woman of indeterminate age, on the plump side and having a presence about her spoke in a clear voice.

'I have looked at the child, sir. I would say that it came into this world far too early. Maybe as much as six to eight weeks early. I could find no marks on its body. It would have been a girl and in my view it is quite likely that it was either stillborn or died very soon after it was born. The child was had outside of wedlock and that is an evil sin but I cannot say to you, sir that she, the mother, was responsible for the death or the killing of the infant.'

Pelham thanked the midwife before turning to Mary Thomas.

'I have heard and accept what this wise woman has said and I will not send you to the hangman. You are nevertheless a wicked woman for conceiving a child and then trying to bury it to hide your crime and shame. I must know, who is the father?'

Mary Thomas replied: 'I cannot tell, sir.'

Pelham again demanded that she answer his question and she gave the same reply.

'Very well,' said Pelham, 'you either cannot or will not tell me who the father is. For your crimes I am sending you to the House of Correction for one year. You are not from this village and you are never to return. You are a base woman and I do not want the likes of you around here.'

Turning to George Wright, the innkeeper of the Plough, Pelham said: 'You will keep this woman locked up and under the supervision of the Parish Constable. I will send word to the House of Correction in Dorking and they will come for her. No harm is to come to her. I have said what will be done with her.'

Everyone then dispersed with Henry and William Weller setting off for the woods again just as they had done in the morning. This time they would find no distraction along the way.

Chapter 13

The Reverend Williams did not stay away from his church and Rusper for long. Whatever business had called him away must have been completed. Over the past few years many clergy had been examined and called upon to give account of themselves to find whether they had been doing their job well enough to be allowed to keep it. Many clergy had deservedly been thrown out as being either corrupt or incompetent, yet others who may have been just as undeserving, seemed to have worked a deal to keep their positions.

During the earlier days of the Civil War lay preachers and lecturers had travelled the Weald preaching their own version of how to honour God and keep to His laws without the need for a church with all its bishops. These 'Puritans' were seen less and less now and their influence had waned, with many leaving for the New World. True, there was no bishop any more but most of the people of Rusper, perhaps reflecting the size of the community and its relative remoteness, adhered more to the traditions of the church. This is what they knew and this is what they were more comfortable with.

The Commonwealth remained in the ascendancy. While as the Scots had proclaimed Charles II, the son of the executed King, as just not their monarch but also as the monarch of England and Ireland, the English parliament passed a statute that made any such declaration unlawful in England and Ireland.

Then at Worcester the forces of Charles II were routed and Charles was forced into exile. Even with the fighting in England over, Pelham's ironworks remained busy what with new wars being fought by the republican Commonwealth under the Lord Protector, Oliver Cromwell. First, there was Ireland and then fighting between the Commonwealth and the Dutch as well as with the Spanish. This had secured employment locally for the likes of Henry, but the landscape had changed over the years as yet more and more woodland disappeared.

Since the loss of his wife Mary and their stillborn daughter, Will had suffered a loss of faith and he still felt the same even now some years after their loss. Will attended church only often enough to stay within the law and avoid being fined for non-attendance. When they were growing up Will would always find time to see his children Sarah and Billy on Sundays and, if it was a day that he was not going to church, the children would go with Henry and Fortune and he would see them all afterwards. The children would also come to the stable yard at the Star, particularly during the lighter evenings, to watch their father at work even if he was too busy to pay them much attention.

Sarah later secured a permanent position as a domestic servant at Faygate Farm, a credit to her given the difficulties people from the village had in meeting the particular demands of their employer.

Billy was now working as a stable lad for Mr Pelham and his son. Will had not only taught Billy the basics of looking after horses but had shared with his son all that he had learnt over the years. Edward Grimes was in charge of Pelham's stable and had remained of the Puritan persuasion. To Puritans education was extremely important and part of a Puritan's conviction was that every man and woman should be able to read the Bible for themselves. Grimes was teaching Billy to read, something that Will had never accomplished.

Will was now beginning to feel his age, particularly on cold or wet mornings. Francis Wickham's son Richard now mostly ran the Star, although old Mr Francis was to be seen shuffling around and doing the odd little job to keep himself involved and occupied.

The past couple of years had been particularly hard. Although the land around Rusper was not good for growing crops to start with, the harvests had been poorer than normal on the Weald and poor across the country. Food was again so expensive that many of the poor struggled to feed themselves and their families. Taxes on landowners, merchants and businesses were high because of the ongoing Spanish war and then came the news of the death of Oliver Cromwell. Also came the news that, because there was no one else and there was virtually no parliament other than a discredited bunch of politicians from the so-called 'Rump parliament', Cromwell's son Richard (only because of sharing his father's name and he was very soon to be called 'Tumbledown Dick') had been appointed as successor Protector under the Commonwealth.

The army had refused to recognise Tumbledown Dick Cromwell and, with the Long Parliament being recalled only to be dismissed again, it was clear to all that the days of the Commonwealth were numbered.

At the end of May 1660 news reached Rusper that the 'King' was to return from exile and take up his proper place on the English throne. Everyone rejoiced and joined in the celebrations with very few exceptions, such as Edward Grimes up on Pelham's Estate, joined in in the almost spontaneous festivities. Pigs were slaughtered for the spit. Hogsheads of ale beer were opened and there was much dancing.

Later that year smallpox was to ravage the country. Many of the very old and very young were lost, but also some of those who seemed fit and able adults, or at least as well and as fit and as able as their diet and conditions of living would allow.

Will, Mr and Mrs Wickham and Fortune were among the villagers to perish. Even the King was to lose his younger brother Henry and his sister Mary to the epidemic. Neither wealth nor privilege were a guarantee to escape the ravages of the disease.

Chapter 14

Farming had always been a somewhat precarious way of life. The soil was poor and crop yields were sufficient only to bring home a very modest income in the best of harvest years. As generations of yeoman farmers died off or moved away, Squire Pelham had seized the opportunity to acquire more land. The reasons for this were lost on most people who could only assume that the squire wanted to rebuild his status after going into a junior partnership with Sir Stephen Bowyer in his iron-making activities.

Things in England in the countryside had reverted to type, although some argued there had never been much of a change anyway. By and large, with the exception of people such as the blacksmith or those running a business such as the Star or the Plough – and even they paid rent to Pelham – the position of Pelham as squire and of other country squires was paramount. The lifestyle and comfortable existence of the squires with their estates compared harshly with the lives and conditions endured by the tenant farmers and the mass of landless labourers seeking work where they could.

Yet other things had changed since the restoration of the King. Edward Grimes could not swallow the re-establishment of the traditional Church of England. He decided that England was no longer his country. He had heard that Puritan communities had set sail for the New World to establish their own societies based upon Puritan principles for worshipping God and doing His will. Billy was now the senior stable hand and, under some direction, was responsible for day-to-day running of Squire Pelham's stables and the upkeep of his horses.

Walter Holcombe, the Squire's estate manager, came to Billy one morning with some news.

'Next month the Squire is to receive a number of important guests. Some will come by coach and some on their own horses. They will stay for maybe a few nights. The Squire wants everything to be perfect. The coachmen will look after their own coaches and you will be responsible for ensuring the horses are well cared for. If it looks like a horse needs a new shoe you will send for the blacksmith and the Squire will pay. You will ensure that all the tackle and saddles are maintained and made to look like they have never looked before. The Squire has impressed upon me just how important his guests are and how important this occasion is to him. Now I am telling you just how important what you do is to me. If I am not satisfied then you are finished here. I have made arrangements for the stable lad at the Plough to come and help for a few days.'

Billy opened his mouth as if to protest. Holcombe raised

his hand and Billy kept his silence. Holcombe continued: 'Up in the house the Master is bringing cooks from London and all manner of strange foods will be prepared. That is a sign of how important things are and of the standing of the Master's guests. Anything you see or hear whilst the Master is receiving his guests you will not tell anyone and you will not speak about it. Is that absolutely clear to you?'

'Yes, sir,' answered Billy. 'I will not let you or the Master down and if the lad you send me from the Plough thinks he can get away with anything then he will have another thought coming.'

The anticipated guests never did arrive. In fact, the only arrivals for some considerable time were the Squire's son John and his wife and their young child. They had fled London in terror. Those that could, and were rich enough, left London. The King had moved his Court to Oxford and, following the King's example John, Elizabeth and their daughter Hannah had sought to escape and to seek refuge away from London at the Pelham Estate in Rusper.

What drove them away was the Great Plague, the Black Death. So called because those that caught it saw their skin turn black in patches together with outbreaks of buboes, swollen tongues, compulsive vomiting and the certainty of death. Once anyone in the household showed signs of the plague the house was sealed and a red cross was painted on the door along with the words, 'Lord have mercy upon us.'

This is why John Pelham and all his friends and acquaintances with homes in the country fled London upon hearing the first news that people were dying from this killer disease. It was the wisest thing John Pelham was to ever do in his life, as within weeks of the outbreak the Lord Mayor ordered the gates of London to be locked and no one could leave the City without a certificate of health.

Squire Pelham summoned his estate manager Holcombe

and his agent Simons within an hour of John arriving back home.

'London is being visited again by the Black Death. We must do what we can to have no contact with persons or things coming from London. My guests that we have been preparing for must stay away and now that my son has arrived home no one else will be welcome at the house. In fact, there are to be no visitors allowed whatsoever on the estate and I forbid anyone living or working in the house or in the outbuildings to leave. This even means it is forbidden for anyone, including myself, to leave the estate to attend church. The Reverend Williams will come each Sunday, but is only to be admitted onto the estate if he is clear of any signs of skin discolouration and swellings.

'I will discuss with Mrs Rodgers, the housekeeper, what arrangements need to be made for those who work in the house. She will advise as to those persons she thinks she needs to keep here to maintain the running of the house. Those that are not essential for the running of the house will return to their homes and stay away until I say otherwise. As for those workers attending the estate outside, they will not come within half a mile of the house. No goods or matter of any description will be allowed on to the estate. Even letters addressed to me or to my son are forbidden entry and are to be burnt. You will tend to this, Holcombe, and ensure that my instructions are carried out.

'Simons, you are to go to the Star and to the Plough and forbid them in my name to accommodate any travellers and tell them that anything they receive is to be well and truly aired or burnt. If they claim hardship then I will give them hardship when I close them down.'

'Let us pray that the pestilence stays away.'

Billy was not unduly concerned when the Master's instructions were made known to him. He was a temperate man and did not frequent the Plough or the Star. Whilst Billy did not hold with all of Edward Grimes' Puritan principles, he was content, with grateful thanks to Grimes' tuition, to read the good book for himself. Like his father, Billy attended church only enough to avoid being fined, but unlike his father this was not because of a crisis of faith but because he did not like the way that the church was run and what it stood for. He did not need to have another person to communicate with God for him.

Billy was also pleased to later hear that Mrs Rodgers had decided that Anne Gunter was one of the chambermaids that she needed to live in to help her to run the house. Billy was rather taken with Anne and he was intrigued about the opportunities that might present themselves to help him better to make her acquaintance.

That late spring and summer were hot. Hotter than usual. Even living in a semi-isolated state as they were on the estate, news came through that things most dreadful in London and that deaths from the plague were occurring in the countryside as well as in the towns. Some were blaming the wickedness of man for bringing first the pox and now the Black Death upon them and that the only way to earn God's forgiveness was through greater piety. Only then would God lift this curse from mankind. Others, like Billy's late father, questioned how an all-merciful and forgiving God could do this to his children. Some houses in Rusper contained victims of the plague and had been sealed and guarded to make sure the occupants did not escape until things had run their course. On a few occasions someone might live through the ordeal and recover, but for most there was only one fate. A most painful and awful death.

Rusper did not escape its share of pain and grief. Some were to perish, including some that worked before on the estate but were excluded and now lived in the village. Apart from his sister Sarah down at Faygate, Billy was not that close to anyone in the village, although he considered he still had some sort of connection with Mr Wickham at the Star as his father had worked for Wickham's father. His uncle Henry had passed on peacefully one night the previous winter so he had little in the way of family ties and no real friends.

It was approaching autumn and the days were getting shorter and colder. His friendship with Anne was though growing warmer and deeper. Anne was an attractive girl with long black hair, a clear complexion and a full figure.

Billy had offered to teach Anne how to read. Anne had replied:

'Don't be silly, Billy! What would I want with reading? Reading is not for the likes of me. Anyway,' she said with a full smile and looking Billy full in the eye, 'you are going to tell me all I should know, aren't you, Billy?'

With autumn turning into winter the devastation and dying from the Black Death had all but died down. Pelham had decided to remove all restrictions on the movement of people and goods, and both the Plough and the Star were cleared to accept travellers as guests. With some reluctance John Pelham had agreed to his father's request that he and his granddaughter, and his daughter-in-law Elizabeth of course, would spend the winter with him before returning to London in the spring. With Master John and his family staying through the winter Mrs Rodgers decided that the house would run better if Anne were to stay rather than be sent back to live in the village.

The following year with the coming of spring and summer Pelham also began to turn his thoughts towards re-kindling his interest in the postponed gathering together of certain important people from in and around the Weald and with the contacts that he and his son John had made in London. For quite some time now he had been regretting his decision to become the junior partner to Sir Stephen Bowyer's enterprises. Their interests now lay in different directions. The long winter nights had given Pelham and his son ample opportunity to talk through their concerns, and this built further upon their own insecurities arising from what they perceived to be a threat to their position and to the traditional way things ought to be as far as squires and their like were concerned.

The likes of Bowyer, the financial and merchant classes and such magnates as the Dukes of Bedfordshire and Devonshire, who were strong enough not to need to look to the Crown to support their position and status, were a threat to the old squire-led order. Sir Stephen and the merchant classes had vast interests in trade overseas in places such as India, the islands of the West Indies and the New World more generally. Disruption caused to trade, such as the wars against the Dutch had brought about, went against their interests. These Whigs, supported by what was left of the Puritans and the republican supporters and sympathisers from the Civil War, thought they were the new order.

The Squirearchy like Pelham and the other landowners with less of an internationalist interest, together with the Anglican church, felt vulnerable in the face of the so-called 'new order', and sought to protect their interests by aligning themselves with the Crown. The threat of a return of Catholicism was also in the back of their minds.

Master John and his family stayed until Easter and then returned to London. At this point Mrs Rodgers decided that Anne should return to the village at nights. She was also aware of and concerned about the possible consequences of the fondness that her chambermaid and Billy had developed for each other.

Then, in September of that year alarming news began to circulate. The news was that London had burnt down. At first, there were fears that the country was under attack and people kept themselves on the lookout for foreigners and arsonists. When a clearer picture started to emerge, it was obvious that no foreign agencies were at work after all, but the result of the Great Fire was plain for all to see. One-third of London and four-fifths of the City of London were gone.

Chapter 15

It had been almost six months since Anne had returned to the village each night. Anne and Billy in the meantime saw each other for brief moments only, except on Sunday afternoons. These less frequent encounters helped them both to realise that their hearts and futures lay with each other. They decided to marry the following spring.

Billy still lived in the stables whilst Anne was obviously now living in the village. Billy decided to approach the estate manager Holcombe.

'I and Anne Gunter are betrothed and are to marry soon. I would like to ask if it is possible for me to move to the village when we are married and if there is a place that we can rent?'

'Out of the question!' said Holcombe. 'You are needed here on the estate and to be available at all times. This may sound hard but my first duty is to ensure that everything is run to the Squire's satisfaction. There are no dwellings available on the estate at present as they are all occupied. Perhaps in the future something may become available but I make no promises. There will be no further discussion on this matter.'

Living in the village, Anne was more au fait with what was going on. The number of deaths resulting from the plague meant that there were more opportunities for work to be found, as fewer people were available for employment and those could consequently be more particular when it came to looking for work. It was easier for people to move from job to job. In Rusper itself eight families had perished entirely, except for a son of one of these families who spent a large part of his time in the woods burning charcoal.

Despite the disruption of affairs caused by the Great Fire in London, some semblance of normality had returned and business at both the Star and the Plough had picked up.

Anne in some ways was a forward woman, even though she had no interest in learning to read. She took it upon herself to go and see Mr Wickham.

'Mr Wickham, you will probably be aware that Billy Weller and myself are to be married. Billy has asked Mr Holcombe for permission to move away from the estate and for us to rent somewhere to live after we are wed. That permission was refused. Billy has not asked this of me and I am doing this on my own accord.'

She paused to take a breath.

'You know, Mr Wickham, Billy and his father worked for you and for your father as stablemen. I was wondering, sir, if, knowing Billy as you do, you are in need of a good stableman, so Billy could have the opportunity to release himself from the Squire's service?

'I know that this could cause you difficulties with Mr Holcombe or Mr Simons and, possibly, with the Squire himself, but perhaps if you have a business interest at stake you could talk to Mr Holcombe or to Mr Simons on our behalf and maybe he could let us rent one of the empty cottages? You may also know, sir, that now things are returning to where they were before the pestilence that I could be a good worker for you as well and you know that I work for Mrs Rodgers up in the big house.'

Wickham tugged at his ear and was silent for a moment.

'It must have taken some character for you to come to me like this. I do need a good stableman, as it happens, and Billy certainly fits the bill.'

He smiled to himself at the unintended pun. Anne did not seemed to notice.

'Oh, I nearly made a joke there! Yes, I could also do with some help inside and, if Mrs Rodgers has found you satisfactory, then you must be some good. Mr Simons comes here some evenings. Leave things with me and let's see what can be done.'

Anne could scarcely contain her delight.

'Oh, sir, thank you, thank you! I will not say anything to Billy for now but perhaps I can tell him some good news after you have seen and spoken to Mr Simons. May God bless you sir and a very good evening!'

She turned and left the yard to go home.

As good as his word, Wickham did see Simons three nights later. He explained his own situation and his need to have an experienced and capable stableman. Wickham also spoke of his willingness to take Anne on and that, with the losses suffered by the village, how good it would be for the community to welcome a new married couple. Mellowing with the benefit of a few ales on a Saturday evening, Simons promised to see what he could do. In any case, he and Holcombe had one or two run-ins of late and Simons saw this as an opportunity to put another one over him.

Things were set in motion. Billy and Anne first served notice to quit the Squire's services and, true to his word, Mr Simons delivered and they were promised that they would be able to rent a cottage in the village.

Billy and Anne were married soon afterwards. Billy's sister Sarah was there and Mr Wickham and his wife were also invited to the wedding and they had their wedding supper in Mr Wickham's private room. Things had come full circle.

Chapter 16

Away from 'The Big House', life for Billy and Anne was busier but more enjoyable. Working for Mr Wickham was relatively pleasant with far less formality and a more relaxed atmosphere.

Anne was to lose her first baby and then their firstborn child whom they called William was to die after just two months. These heartbreaking setbacks were to be compensated with the joy of Sarah, another William, John, Anne and James coming into this world at fairly regular intervals. and then last of all the surprise of little Thomas who was lost to them just two days after his first birthday.

Upon reaching an appropriate age, Sarah and William were to go and work at what was now Sir John Pelham's house. Whilst Sarah was only a parlour maid, as opposed to her mother's former position as a chambermaid, William assumed duties in helping to look after the stables. The family tradition seemed to be well in place.

Upon the death of his father Sir John Pelham decided that he needed to further consolidate both his prominence on this part of the Weald and his alliances in London. It was through these alliances that Sir John was awarded a Baronetcy bestowed upon him by King Charles himself. That was a few years back now and things these days were very different, with King Charles' Catholic brother James now being on the throne. Sir John felt he was vulnerable if not as yet directly under threat now that there was a Catholic King.

Chapter 17

Billy was standing in the yard at the Star one evening puffing away on his clay pipe. He was in conversation with Richard

Wickham. They had become firm friends over the years and this extended beyond the normal employer and worker relationship.

'I see another band of those Frenchies have arrived this afternoon, Richard. Just how many more of these Hugonets, or whatever they call themselves, are we going to see? They can't speak a word of English between them and Sir John cannot be making rent out of them if they have no work. It is true that we do not have as many people working for the ironworks these days and there have been some empty cottages, but what is the sense in filling them with these foreigners?'

'All I know, Billy, is that Sir John has great sympathy with their plight, what with him being so strongly connected with the Protestant church. These are Huguenots, Billy. They are like us and follow the Protestant faith. Those French Catholics led by their king have persecuted them and have driven them out of France and they have fled here and elsewhere for their lives. What I want to know is whether the persecution of Protestants in France is all part of a Popish plot to destroy the Protestant faith all over and that king of ours will sell us back to Rome and England will become Catholic again. This king of ours is too much in league with the French and far too Catholic for my liking and now he has produced an heir to the throne and he is Catholic as well.

'That aside, from what I have heard off of the estate these people are skilled and clever persons and Sir John has no plans to keep them here but is letting them stay as a sign and signal of his faith. They will disperse, I guess, as soon as Sir John can sort something out for them, probably in London.'

'Well, I hope you are right on that last account,' said Billy. 'As for the rest of it the very last thing we need is for England to have another war in our own country and if things started to go bad for the King then would he turn to France for aid? If he did then that would be the end of it for me. I would do as Edward Grimes did and take my family off to the New World rather than stay here. Anyway, it is getting late and I should be getting home. By the way, I would like to get my son James to know about horses so, unless you object, I would like to bring him to work with me.'

'Getting to feel your old age are you?' quipped Richard with a smile.

'I can beat any man half my age,' snapped back Billy. He was in fact in his forty-eighth year.

Chapter 18

The standing and unpopularity of King James was to get worse. He had abolished parliament and had replaced his previous Protestant ministers with Catholics. True, these events had little direct consequence for the ordinary people of Rusper and for the likes of Billy and his family, but news of these developments did play on people's fears about a Catholic takeover and the prospects of foreigners, including the Pope in Rome, interfering in the affairs of England and Englishmen. They may not have had much say in how their lives were run, but at least the likes of Squire Sir John Pelham were Englishmen.

For Sir John Pelham things were more serious. As a member of the squirearchy, a magistrate and now titled gentry things were clearly getting out of hand. What Sir John saw as a further afront was to see the King replacing Anglican bishops in the Church of England with Catholics. An outrage. Sir John had also seen friends and acquaintances displaced as magistrates and Catholics put in their place. His own position was threatened. The time had come for open action for the Whigs and the Tories to set aside their differences and to do away with this unwanted and unpopular King.

Sir John was to stay away from Rusper all that summer and into the autumn. His place was at the centre of things in London. Sir John was to be part of the party to open and hold negotiations with representatives of William of Orange, nephew of the Catholic King James, and his wife Mary, daughter of King James but both staunch Protestants. Following this, an invitation was sent to them to accept the crown of England, Scotland and Ireland.

Everyone's fear was that King Louis of France might intervene and attack the Netherlands to prevent William of Orange and his fleet and army from setting sail for England. On the anniversary of the Gunpowder Plot, still celebrated in villages like Rusper throughout the land by the burning of effigies of Guido or 'Guy' Fawkes, William landed in the West Country. One by one King James' supporters either fled abroad or came over to William's side. Early in the following year formalities were completed for a joint monarchy of King William III and Queen Mary II. With a new Bill of Rights the gulf between the Whigs and the Tories was narrowed. James II was the last absolute monarch England was ever to see. Some free-thinking and liberal-minded people with an interest in affairs abroad wondered whether the lessons from England's Civil War and the ousting of the last absolute monarch in the person of King James would inspire a desire for change in other countries having absolute monarchs such as was the case with France.

On his return to Rusper Sir John ordered a mass celebration and contributed two pigs and two sheep for the spit. The villagers were to make merry with great enthusiasm. Even Billy was seen to partake in the odd beer or two.

The ousted King James did try and make a comeback to regain his lost throne the following year but he and his army of supporters in Ireland were defeated at the Battle of the Boyne. William's sovereignty was now undisputed across the British Isles. It was the summer of the year 1690 and for most

Protestant Englishmen at least it was a good year. The vast majority of people in Catholic Ireland thought otherwise. King William had good intentions for his Irish people and for religious freedoms but the men with property, influence and the real powers behind the throne were determined to keep those troublesome Irish in their place and they did with cruelty and brutality that was to resonate down the ages.

Chapter 19

Richard Wickham and Billy were sitting out in the yard one fine evening whilst Wickham was taking a break. As usual, Billy was tugging on his pipe; his lined face becoming even more creased as he inhaled his smoking tobacco. Billy's grey hair still had a few flecks of colour. Wickham was neat in appearance but not smart and he was now almost totally without hair. He turned to Billy.

'Running this place is getting too much for us now, Billy, what with Mrs Wickham and myself having never being blessed with children (for Billy it had always been Mrs Wickham and not Elizabeth). 'I have been in discussion with Sir John's new agent, Maynard, and we've agreed that there is no one in Rusper ready and able to take over the running of the Star. I have agreed to stay on another month or two to enable Sir John, or more likely Hugh Maynard, to get someone installed here. They may have to bring someone in from Dorking or even further away.'

'Where will you go and what will you do?' asked Billy.

'Mrs Wickham and myself have a fancy to go and live by the sea. I have never seen the sea and we have saved enough to get by on. Other than cousins who we have not seen for quite some time, I have little in the way of family. Mrs Wickham does have a younger sister living down Brighton way so we are thinking of finding somewhere nearby so that they may visit each other.

'I have put in a good word about your boy James and about how he is capable of tending the horses and running the stable. I know that you like to come in for an hour or two each day, Billy, and I am able to offer you some small consideration for that, but I fear that this will come to an end when the new proprietor is here. Anyway, that is some weeks away yet so let us enjoy each other's company in the meantime and depart as the best of friends.'

'I will miss coming here each day and of course I shall miss our friendship,' said Billy. 'We have seen and heard of so many changes, you and I. Sometimes it seems like one week in a season is just the same as another, but then big things happen that affect us here in Rusper in the same way as they do in London or elsewhere and then we hear about so-called "big things" happening elsewhere and we just continue to go about our daily business as normal.

'Look at the changes that have taken hold of the country. After the war Edward Grimes could not take to the changes and he left for the New World. I hope that things worked out for him. It was a desperate but brave thing to do. He taught me to read the Bible and I will be grateful until my dying day for that. We saw the King come back after Cromwell and then another Catholic king come to the throne and new fears about another civil war, only for him to be replaced by a Dutchman and a Protestant daughter of the Catholic King that we wanted to see the back of. Now you say that you and Mrs Wickham are off to live by the sea. You'll be sailing round the world next!'

He laughed.

'Then may the Lord have mercy on us!' laughed Wickham in turn. 'At least I am too old, or at least I hope I am, to be pressed and forced to go to sea in the navy but then Mrs Wickham may pay to have me pressed so she and her sister can spend all the time chattering and gossiping to each other!'

They both laughed together.

Richard and Mrs Wickham were to leave during the week after Harvest Festival. Before they left, the Wickhams and Billy and his family had one last evening together. Billy and Anne were there of course, as was James and his betrothed Sarah, whose family originally came from Capel way, that being a good walk from Rusper. Billy's children, Sarah and William, were up at Pelham's house and the other two children had moved away and were unable to join in.

The following morning those possessions that the Wickhams decided to take away with them were loaded on to a cart. They had yet to find accommodation down where they were going, so they had decided to take only those personal items of significance and clothing that they obviously needed or items that were of sentimental importance. They would sort out furniture and such things later.

Chapter 20

James and Sarah were to wed on a cold snowy Saturday in February. The wind was coming from the north-west and with the church of St Mary Magdelene being the highest point for miles around they were chilled to the bone during the walk to and from the church. It was not that much warmer inside the church but at least they were out of the wind.

Not this time, though, the privacy of Wickham's private room, but James and his bride and her parents George and Sarah, Billy and Anne and together with Sarah and William having been allowed a half day off from service on the Pelham estate, formed a small but intimate party. They found a corner in the warmth of the Star for comfort and for conversation and a relatively rare opportunity for all to be together and to enjoy each other's company.

Chapter 21

King William departed this world having being killed in a riding accident. Queen Anne, the Protestant-reared daughter of the ousted Catholic King James and cousin to William of Orange had come and gone and, as she survived her own children, the throne passed to the House of Hanover in the shape of Queen Anne's second cousin who became King George I. In reality, as for generations before, these big events outside of the High Weald did little to affect everyday existence and life for ordinary poor working people in Rusper. It was partly for this reason that James and John, the two eldest sons of James the stableman at the Star and Sarah, became determined to escape the tedium and predictability of an existence that was mapped out for them almost from the day that they were born to the grave, if they stayed in Rusper.

The trees continued to disappear despite attempts to revert back to the old ways of good husbandry through coppicing and pollarding. There was still some work to be had at the ironworks, but it was clear that this was no longer at the same level that people knew and understood to have been undertaken a generation earlier.

London was calling to James and John. They wanted to see something of the big city. They were eighteen and seventeen and therefore old enough in their minds to go out into the world beyond the Weald. For the past five years James and John had only ever found irregular and unappealing labouring jobs. Their brother George seemed to be the one interested in following the family tradition of tending horses and working in a stable yard. As far as James and John were concerned, their younger brother was welcome to it. Let London give us a chance, they thought. If the worst did come to the worst, they could seek adventure elsewhere. They decided they would tell their parents one Sunday after supper.

John, although a year younger than his brother, had more spark and was clearly the brighter and the more confident of the two brothers. He had taken more easily than his brother James to his father teaching him how to read and write. A proud tradition, John had been told by his father, and he had his grandfather to thank for it. This facility of reading and writing, he was repeatedly told, would hold him in good stead and would set him apart from others who couldn't read nor write their own name. The one thing James did counsel his children, though, was that they should sometimes be wary of revealing this skill to others.

'There are some men that do not stand for the likes of us ordinary working people being able to read or even write our own names. Those people see us as a threat to them and to their position just because we can read the Bible and write and spell even the simplest of things such as our own names.

'Then there are others who think they should deny education to those whose place in life is but to labour away for others and for whom any degree of learning will just make them unhappy with their lot.'

All five of James' eldest children could read to differing levels of ability corresponding to their ages. No doubt later the three young'uns would take to it when they were old enough.

Supper over, and with their mother clearing things away, John turned to his father.

'Father, mother, you know that we love you, but James and me are not happy here any more. We get work as and when we can, when it's about, but we want more out of life than this. We have been thinking about this for quite some time, and now we are old enough we want to go together to London and see what life is like there and if we can make our own way in the world. We want some adventure. We don't want to be here for the rest of our lives waking up every morning knowing that today is likely to be the same as yesterday and likely to be the same again tomorrow.

'London must have something better to offer. You have taught us to read and write, father, and this is something I would rather be taking advantage of than labouring away down here. If things do not work out then we could always become enlisted men in the army.'

At this their mother protested loudly.

'You will not be joining any army! I will not have you going off somewhere and fighting and getting killed. You should stay here on the Weald. It has been good enough for our families for generations and it is good enough for you.'

Their father decided on a different tack.

'Your mother is right. You are not going into the army, not least because you might get killed. You do not know where you may end up, when you may get your next decent meal or even when you will get paid, not to mention when you may be given time to spend money even when you get it. Get that idea right out of your heads now the pair of you!

'As for the rest, where will you go in London? You know no one. You have no introductions. Who is going to give two bumpkins from the country a second look let alone a job, and come to that where do you think you are going to live? Tell me that, eh! Your Sunday best here is likely to stick out like a sore thumb. You do not stand a chance. I guarantee you will be back here within a month expecting your mother and me to pick up the pieces of your folly. Stay here sons. This is where you belong.'

It was James' time to chime in.

'We don't want to upset you both but this is something we

must try. Can you not see that? If we promise not to join the army, would that set your minds at rest? John has always been more clever than me and maybe he deserves a chance to see what he can do away from here. If we cannot find work within a month or if we are unable to support ourselves then we promise to return. What say you to that? If we go together then we will not be alone and we can look out for each other.'

Their father now had some more sympathy for what they had to say but was not prepared to let things go at that.

'And what do you expect to live on? Air and water alone won't keep body and soul together.'

'That's right,' Sarah chimed in. 'You two haven't got two beans to rub together.'

'We have saved some,' said John. 'Can you not see that this is something we must do. If we try and fail then all very well we will come back here and do our best but if we don't go how can we ever be happy? We will always be wondering what might have happened if we'd tried.'

'And when did you intend to set out on this ridiculous idea of yours?' asked Sarah.

'Just before first light in the morning,' answered John.

Sure enough they did. They gathered their belongings together before going to bed. His father came up to James when John was out of earshot.

'Son, you are the level-headed one out of the two of you. You must not let your mother know that I am giving this to you, but here are two sovereigns, altogether all I have ever managed to save all through my life. You must spend the money only if you absolutely have to. If you end up being away for a month or more you must write to us. If you cannot get someone to deliver to the Star then write through the Talbot in Cuckfield and they will pass it on to me at the Star as we still have a posting-house connection. I am relying upon you, James, to look out for your brother. He may be bright but you are older than him and should have more common sense,

73

although I must say I don't think either of you is showing an ounce of common sense between you at the moment!'

James and John were already on the road leading out of Rusper as the sky was getting brighter in the east. They would follow one of the trails through the ever-shrinking woodland and pick up the road to Dorking and then on towards London. Neither had ever been as far from home as Dorking. London was another world away.

Chapter 22

James and John were into the second day of their journey having slept the night rather fitfully in the open. It was approaching the middle of the morning and they had been walking since the first signs of daylight. From time to time a lone rider or a cart would pass them in either direction without a word said. That morning they had yet to come upon anyone else on foot.

They came to a stretch in the road where the trees on either side met in the middle. It was considerably cooler out of the sunlight and under the shade of the trees, although James and John were warm enough from their exertions. The cooler feel was welcome.

Then suddenly to one side of them came a stirring and some movement amongst the bushes. Startled, James and John came to a halt and turned to face the disturbance. A man emerged, and from the look of his fine shirt and breeches, a gentleman at that. He was holding the top of his left arm with his right hand and was unsteady on his feet. John was first to react. Dropping his bundle he moved towards him.

'Sir, what has happened? Can we be of help?'

'You might well ask,' replied the gentleman. 'I have been

set upon by two villains. Footpads. They jumped out in front of me waving sticks and shouting. My horse reared up and threw me, causing me to fall on my shoulder. They then pulled me into there ...'

He nodded in the direction from which he had emerged.

'... taking my purse and even pulling my jacket from me. If you two fellows think you can take advantage of me then you will be disappointed. I have nothing but the clothes I stand in, unless it's my boots you are after.'

'You need have no fear of us,' retorted James. 'My brother asked if we can be of assistance. We have not seen your horse and I doubt if it would have run off into the wood so it must have turned back in the direction you came. If you can walk then we can help look for the animal in case it has stopped nearby. From the way that your arm is hanging down, you will need a doctor to set your shoulder right. Now, do you want our help and our company or do you want to wait for the next person to come along?'

The gentleman could now see that he had caused offence. He spoke this time more gently.

'I would be grateful for your help and, if I have caused offence by what I said, then I'm sorry. My shoulder gives me so much pain when I move I cannot walk with it. Back that way about two miles on there is a small hamlet and some sort of an inn. If there is no sign of my horse then will one of you go back and bring a cart or something for me? I will then be in your debt.'

Without further prompting James said: 'Then I will go for help and John will stay with you. A few hours delay in our journey is of little consequence and I do not want it on my conscience that we left an injured and unfortunate man unaided when we could have done something. I suggest you try and walk a little way so that we are out from under these trees and in the open. The two of you can wait for me then. I doubt if those villains that set upon you will bother us again.

It would be lean pickings indeed if they did, for we have little of value.'

As James walked ahead to find help, John and the gentleman followed behind slowly in order to cause as little discomfort to the gentleman as possible. When clear of the trees and out in the warming sunshine John and the gentleman settled down to await James' return.

'May I ask where you have come from and where you and your brother are headed?' enquired the gentleman.

'We are from off the Weald, Rusper to be exact. We have decided to try our luck in London,' replied John.

'Rusper! I know it well. My uncle is Sir Clive Pelham. I was on my way to visit my cousins. London, you say? You are wanting to try your luck in London? You will not find it easy. There is work there but there are also many labourers not working who have come to the city from the country. You may well find it hard to find regular work.'

'Our sights are set higher than that, Sir' replied John. 'I would like to find a position as a clerk or something similar. If we were content with labouring we might just as well have stayed in Rusper.'

'A clerk you say?' said the gentleman. 'Then for the second time I might have reached the wrong conclusion about you. Forgive me for saying but it is though unusual to come across ordinary-looking fellows who can read and write.'

'My father taught us and our grandfather taught him,' said John proudly. 'My grandfather ran the stables on your uncle's estate and it was a puritan who taught him to read so that my grandfather could read the Bible for himself.'

'So, your grandfather probably worked for my great uncle and here today you have done my family yet another service,' replied the gentleman. 'It may be I can do something for you in return for your trouble and kindness. When we get to what passes for civilisation out here I can write for you a letter of introduction to one of my uncle's managers. I can ask him to offer you and your brother a position – on a trial basis, mind you. It will then be up to you to make the best of it.'

'Oh, sir that would be wonderful!' exclaimed John. 'That is all I ask in life. To be given the chance to make something of myself.'

They lapsed into silence for a while. Then the gentleman started up again.

'So, you have family in Rusper? Do any of them now work for my uncle?' he asked.

'My brother helps in the stables and my sister works inside the house. My father James Weller runs the stables at the Star,' John replied.

'Then, when I get to Rusper I shall send word to your brother and your sister explaining how you helped me and that I have given you and your brother a letter of introduction so that you may find employment. I am sure that will set their minds at rest.'

'Thank you for that, sir. Yes, my mother in particular was most anxious about us leaving for London. Both James and myself will do our very best to make our family proud and we will not let you down either as you are making all this possible.'

They then fell back into silence again. The occasional rider and cart passed them by, coming from the direction of the Weald carrying goods from the ironworks or timber, and carts headed the other way carrying anything that there was a market for. It was well into the afternoon before James returned with a horse-drawn cart and its owner. James reported that he had seen no sign of Master Pelham's horse. John, James and Master Pelham climbed into the back of the cart. There being no doctor at the small hamlet, the cart owner, on the promise of handsome payment later and the added assurance of the family name of Pelham, took them a few miles further on to the village of Warwick, still on the road to London, but a place John and James had never even heard of.

Master Pelham took a room at the King William inn. A doctor was sent for to reset his dislocated shoulder. He ate alone but he did send out a meal for John and James together with the promised letter of introduction addressed to Mr Hammond Radley at The Minories Coffee House in the City of London.

Two days later the two boys arrived at the door of the Coffee House and handed over their precious letter of introduction for Mr Radley's attention. A message came back to them that Radley was not prepared to see them, but instead the letter was returned to them with instructions that they go to an office a few hundred yards away where they were to give Hammond Radley's compliments to a Mr Dawkins.

Clearly put out, and with obvious reluctance, Mr Dawkins ordered them to report for work at eight o'clock prompt the following morning. Now, all they had to do was to find accommodation. The result was in the early forfeiture of one of their father's sovereigns as rent in advance was demanded. This was not something the brothers had allowed for. Still, they had enough of their own money to buy food to eat.

Chapter 23

The weeks went by and the weeks turned into months. Originally both James and John had been set the task of copying documents. From their first few weeks' wages they bought clothing more suitable to their position as clerks than their previous country-style Sunday best.

After the passing of the first few nervous weeks at work, John began to show that he was interested in more exacting work. Mr Wyatt set, organised and checked John's work and set him more and more challenging tasks. As a consequence,

John was also was shown how to draw up and work out ledgers. This is when John first became more aware of what the East India Company was involved in. James continued, as before, with copying documents.

London was a place of awe and wonderment to James and John. They never knew that so many people could be in the same place at the same time. Many times did they get lost in the ramshackle parts of the City, but some of the sweeping avenues and streets with their stone buildings never ceased to amaze them.

They were not tempted by the more bawdy revelling side of life, and they saw much of that particularly amongst the poor who surely must have been the least able to find the money to indulge themselves. For James in particular he found the seedier side of London life distasteful and he was slowly becoming more disillusioned and bored with his routine document-copying work.

Chapter 24

John and James no longer worked in the same office. Indeed, they were now not even in the same building. In the almost two years that they had been in London John had seized every opportunity to excel and impress, often working late well into the evening. James was beginning to tire of it all. He missed the family and, to his surprise, he was even missing Rusper. He stayed because of John and because he had promised his father that he would look out for his younger brother.

One evening, John returned earlier than usual to their room, bursting through the door, out of breath, but obviously delighted about something.

'James, James you won't believe what I have been offered!

The Company have offered me the chance to go to India. They want Englishmen out there before, as everyone says, we are at war with France over India. India! Me and India! It is beyond belief!'

James was dumbstruck.

'James? Did you not hear what I said?'

'Of course I heard you,' said James. 'Half of Clerkenwell heard you and I suppose by your manner you are intending to go to India. If that is what you want, then go. At least I won't have to look out for you any more. What have you told them? What about our parents? What are they going to think? I don't think I know you any more, John. You have changed and I have changed. I don't want this life any more. I miss the Weald and maybe now I that I can show that I can do something more than just labouring, I can return satisfied.'

'Of course I have said yes, James!' John cried. 'A young man from the Weald does not get this sort of opportunity offered to him and then turn it down. That would be madness. My ship sails within a month. If you miss the Weald that much then serve your notice and let's go home together so I can say farewell to all our family.'

They were to set off for Rusper the following week. James had served his notice and John had permission to take two weeks out without receiving pay. They were not to walk this time. They would ride in style and hire two posting horses. John could not wait to see the look on his father's face as he and James arrived at the Star unannounced and on horseback too. James was just pleased to be going home but was worried about what opportunities there would be for him. He had a reference to say that he was a good time keeper and that his document copying was to an acceptable standard, but this was not exactly a glowing commendation. On the other hand, he said to himself, how many people down on the Weald could say that they had worked for two years for a company in the City?

The ride to Rusper was uneventful and they did take a room for the night along the way. John's vision of the look of surprise on his father's face as they rode into the yard at the Star went unsatisfied. It was late evening when they arrived at the Star. Their father had gone home and it was their younger brother George staying on to tend any late arrivals that was the one to be surprised by the nature of their arrival.

Leaving the horses at the stables, they went on ahead of George. Thanks to his brothers, George now had some more work to do.

'Shall we knock first or just walk in?' asked John. 'Perhaps we should have given notice of our coming.'

'It's our home, John. We shouldn't see the need to knock when calling on our own.'

They knocked anyway, but opened the door rather than wait for their knock to be answered. The scene was like a tableau, with everyone standing like statues. It was their mother Sarah who reacted first.

'You two! My boys! Just look at you dressed up all fine. Why could you not tell us you were coming? Giving your poor old mother such a shock like this. Oh, just come here both of you!'

Sarah tried to hug both of her sons at the same time and she started to cry.

'Welcome home boys,' was all that James the father could say. Of their brothers and sisters only not-so-little Anne was there but she was soon to be joined by George when he had finished at the stables.

Of course, there were lots and questions about what John and James had been up to. There was a total lack of comprehension when John told them of his forthcoming adventure to India. He had to tell them at least three times before it all sunk in and they were sure he was not spinning them a yarn. For their part John and James wanted to hear about what was happening with their other brothers and sisters. James, but not John, also wanted to know about what had happened locally since they had left.

It was getting late when George asked James a question. He still looked up to his oldest brother even if John was the smartest.

'Tell me, what was the worst thing you saw in London?'

'The worst thing?' started James. 'Well there is the filth and the stench and the poverty, and the poor that cannot find work, and the drunkenness. That is bad enough but then you see some wonderful things. If we had not had those opportunities presented to us following our chance meeting with Master Pelham I don't know if I could have stuck at it. As for the worst things, we saw, I don't know if Annie or your mother will thank us for telling of them.'

'Go on,' urged Anne 'I'm not your baby sister any more. I may even be getting married soon.'

'Very well then,' answered James. 'Without doubt, and this is all beyond my comprehension, it is the scene and the spectacle that is created by the hangings and what goes on around them.

'Imagine this. At Tyburn and at the Old Bailey there would be twenty or more people standing in line down the middle of this long tall wagon. They are on their way to be hanged. The prisoners would have their hands tied together in front of them so that they might raise their hats to the cheering crowds as the wagon passes along its way from the prison to the place of their deaths. The one and only time your brother and me saw this happen, and we didn't have the stomach to see it again, the condemned were singing and making jests to entertain the crowds that had come to watch them die. Some of the prisoners were accompanied along the way by their friends to help make the event even more merry. They call all this "gallows humour".

'The wagon then pulls up under the gibbet. The prisoners already have a halter around their necks and the hangman will then start at one end of the wagon and move along down the line of prisoners, attaching the halters to the gibbet. When this is all done the wagon driver will then move the horses and the wagon away and the prisoners are left hanging there from the gibbet and everyone is cheering ... well, everyone except the prisoners. They have finally gone quiet.

'Then friends or relatives, or a stranger if he has been paid, will pull on a prisoner's feet or smash a large piece of wood against a prisoner's chest to hasten their going. The unfortunate ones are just left there to dangle. They die hard and take a long time doing it.'

'This is a gruesome picture indeed,' said James the father. 'We are no strangers to hangings here on the Weald but unless the person sentenced to die is of the most horrible kind, or his crimes are that terrible, it is not a cause for celebration.'

'Wait until I tell my friends,' George blurted out.

Everyone gave him such a look that he wished he had kept his thoughts to himself.

John was to stay for the week before returning to London and then leaving on his great adventure. His parting was particularly emotional. His parents, brothers and sisters knew that they would never see John again.

For James at least he was able to secure some office work at Pelham's ironworks. His good character and the fact that he had come to the aid of Sir Clive's nephew ensured this. As for the rest of the family, James the father stayed on at the Star as long as he could, but in the latter years it was George that did most of the work and eventually assumed full responsibility for running the stables. William stayed at the stables on the Pelham estate but did not have control of them. Sarah continued to work in the Pelham household but never achieved her goal of being a lady's personal maid. For the others, they lived and died in much the same way as the generations before them.

Part III

Time to Leave the Weald Behind

Chapter 1

And twenty years on

George Weller, stableman at the Star, had courted and married Sarah Short from Newdigate some years before at her parish church of St Peter. They had met at one May Day celebration and things moved on from there. The walk between Rusper and Newdigate could be done in just over an hour so they were able to meet during their courtship on Sunday afternoons and occasionally at other times, particularly during the longer hours of daylight in the summer.

Their two sons, James, and then George, were finding work as lads at Pelham's ironworks. Like many families, it was as if it was only right and proper to continue passing the same names down through the generations.

On a clear night for the past two days there had been a strange and bright light in the sky. In the village people did not know what to make of it. At first a blur and then a more distinct light with a dusty sort of tail behind it. It was approaching the middle of March and there was still a distinct nip in the night air. It was almost dark when a rider entered the yard at the Star. George came out to greet him and held the reins as the rider dismounted.

'Good evening, sir,' said George. 'You have done well to reach us before it is completely dark and with that infernal light in the sky these days who knows what devilry and mischief is about. It must be a bad omen of worse things to come, as if things are not bad enough hereabouts. I will tend your horse, sir. Why don't you go into the warmth and find some supper?'

I will, I will,' said the stranger. Having dismounted and moved more into the light from the lantern by the stable door he was obviously a man of quality and a gentleman.

87

'That light you talk of has nothing to do with the devil or the underworld and it is pure superstition to think it is a sign of coming misfortune. Let me assure you that there are noted men of science that can explain this object and my father was associated with a man called Edmund Halley who predicted many years ago that this object was going to appear in our skies again almost to the week. In fact there are ancient writings that record regular visits from this object that we call a comet. Be at rest man. We should be in awe at yet another example of God's work and not in fear of it.'

Upon which the stranger headed for the warmth inside.

Chapter 2

George was not alone in worrying about the future for his sons. Despite the conversation with the gentleman at the Star a few weeks previously, George was not convinced that this supposed scientific and natural phenomenon was anything other than bad news and a sign of worse things to come.

In common with other iron-making communities across the Weald, Rusper folk were aware that new iron-making techniques had been found using a new material called 'coke' that was produced from coal. From what they had heard, this new method was far more efficient compared with iron making based upon the use of charcoal to fire the furnaces. There was no coal on this part of the Weald and it was plain for all to see that the trees were disappearing. Charcoal burning was being carried out farther and farther from the ironworks than before as local supplies were becoming less and less as the area of woodland continued to diminish.

The effects were felt by everyone and not just the charcoal burners and ironmasters. The costs of wood for cooking and for keeping warm in the winter had increased at the same time as the price of grain and bread also increased. At certain times of the year when food costs were highest, families and individuals in town and country alike fell on particularly hard times. The situation in Rusper was no different from elsewhere. Often both the able-bodied who were unable to find work and the so-called 'impotent poor' such as elderly widows who were also unable to work and to support themselves had to call upon the Parish Overseers to provide poor relief to buy the food and wood needed to exist.

One day, as the family of George and Sarah and the boys James and his younger brother George, or rather the soon to be young men, had gathered for an evening meal, George the father cleared his throat and began.

'Boys, I worry for the future. I worry for the future for folk here on the Weald but in particular I worry for your future.'

'Why should that be, father?' asked James.

'You must have heard it yourself from other workers that further up the country they have found ways to make iron without using charcoal, that makes the whole business bigger, more efficient and costs less than it costs here. They are doing something to coal that means they can use coal rather than wood to fire the furnaces. If iron making on the Weald was to scale down or cease altogether, where would that leave people? How would they be able to earn a living for their families? James you are the eldest. What I want you to do is to come and work with me at the Star. I will ask Mr Maynard if he will agree to take you on at less than a full wage. You can then learn from me how to tend horses and maybe this will stand you in good stead in the future. To help persuade Mr Maynard you will also have to agree to do other things to help him run the Star. This means that there will be less money coming in but I think we should prepare for the future rather than wait and see what happens.'

'Your father is right, James,' added Sarah. 'You will want to get married yourself one day and have your own family. Start thinking now as to how you may provide for them. If and when you do I hope that your marriage will be as happy as mine is with your father. As for you, George, I don't know what we can do. You will just have to stay where you are for as long as you can.'

James had been staring at his empty plate. Then he looked up and spoke to his father.

'There has been some talk up and around the ironworks, father,' said James. 'People have heard about new ways of iron making and do worry for the future. I will not miss the ironworks but then I do not fancy working for less than a full wage not least because this will affect the four of us. I will though take your advice, father.'

'That is settled then,' said George. 'I will speak to Mr Maynard tomorrow and try and persuade him to take you on.'

'Let's change the subject,' said George. 'It came to me again today. I wonder whatever happened to my uncle John, the one that went to India. I think my father only ever received one communication from him since he left England all those years ago.'

Britain and France had been at war. First in North America and then, as George's uncle John had predicted, in India. The question on everyone's mind now was when would England and France next go head-to-head and fight a European war on land and at sea. France was after all the old enemy and always would be. Never to be trusted even in peacetime.

George continued.

'Did uncle John fall ill? Was he caught up in any fighting with the French? Then maybe things went well for him. We will never know. Whatever happened he must be dead now by any estimation. If he is alive today he must be well into his seventies.'

Young George did not sleep very well that night. He lay there awake recalling his father's words from earlier and wondering what the future held for him if he was thrown out of work as would be more than likely to happen.

Chapter 3

James did take up a position for a few years at the Star on less than a full wage. He learnt what he could from his father but James was always determined to find a full living wage elsewhere. His father's advice had been sound. James had become associated with working with his father who had the position of stableman at the Star. On that basis and with that reputation, James was to obtain work at Cudworth Manor House in Newdigate.

George, on the other hand, had been one of the lucky ones. Some iron making had continued at Pelham's works owing largely to the seven years of fighting involving Britain, France and a number of other countries that George had not even heard of, let alone worked out where they were. As far as he was concerned, it was something going on in Europe and he was grateful to still have a job. George was now betrothed and he was sitting in the Five Bells Inn in Newdigate with his brother James.

'James, Ruth and me have settled on a wedding date towards the end of May,' George announced. 'It should be a beautiful spring day and an ideal day to get married. I would like you to be the witness at our wedding here in Newdigate.'

'Of course, George, I will be delighted. What about Ruth's family? Who is coming?' asked James.

'Well, brother of mine,' said George, 'only her father William Palmer from over Capel way. I am sure I told you that Ruth's mother died giving birth to her and it was her aunt that helped her father to raise and care for her. Now her aunt too has gone. Dear Ruth has not had things easy. Anyway it will be just our parents, us two and Ruth and her father at the wedding.

'Here is more good news. I have got work at Ewoods ironworks here in Newdigate. Things here may be not as big as at Pelham's but it is time to get away from Rusper, and Ruth can also be nearer to her father in Capel if we rent a place here. Now that it seems there may soon be peace for the time being in Europe. Then if the ironworks on the Weald are to go then it matters little whether I am at Ewood's or at Pelham's. If I just worry about what may happen then I will end up doing nothing. If the worst comes to the worst, at least Ruth and me can be poor together.

'What about you getting married, James? Any secrets you have been keeping from us?' asked George.

'Nothing yet,' was the noncommittal reply.

George and Ruth married as planned in May on what proved to be a beautiful spring day. By the time George and Ruth had their first child, a daughter Rebecca late the following year, George was finding it more and more difficult to find steady work. The ironworks business had indeed dropped right off and such business as there was involved only the making and casting of small items for everyday use and farming tools and implements.

Ruth was heavily pregnant when, at last, James got round to marrying Mary Wright after an on-off courtship of almost a year.

George and Ruth's joy at the birth of their first son was short lived. He was a sickly child and they arranged for his baptism when he was just three days old. They called the infant James and the poor mite died the following day, but at least he was in God's grace.

Chapter 4

The following year was another bad year for George and Ruth and for young Rebecca. They found themselves before the Parish Overseers seeking relief. As was the usual custom, they were to queue up with other hopefuls outside the vestry after Sunday Divine service.

'For the record you will confirm that you are George Weller of Newdigate?' George was asked.

'Yes, sirs, I am George Weller.'

'You will explain your status and situation and why you think you should be a burden on this parish.'

'Sirs, I was baptised in Rusper exactly thirty years ago and there I worked for the Pelham family ironworks. In May of 1762 I married my wife Ruth here in Newdigate and I secured a job at Ewood's ironworks. Now there is no work for me there and I have no means to support my wife and our daughter, Rebecca. I am at my wit's end sirs. I just cannot find work and have no money for food or wood or for rent and my daughter has no shoes and mine are beyond repair.

'We have lost an infant son after just four days through our miserable condition. I find myself without hope and in desperate need and to my shame that is why I am before you today. The harvest is in and there is now even less work available and winter will soon be upon us.'

The examination was fair and the Churchwarden and Overseers were persuaded that without aid the family would surely perish. The Overseers granted to George on that occasion a sum of money to pay for the rent of their cottage and to enable them to buy food and wood for fuel and even the shoes that he and his daughter so desperately needed.

More often than not George would have to do some work of benefit to the parish such as clearing roadside ditches. After all, it was the richer people within the Parish that the

93

Overseer collected the rate from, so it was only right and proper to make them work for whatever they were awarded and to the improvement of the parish.

Even so what they were granted did not go far and it seemed that they always went to bed hungry, but George and Ruth tried to ensure that young Rebecca did not cry through hunger. Ruth had become thin and the following year she gave birth to another boy that they baptised George. He too was to die young. George was again to find himself before the Overseers pleading for relief. Sometimes it was for money or for bread or even for a pair of boots to keep the weather out.

There was little that James could do to help his brother. He was the sole earner these days as Mary had produced two daughters Sarah and Mary in quick succession.

Chapter 5

James and Mary were to fare better than James' brother George. They were to have four children. First, two daughters, Sarah and Mary, and then two sons Daniel and William. James brought in just enough to provide money for rent, food, fuel and when absolutely essential clothing for the family, and it distressed him greatly that he could not provide for his brother and family as well. William was the youngest of James' children and an unexpected late addition to the family, there being some eight years' difference in the ages of Daniel and William. William was not to know his uncle George as he was to die at a relatively young age in the same year that William was born.

Daniel was the apple of his father's eye. James worked long hours and was determined to continue the proud family tradition of being able to read and write.

'Daniel, I want you to ask to join the choir. I have heard

you sing in church and when you are in a joyous mood. You will respect my wishes in this regard.'

'Yes, father.'

'This is no passing whim of mine, son. I want you to take a place in the Free School. There is a limit to both the time that we have for me to be able to show you reading and writing and you will learn faster and better by going to school.'

'Yes, father.'

The Free School, like other establishments of its type, was there solely for the benefit for education of the poor so that they should learn to read and write and learn those other good lessons of importance to young people of their class and station in life. Through increased income from a trust comprising property and investments, the number of pupils that could be taken in at the Newdigate Free School during any one year had now increased to fifteen.

James and Daniel were waiting their turn to see the Overseer of the Poor, who was also the schoolmaster as well as the Parish Constable. James was able to read a memorial in the schoolhouse.

'*This schoolhouse was endowed by the Reverend George Steer Rector of this parish from 1610–1662 for the education of children of the poor.*'

Beneath this memorial was another.

'*This memorial is dedicated to the memory of and by the wife of George Booth who established a foundation for the benefit of education of the poor of this Parish. May God bless and care for his soul.*'

James and Daniel were called in by Mr Thomas Chart.

'We will waste as little time as possible. I know you, boy, from the choir. I see your family in church regularly.'

Looking directly at Daniel, Chart continued:

'Why should I spend my time teaching you to read and write?'

James answered on his son's behalf.

'Mr Chart, sir, I have had the good fortune to have some

ability to read and write. I see these qualities as important for my son as I would want him to be educated enough to be an advantage to his employer and to reduce the chance of him falling upon hard times.'

Chart looked over the top of his glasses at them.

'I want the boy to answer this time,' he said. 'Will you promise to work hard and to attend school every day unless you are too sick to get out of bed or you are required to take part in the choir? It is a privilege to attend this school and I only want children that are prepared to listen to my instruction and to work hard. Is this you?'

'Oh, yes, sir,' replied Daniel. 'I will work very hard, sir.'

Turning to James, Chart said, 'I see you in church, which is one thing, but do you promise that at home you will say grace before meals and that you will raise your family and conduct yourself in a godly fashion?'

'Yes, sir, I do,' replied James.

Daniel was forever grateful for what he took away from the school. Difficult as times were, with a number of people in Newdigate being unable to find work, Mr Chart had installed himself as schoolmaster and he was considered by most to be a man of some learning. Chart also took it upon himself and considered it to be his Christian duty, but also perhaps to his personal satisfaction, to try and find positions for those pupils who took their learning seriously.

In Daniel's case, he was to be found work as a servant for William Humphrey of Charlwood, an adjacent parish.

Chapter 6

Daniel could not be happier. He was seventeen, desperately in love and with a kind and considerate employer in Mr Humphrey for over two years now.

Daniel and his cousin ... well, his second cousin ... Sarah had always been very close as children. They sought each other's company whenever they could whilst they were growing up. Now they sought each other's company because they loved each other so much – too much, in fact, as they could not resist the temptation to become intimate. They knew that their parents would be angry and disappointed but they needed their consent to get married. Sarah thought she was going to have a baby. At first there was a lot of shouting and outrage that they should have let themselves go and now had to face up to the consequences, but after the initial upset both sets of parent agreed to give their consent for Daniel and Sarah to be married.

Daniel thought that Mr Humphrey may take exception to him marrying so young, particularly as Daniel had lived in since joining Mr Humphrey's service and there was the issue about what would happen when Sarah had the baby.

Whilst Daniel did not like to deceive Mr and Mrs Humphrey, after talking things over with his father James and then with Sarah, he decided to tell Mr Humphrey about the wedding plans but not about the forthcoming baby. This was just as well, as it turned out Sarah had been mistaken and she was not carrying a baby after all.

Mr or Mrs Humphrey could have proved awkward about the marriage but this was not in their nature and in any event they and their two young daughters Sarah and Jenny had other things to worry about.

Mr Humphrey was not at all well. Daniel did not have much money put away, but with a little help from his father, and with the agreement of the Humphrey family, he and Sarah were able to rent a cottage just a few minutes away from the Humphrey residence, and so Daniel moved out. The few sticks of furniture they acquired were very basic but at least they could start their married life together under their own roof.

Within two months of them marrying, poor old William Humphrey passed away quietly in his sleep. No one ever really knew what was wrong with him. Daniel was assured that for the time being the family still needed his services. There were consequences, however. Now that Mr Humphrey had died and, given that he was the one who had been responsible for giving Daniel a position in his household, Daniel, and by extension Sarah, needed now to be termed as 'settled' in Charlwood. To this end Daniel had to approach the Overseers of the Poor in Charlwood arguing his case on the basis that he had been in domestic service for over one year.

Daniel returned home after being before the Overseers. He kissed and held Sarah in his arms as soon as he was through the door. He gently pushed her away and holding up a folded piece of paper said:

'Well, my love. They have given me the settlement certificate confirming that we now can legally stay in Charlwood.'

'What does it say? Tell me,' she asked. 'Read it to me.'

Unfolding the paper Daniel started to read out loud for Sarah.

'It says – "We the Churchwardens and Overseers of the Poor of the Parish of Charlwood in the county of Surrey do own and acknowledge Daniel Weller late servant of William Humphrey of Charlwood aforesaid to be legally settled in the said Parish of Charlwood in the County of Surrey aforesaid and we do promise and agree to save harmless and keep indemnified the Churchwardens and Overseers of the poor of the Parish of Newdigate in the County aforesaid from all costs or charges which they or any of them may sustain on account of the aforesaid Daniel Weller. Witness our hands this 27th day of March 1791 George Jackson Churchwarden, David Constable and William Holliday Overseers". There. What do you think of that?'

'Oh, Danny,' said Sarah 'You can read all them words like that. You are so clever. I can hardly understand what it is they are saying.'

'I have often said, my love, that I can teach you to read and to write your name but you will have none of it.'

'I know you have,' said Sarah. 'I just don't see what use it is for me. You can read for both of us. That will do me.'

And so it was for the next few years Daniel continued to work for the widow Humphrey's household and Daniel and Sarah lived in bliss in the simple cottage that they called home. On one occasion Sarah thought she was again going to have a baby but this proved to be a false alarm and on another occasion she was to miscarry but despite these disappointments they thought they were the happiest couple in the whole world.

One day Mrs Humphrey summoned Daniel, the cook Mrs Tidy and the parlour maid Margaret Sumner into her presence.

'I have to let you all go,' started Mrs Humphrey. 'I am taking my daughters away from here to be properly educated as young ladies. It will have to be to London and other fashionable places in this country given the terrible things going on in revolutionary France.

'I do not know how long we will be away from here but it will be for some time so I won't be needing you, Mrs Tidy. Nor you, Weller, but my friends Mr and Mrs Charrington in Leigh are prepared to take you on until we return as they have told me that they are interested in taking on some extra help. My dear late husband took a shine to you and you have served us well and faithfully and you have that pretty young wife of yours to look after. That is the best that I can do for you.

'As for you, Sumner, I can pay for you to come in once a week to keep the place clean and clear of dust.

'We will be away next week. So, would you, Weller, arrange for our transport to London. Perhaps your father can be of assistance there. That is all. Please now go about your business.'

Daniel expressed his thanks to Mrs Humphrey for her kindness and consideration before leaving the room. Mrs Tidy had a face like thunder and did not speak to anyone for the rest of the day. Her pots and pans said it all for her as she moved about the kitchen making much noise.

Daniel was not to see them again after they left in their carriage the following week.

Chapter 7

Leigh is another parish adjoining Newdigate but to the north, whereas Charlwood lies to the south-east, Rusper to the south but a slightly longer distance away from Newdigate than Charlwood. Daniel and Sarah moved to Leigh but this time without feeling the need to seek a settlement certificate as they intended to return to Charlwood.

Given their previous disappointments, Sarah had held back from telling Daniel that she believed once again that she was with child. It was only when she was absolutely certain that she told her husband. As Daniel went to kiss her neck and put his arm around her, she said: 'Danny dear, I think you will have to learn to be patient unless you want to risk us losing another chance for a baby. Don't look so surprised. You should know what you have been up to!'

'Oh my love,' said Daniel. 'Can we be certain this time? Boy or girl, I don't mind, then we can be a family just like everyone else around us.'

'There is no doubt this time, Danny. I just need to ensure that I hold on to it this time.'

They were so full of joy and love when, at the beginning of May, that time of the year associated with love and romance and the beginning of summer warmth Sarah gave birth to a beautiful baby boy.

On a hot July day the baby was baptised as 'Daniel' at Leigh parish church. The event was the cause for quite a family reunion. Although the infant Daniel was oblivious to who was there and what was going on, he was in the good company of his grandparents James and Mary Weller, his aunt Mary and her husband Benjamin Lucas and his uncle William. On Sarah's side of the family were her parents James and Hannah Weller and her brother Peter. When they had finished in the church they all found a place under the shade of some trees to share some food and to talk the afternoon away.

James – that is, Daniel's father James and not Sarah's father James – had borrowed a horse and cart to take the party from and then back to Newdigate. Benjamin Lucas piped up.

'You Wellers like to confuse everyone, don't you? I mean, look at you. We have amongst our small company two James and two Marys and now two Daniels and if you include Mary's sister who is not here we have two Sarah Wellers as well. Give this poor lad a chance for heaven's sake! By all means keep to his baptised name but can't we give him another name as well? You lot might know who you are,' he said with a grin, 'but for the rest of us mortals it is not that easy.'

Everyone had a suggestion, but out of all of this came finally 'Sam'. This was to stay with him for the rest of his life.

Daniel had forced himself not to think about the consequences of the news that he had received the previous day that Mrs Humphrey was not to return to Charlwood. She had followed her husband to the grave. The Humphrey daughters Sarah and Jenny were not yet of an age or a position to return to and run the house in Charlwood. The house was to remain empty and Daniel, Sarah and now baby Sam were reliant upon Daniel's continued service to the Charringtons.

Chapter 8

'Sam' was growing fast and even at this young age it was clear that he would develop into a strong fellow. The Charringtons had organised a family gathering to see in the new century. Permission had been given for the staff and their close family to hold their own celebration in the servants' quarters from ten o'clock. After that time the 'family' would tend to their own needs and serve their own drinks and refreshments. Just after midnight the Master and his Lady came downstairs. Everyone fell into respectful silence.

'My husband and I just wanted to come down and wish you a Happy New Year,' said Mrs Charrington.

Then she added rather cryptically:

'We are at the start of a new century and no doubt we will see a number of changes. For this reason I want to wish you all the very best for the future. Please carry on and enjoy yourselves. We will be taking breakfast an hour later than normal tomorrow, but in all other respects I expect the house to be maintained and run as normal so I suggest you do not leave it too late before you go to your beds.'

Over the coming weeks Daniel could sense that there was some tension 'upstairs' between members of the family. He did not know what was troubling them at first but it was soon to become clear.

Chapter 9

News was spreading around Leigh and the surrounding communities that would put their very existence at risk. Enclosure, long affecting other country areas, was now coming to their part of the Weald. The land around these parts, even with the aid of the new habit of liming intended to improve yields, was still not good. Nevertheless, moving away from strip farming or creating larger parcels of land were seen as ways for growing more crops and for landowners to make more money. The word was that the Duke of Norfolk was on the move, as had previous Dukes been before him.

First to go would be the common land from which ordinary folk could gather tinder and wood for their fires or even graze animals if they were fortunate enough to possess any. The Pelham family also was aggressively looking to acquire more land and had no intention of losing out to the Duke of Norfolk when it came to acquisitions. Pelham's iron-making activities had continued to diminish further and were now being conducted at a basic level only.

It was clear to Daniel and other intelligent or observant people that the likes of the Charrington family were to be squeezed and pressured into selling land either to Pelham or to the Duke of Norfolk. The tension in the family that Daniel had observed must obviously have been caused by the need to decide who to sell to and how much land would they let go. If they stood out against selling any land, then there was no guarantee that they would not be forced to sell if a private Act of Parliament was passed and the majority of other landowners in the area were in favour of sale for enclosure. In the end the Charringtons opted for sale of a considerable part of their land to the Duke of Norfolk. Whilst the sale would bring in an immediate income, the consequences for the Charrington family in the longer term would be for a reduced return on their estate. They would need to follow that old adage 'cut your coat to suit your cloth'.

The act of enclosure was to bring hardship to many both through the loss of the use of common land and less work being there for agricultural labourers. For Daniel and Sarah and for young Sam the consequences were indeed grave. Daniel was very worried about Sarah. She was frightfully unwell and carrying a high temperature and sweating profusely at the same time.

Daniel was one of two other staff to be told by Mrs Charrington that their services were no longer required and they had been given a week in notice. At least in Daniel's case Mrs Charrington promised a reference to the effect that he had come to her on high recommendation and had performed in a satisfactory fashion during his time with the Charrington household.

Chapter 10

Daniel's beloved and beautiful young wife succumbed to her fever. She was only twenty-five and now Sam was without his mother when he was only five years old. Daniel was heartbroken, without work and with no prospect of finding any. Sam deserved a better start in life than this. What was needed was a family meeting.

Present back in Newdigate were Daniel's father James and his mother Mary, his brother William and his brother-in-law Ben Lucas. Daniel's sister Mary was outside looking out for Sam and her own children.

Daniel opened the discussion.

'Sam is all I have got now. He is my only reason for not giving in and I must secure a better future for him. I can't stay in Leigh there is nothing there for me except memories and reminders of Sarah. Things are too raw at the moment and I cannot stay there. I have a settlement certificate for Charlwood but there is nothing there for me either unless I ask the Warden and Overseers to be relieved. I cannot stay here in Newdigate and there is no work to be had. I think all that I can do is take Sam with me to London. At least there must be chance of earning a living there. What do you say, father?'

'Things are black indeed!' said James. 'Try London if you must. There is nothing for you on the Weald since everything has changed now and none of it for the better. Leave the lad here though, son. We will look after him. He has lost his mother and needs a woman to be there for him. What do you say to that?'

'No, thank you, father,' said Daniel quickly. 'Sam stays with me. I will not have him lose both his father and his mother. It won't be easy with him but it will be harder for me still to be without him.'

William, or rather Bill as he was known by, Daniel's youngest brother, then joined in.

'Let me go with you, Dan. I am eighteen now and like you there is nothing here for me, apart from the family, of course. Let me come with you to London and I can help you look out for young Sam as well.'

'I will be glad of the company and companionship, Bill,' said Daniel. 'You are most welcome to join us. So things are settled then.'

'Well,' said James. 'It is pointless trying to stop you, although I do wish you would leave Sam with us for now and send for him later. You are after all following a family precedent when your great uncles James and John left Rusper for London all those years ago. Unlike grandfather I am not able to give you two gold sovereigns. I am well into my sixties myself and your mother and I will need to keep what we have for when I am not able to work any more. What I can do though is let you take one of the posting horses as far as the Bull's Head in Dorking so as to balance the number of horses available for hire. Dorking is only about seven miles from here but it is on a road to London, so this should suit you fine. That way you will be spared having to carry Sam all the way and one of you can ride with him seated in front of you. Mind what you say when you are in Dorking. The Duke of Norfolk lives there and the last thing you want to do is get thrown in gaol for speaking out or saying anything against him. Instead of finding yourselves in London you might end up being deported to Australia.

'I see little point in hanging around before you embark on this adventure. I suggest you set out in the morning. The weather seems set fair enough for that. Remember the road beyond Dorking has been turned into a turnpike by that Duke. This will be after the Bull's Head but give the start of the turnpike a wide berth just in case some corrupt bugger tries to charge you for walking down the Duke's road. I've heard that one before.'

And so it was Daniel, Bill and young Sam set out to leave the Weald behind them.

Part IV

Pastures New

Chapter 1

Dorking was reached without incident in a little under two hours with Daniel and Will taking it in turns to ride with Sam. Just before Dorking Bill, who was by this time taking his turn to walk, looked up at Daniel and said: 'Look Dan, we are set for London and that is fine by me but why don't we at least enquire about work along the way? You never know. We might strike lucky.'

'You always look on the bright side don't you, Bill?' replied Daniel. 'No harm in trying though but there will be others looking for work given all the problems there have been back there.'

He turned his head and nodded vaguely in the direction they had set out from.

The novelty of riding on horseback was wearing off for young Sam. He was uncomfortable and fidgety. He started to get the grizzles and by the time that they pulled into the Bull's Head Sam was in full song. He was crying, choking and calling out for his mother by the time that Daniel handed him down to Bill to set on the ground.

Daniel presented himself at the stables and was before a peculiar individual sporting a mustard-coloured waistcoat over his collarless shirt. Daniel explained.

'I come from the Star in Newdigate and my father James Weller who asked me to bring this posting horse with me as we are on our way to find work in London.'

'Ah, you are one of James' sons, are you?' the man replied. 'And the other one with you and the young'un making so much noise? I am Thomas Pickering. I have known your father for years, although we have not spoken much of late,' he said with his thumbs firmly planted in the small pockets of his waistcoat.

'You know my father?' said Daniel. 'How curious he did not mention this to me. Yes, I am his oldest son, Dan, and that is my brother Bill and my young son, Sam'.

'Your father and me had a slight falling-out a little while back. A misunderstanding and a small trifle I assure you, well at least on my part. Your father seemed to take a different view and probably still does by the sound of things. Why is that child calling for his mother so? She is obviously not with you,' said Pickering.

Dan went on to explain his circumstance, the death of Sarah, the effects of enclosure following on from the loss of work at the ironworks and his determination to make his way to London. Pickering listened intently, his face becoming more and more serious as Daniel's tale unfolded. Sam continued to blubber and there was nothing that Bill could do to comfort the child.

Placing a hand on Dan's shoulder Pickering spoke.

'This is indeed a sad tale and I am sorry both for your personal loss and for your plight. We must do something to settle this poor child. Let's see if Mrs Pickering can work her magic. We have had nine children ourselves and Mrs P has been a wonder and a marvel. Then let's talk a little bit more. I am concerned about your plans for London and I would like to offer you some advice based upon what I know if you have a mind to heed them.'

Daniel nodded and fell in behind Pickering as he gestured for them all to follow him. He halted just outside the door and went in alone leaving Daniel, Bill and the still tearful Sam outside. After just a minute the plump matronly form of Mrs P emerged. With the biggest smile you can imagine bending down to nearer Sam's level and with soft words that no one else could hear she enticed Sam inside.

With Sam receiving Mrs P's attention, the three men sat down to talk. Pickering began.

'Dan, Bill, you must of course decide your own course of action, but before you do I do urge you to listen to what I have to say. We here in Dorking get to hear and see more of things than from where you come from. Believe you me

110

things are not well in London. People are going there from all over the place and not just from off the Weald.

'You may find that regular work for both of you is difficult to come by unless you are prepared to do the dirtiest and the most foul such as in the tanneries or with dyers and they do not pay enough for anyone to have but the most basic existence. Furthermore, you are men, and boys and girls can do many jobs and at less money as well. Maybe you have had some schooling and things may not be so black as that, but how sure can you be?

'Then you will have to find a room to stay and look after young Sam at the same time. From what I hear conditions are miserable with more than one family to a room in some parts and there is much sickness as well. Would you want to expose young Sam, or yourselves for that matter, to such things?'

As Pickering paused, Daniel spoke up.

'I have worked in good households and I am carrying a reference, so that should stand me in good stead. Not the same for Bill though, as he has done only labouring here and there. We have been around horses since our childhood as well so maybe that is another string to our bow. You are right about schooling, well for me at least. Father taught Bill to read and write but he did not benefit from the good lessons that I had at the Free School. I did not realise that things in London are as bad as you describe and now I fear for Sam's safety and welfare, but what other choice have we got? The Workhouse?'

Pickering listened carefully, then replied:

'I cannot promise that this will work, but I have a proposition for you. I would like to set right any slight that your father may feel I have caused him. It saddens me to think he no longer has a good opinion of me.

'My proposition is as follows. Mrs P's family runs an establishment some fifteen to twenty so miles from here.

That is how Mrs P and I met. Mrs P's father was into growing and now so is his son also. He grows all sorts of vegetables and things that he sends to market in London. Around this time of year he takes on men and boys to bring in what he grows and then these goods go by cart to London. From time to time he will take other people's produce that is surplus to local demand. Another small little sideline so to say.

'With you knowing horses it could be useful and safer to have two drivers making the journey together. With one of you sitting at the back there's perhaps less chance of some urchin trying to steal something as you pass by or when the cart is at a standstill and the other driver is busy or distracted. What say you? Are you prepared to change your plans and at least try this out? I am sure your father will be glad to hear of it if you do.'

'Where is this place?' asked Bill.

'To the west of here through Reigate and Warwick and then on to Limpsfield. Will you give it a try then and will you let me send word or you send word yourself to your father at the Star? Round the back of the stable there is an old hand cart. There may be a couple of boards missing but you can easily fix that and it will be much easier for you than carrying your things and for young Sam as well.'

'Thomas Pickering, you are a truly Christian soul for offering us this chance,' said Daniel with feeling. 'If things do not turn out the way you are suggesting it might, then we will think no less of you for it. If Sam is settled down now then perhaps we should start on our way now and then we should get to Limpsfield the following day if you will give us further directions of where to go.

'It is a strange and happy coincidence that you and my father know each other and that you know people in Limpsfield. I will indeed write a note to my father telling him of what you have done for us and I hope this sets the record straight between you.'

'Excellent, excellent and, you know, it should not be such a strange coincidence to have the connections that you mention as we are all in the same business,' beamed Pickering. 'Let us go and see if Mrs P has worked her magic on young Sam and then we must give you some nourishment before you leave. In the meantime I will write a note you should take with you and I would ask you also to deliver a small package for me.'

Sam was indeed settled down and the missing boards on the old hand cart were easily dealt with so then the small band of Wellers, with some hot pastries taken just from the oven, set out on the next leg of their adventure.

Chapter 2

With the aid of the hand cart, and not having to slow down for Sam or carry him, they made excellent progress. By late afternoon Sam was asleep, resting on their clothing bundles when Daniel and Bill decided on a break. They polished off the rest of the provisions that Mrs P had given them and then set out again for their destination, the Bull Inn, where they needed to search out Luke Corbett.

'Almost the same name as the one we are leaving behind,' Bill had remarked.

They had already passed by some small communities along the way not knowing what they were called. Then they came to part of the track that divided into two.

'He didn't say anything about the road dividing,' said Bill. 'Look though to your left and you can see the top of a church. I would say that is our direction. The other way doesn't look that promising.'

'You're right, I think,' said Daniel. He sighed. 'I still wonder if we are doing the right thing. Still, we are committed now and there is no point in turning back. Where could we go and what could we do?'

Bill did not respond straightaway. Finally he said:

'Dan, you are going to have to decide on other things as well. You have Sam to think of. Two of us is not enough and we both need to find work. I know how you feel about Sarah and that you still grieve for her, but some time you are going to have to face up to whether your son grows up without a woman around him to care and nurture him and that you resign yourself to being without a woman's companionship. Neither is natural.'

'I try not to think about it, Bill,' said Daniel. 'I know I have Sam to think about but I don't feel as though I could truly love someone in the way that I loved Sarah. I miss her so much and I long for her feel, her touch, her scent and the sound of her voice. It is still far too soon to be talking of such things. Come on, I think we should be on our way again.'

So some little time later they found themselves walking down the main street to what was obviously Limpsfield with the church at the end of the street settled within a churchyard. Upon nearing the church they could see the Bull Inn around the corner.

Chapter 3

The peculiar thing about Mr Luke Corbett was that he wore almost the identical mustard-coloured waistcoat as Thomas Pickering. Did they have the same tailor, was Daniel's first thought to himself? Putting this to one side Daniel introduced himself, Bill and Sam to Mr Corbett and gave a brief account as to how they found themselves to be at the Bull Inn, before handing him Pickering's letter and the small package that he had also been asked to deliver.

Mr Corbett said nothing at first. He just held up his hand, clearly indicating that they should stay where they were and then he went inside. It must have been well nearly a quarter of an hour or so before he stepped outside again and by this time there were one or two spots of rain in the air.

'Come,' said Corbett and waved them to follow him under the cover of the stable roof.

'This is most inconvenient. Yes, most inconvenient,' he said waving the letter in the air.

Bill's shoulders sagged visibly and Daniel's back stiffened as Sam clung to the top of his leg. Corbett looked down at Sam and for the first time there came a trace of a smile.

'Inconvenient, but that is all,' he continued. 'Thomas Pickering has spoken kindly of you and has explained the circumstances and the nature of your predicament. I am also aware that there is some sort of association between your father and my brother-in-law. Mrs Corbett and me are not a charity but we have discussed this matter together and we are in agreement that we should be sympathetic to my wife's brother's request that we find you some employment, particularly given what has happened to the boy.

'Now don't get carried away just yet. I said we would be sympathetic but that does not mean I will take you on without first knowing if you can be of use to me. Now you,' pointing to Bill, 'tell me what you can do.'

Bill replied: 'I have done many labouring jobs some on the land and some off it.'

'That's nothing special to me,' said Corbett. 'Two a penny your sort around here. What about you?' he said, gesturing to Daniel.

Daniel knew he had had to sell himself or they were finished.

'The reason why Mr Pickering has spoken up for us is because like him our family has a tradition of horses. My father is a stableman at a posting inn and all us boys are capable and good with horses including carting and more. I have also worked in good houses, including some waiting at table and I have references to that effect. Also, I have received schooling and can read and write, as can my brother here. We are not frightened of hard work and ask only a reasonable payment for it.'

'Well, that's better,' said Corbett, nodding first in Bill's then in Daniel's direction. 'You can both work horses? Can you plough as well?'

'To be honest, sir, my brother Bill is better at ploughing than me as most of my time of late has been spent working in gentlemen's houses, but we are both experienced at driving horses whether it be a cart or a team pulling a wagon and riding, of course.'

'Did your schooling include arithmetic as well as reading and writing?' asked Corbett.

'Yes it did,' replied Daniel, 'and I can ensure that when it comes to selling your produce no one will be able to take advantage or try and short change you if I have any say in the matter.'

Corbett nodded.

'Then purely out of consideration to my brother-in-law I will consider taking you on. Let me then see if you can do the things you say that you can do. Expect to be given all manner of things to do and make sure the boy does not get in the way. You will be paid only for the work that you do and if it is to a level of satisfaction. It is too late in the day to decide anything now. Come back early in the morning and we shall see what arrangements can be made. Be warned though. I am no soft touch. There are rooms for rent across the way. They are nothing to do with me but they should be sufficient for your needs and one of my servants has taken a room there together with her father.'

Daniel, Bill and Sam each said their thank-yous and made their way to the boarding rooms to sort themselves out.

Chapter 4

Having rented a basic room for their intended first week in Limpsfield, the following morning Daniel and Bill presented themselves in the yard at first full light. Sam was left in the room with clear instruction that he was not to venture outside and that they would come back for him as soon as they could later in the morning.

Corbett eventually emerged sporting again his mustard-coloured waistcoat. His manner was as forthright as on the previous day.

'I am glad that you are prompt and early. That at least is a good start. I am intending to send a loaded wagon with produce to Southwark tomorrow or the day after. You,' Corbett pointed to Daniel, 'can then go with Tomkins as he usually drives the wagon alone and we will see if things go better for having the two of you on board. That is Tomkins over by the stable, mucking out.

'For today you can both go down to my fields down the hill from the church and help with the digging up of the first potato crop and other vegetables that are ready. You will be told what to do when you get there. If you bring in enough and we can fill the wagon then we can go to Southwark a day early.'

Again he pointed to Daniel. 'Have you got clean clothing suitable to wait at the table?'

'Yes, Mr Corbett. My previous family were kind enough to let me keep my livery. It just needs pressing,' replied Daniel.

'Good,' said Corbett. 'You can ask in the kitchen about pressing your clothes. I want you here by half past the hour at six this evening. The bells call worshippers for evensong at that time so you will know when it is the right time. I never know who may turn up to take dinner and stay the night. When gentlemen call I like to impress in the hope that I will get more of their business when they come this way again. I put gentlemen in my own parlour. Ann Page waits at table normally and she is presentable enough but if, as you say, you have served in quality houses then this may impress my gentlemen more. So, be here at the right time and then I can tell you whether to change and come back and serve at the inn.'

Corbett said no more, turned on his heels and went back inside.

Daniel turned to his brother.

'Bill, please will you go and fetch Sam and I will meet you in front of the church and we can all go down to the fields together. I want to introduce myself to that man Tomkins as it looks as if we will be driving the wagon together.'

Daniel walked over to the stable entrance to introduce himself.

'Good day to you. My name is Daniel Weller and we have just been taken on by Mr Corbett.'

'Oh, yes?' said Tomkins eyeing Daniel suspiciously. 'To my knowledge we are not short of people, and why have you come to talk with me? I know my job and don't need any help.'

Daniel explained the situation and why Mr Corbett had agreed to take himself and Bill on.

'It is Mr Corbett's wish that we should drive the next wagon up to Southwark together. Have no fear. I am not after replacing you. It is just that Mr Corbett can see that there could be advantages from having two wagon drivers making the trip. Now, if you don't mind, please tell me how many trips to Southwark or elsewhere do you normally make and what sort of things do you bring back with you?'

Still with a slight edge of suspicion in his voice, Tomkins replied, 'Well, this is all news to me. I'm Fred Tomkins, by the way, as it seems that we are to journey together. I don't as a rule bring much back unless Mr Corbett has asked me to purchase something.'

A JOURNEY OF ASCENT

'Look,' said Daniel, 'we should know tonight whether or not we are driving up to Southwark tomorrow or the following day. I have to be back here this evening in case Mr Corbett needs me to wait at table. Let's talk more tonight as my brother and me are now to go and help bring in the produce for the journey.'

'Wait at table and dig up the crop as well, do you? Whatever next?' muttered Fred Tomkins. 'Old Corbett usually expects Greg Page, the father of Ann who works here, to do all the digging as he is not known for his generosity. This is a queer situation. Anyway, time enough for that once we are on the road. I expect we will have further words tonight. I took the empty wagon down to the field first thing and was going to bring it back here for safe keeping later on and for it to be filled tomorrow. It sounds as though we can get a full load ready by tonight if your brother and Greg Page keep at it after you have left them to come back here. Let's work on the basis that we will be off tomorrow, then.'

Daniel nodded and left to meet Bill and Sam by the church and to get in their first day's work for Mr Corbett. Daniel returned to the Bull Inn at the allotted time. It was a young woman that answered his knock on the kitchen door.

'Hello,' said Daniel. 'Mr Corbett told me to come here to see if I am needed to wait at table this evening.'

'So, you're the one after my job are you?' she said with a smile. 'Wait there and I will call Mr Corbett.'

She returned a short while later.

'Mr Corbett says to tell you that you will not be needed tonight but that he may send for you if there are any gentlemen arriving late. I'm Ann, by the way. What's your name?'

'Daniel, Daniel Weller and I am here with my brother Bill and my son Sam,' replied Daniel.

'Was that your little boy I saw across the way then?' said Ann nodding in the direction of the building with rented rooms.

119

'Yes, that's us,' replied Daniel.

'Well, I can't spend all day chatting. Mr Corbett will be having my guts for garters,' said Ann with that smile again. She closed the door. It was the first time Daniel had noticed a woman since the loss of his Sarah.

Daniel went in search of some bread and cheese for their supper. As it was the end of their first day at work he decided upon impulse to obtain a cold meat pie as well. Bill returned later with a tired and hungry Sam having first delivered a message to Fred Tomkins that the wagon was indeed full. Greg Page had stayed with the wagon until Tomkins turned up with the team of horses to take the load of potatoes and other vegetables now all in sacks back to the Bull Inn for safe stabling overnight. Daniel and Fred Tomkins would set off just before first light in the morning.

Daniel did not receive any message from Mr Corbett that he was needed that night. Daniel was glad of that. He had not done hard labouring for some little while and was feeling a bit sore. He expected he would also feel a bit stiff in the morning.

Chapter 5

The previous evening Daniel and Bill had discussed what to do about Sam, who had been playing up, wanting to go with his father on the wagon trip. Daniel had to promise he would take him very soon but that this was the first time he had undertaken the journey and that Sam should stay with Bill for now. Bill had not been told he would be needed for work tomorrow and assumed the worst, but at least he was better placed to keep an eye on Sam.

Daniel went to the stable first thing in the morning to find Fred Tomkins was already hitching up the team.

'Ready for the off then are we?' said Daniel in a cheerful voice.

'Soon,' was the brief reply and Tomkins finished with the horses. 'Get on board and then we go.'

Tomkins went back into the stable and came out with two half-full sacks that he placed on the wagon immediately behind his seat.

'What have we got there?' asked Daniel.

'There is personal business and there is personal business and this is my business,' was the curt reply.

Daniel was determined to break this man down. They were to spend a lot of time in each other's company and whilst they may not end up being friends they should at least be able to get on with each other and they had a job of work to do.

They had been driving for ten minutes in complete silence when Daniel took the initiative.

'Tell me, Fred. What is Southwark like and what should I expect from this trip? This is the farthest I have ever been from home and Limpsfield has much similarity to my own villages so this is all going to be quite strange to me.'

For the first time Tomkins opened up.

'Well in that case you are going to be in for a new experience. There is the Cathedral that is far bigger than any church you will have seen. Then there are the two nearby bridges crossing the river. Can you imagine what it is like to have some sixty thousand people or so in one place? There is the whiff of the river of course but mixed with that all sorts of smells like bread baking and that coming from the brewery. I sell our produce there because there are many inns as well as houses and other businesses and ships docked in what they call the Pool of London and it costs to go across the river to the other side. Oh, and there's the Clink Prison there as well so if we get caught doing something then we will end up staying in Southwark for a lot longer than intended.'

'Why should we get caught? asked Daniel.

Tomkins ignored the question and continued: 'Southwark is not for today though. Mr Corbett has an arrangement with the Duke of Devonshire Inn at Tooting. We stable and rest the horses there overnight, and I know that our load will be safe, and then set out first thing for Southwark in time for the market.'

Daniel pressed on with the conversation telling Tomkins about his father and the Star and about the ironworks and what it was like for him to work in good houses. When Tomkins asked about the boy, Daniel went quiet and sad for a moment before telling him about Sarah.

After a few more moments it was Tomkins who continued the conversation.

'You will have seen Ann back at the Bull. Well, everyone knows that she and me have a sort of an understanding.'

'Well, I'm pleased for you,' said Daniel, but strangely enough he didn't feel pleased and wondered why Tomkins should bring Ann into their conversation in the first place.

'How long will we stay in Southwark?' he continued, changing the subject.

'A few hours, no more than that. I have some personal business to tend to as well whilst we are there but that will not take long. Then we head back home,' replied Tomkins.

They continued on their journey to Tooting mostly in silence. Daniel did not like Tomkins and decided that he was not a man to be trusted, and whatever personal business he was engaged in, Daniel thought it better not to know anything about it.

They reached the Duke of Devonshire Tavern in good order. Each took one of the two horses and groomed them well to make sure that any sweat was removed so that the horses were not at risk of catching a chill. With the horses then watered and fed Tomkins turned to Daniel.

'I have some affairs to attend to here. You will have to make your own arrangements for the night but be ready to leave first thing.'

Daniel watched Tomkins drag his own sacks off of the wagon and take them with him.

Daniel wanted to avoid any expense where he could. He went in search of something to eat and had decided that the hayloft looked comfortable enough for the night. He would steal himself back there when it was dark enough to try and avoid being seen.

He slept well that night and was awakened by the sound of a crowing cockerel. He quickly descended from the hay loft and, having splashed water over his face from the hand pump in the stable yard, he went to prepare the horses for the day. Tomkins turned up from Lord knows where, and with just the one sack, as Daniel was leading the horses out from the stalls to be hitched up to the wagon. The exchange of words between Daniel and Tomkins had reverted to type and was minimal. As they drove on towards Southwark Daniel finished off the food he had purchased the night before for his breakfast.

Chapter 6

The journey from the Duke of Devonshire to Southwark took about an hour and a half. Tomkins obviously knew where he was going so he drove them all the way. Daniel was told he could take his turn for the journey back to Limpsfield.

Daniel was awestruck. He had never seen so many houses and so many people together in one place. The two houses he had worked in were of stone and brick and had a ground floor and an upper floor, but here were buildings all close together having a further floor. They all joined on to one another making streets full of houses and nothing else, whereas back home apart from a few rows of cottages and business premises in the main streets most dwellings stood apart from one and other. And then there was the Cathedral itself and they went close by it on their way to Borough Market. To Daniel though the atmosphere was foul. The streets were full of rubbish and worse. At least back home people were more discreet about disposing of their traces. Added to this was the smell from the brewery and the odour from the river itself.

'If this is London,' Daniel said to himself, 'then dear old Thomas Pickering had done the place a disservice.' It was far worse than he had told them.

As they pulled into Borough Market Daniel could see a high wall ahead of them.

'Is that the Clink Prison, you mentioned?' asked Daniel.

'No. Not that one. The Clink is back down by the river. This one is the Marshalsea. It's where they send debtors,' answered Tomkins.

Reaching back for his sack that had been restored to its former place when he turned up in the yard of the Duke of Devonshire that morning, Tomkins got down.

'Stay here until I come back. You can start unloading over there. No one is likely to want to pilfer a sack of potatoes as they are far too heavy, but that's not to say they won't try when we are carrying loose produce. I should only be ten minutes.'

Daniel watched him disappear into the relative gloom of the Market Porter. True to his word Tomkins came back out within a few minutes minus his sack.

The apparent chaos of the market had some order about it. The sacks were selling well and Daniel soon picked up the way of market trading. There was a degree of haggling but that was as much for show as anything else. Within the hour everything was sold and the remarkable thing was that Tomkins actually had a smile on his face.

'Time to go?' asked Daniel.

'Time to go,' replied Tomkins. 'Let's just pick up some victuals for the way home. With an empty wagon the horses won't need many stops and we might even make it back by nightfall. That will make a nice change. It seems that working two up may have some advantage after all. Your turn to drive. I shall show you the way.'

Over the next few weeks the routine was repeated. Daniel did not enjoy Tomkins' company but the feeling was mutual. On each occasion Tomkins was carrying his customary two sacks – one that he parted company with somewhere in Tooting and the other he disappeared with into the Market Porter. Daniel just turned a blind eye.

Daniel and Tomkins were back in Borough Market. Tomkins as usual disappeared into the Market Porter with his sack. Out of the corner of his eye Daniel noticed that Tomkins was followed inside by three burly men. He thought little of it at the time and continued to unload the wagon. Suddenly there was a disturbance at the entrance to the Market Porter. Daniel turned and could see Tomkins being restrained and manacles being placed on his wrists. Daniel stood stock-still as first a man with a red tunic beneath his cloak and then Tomkins held firmly by the two men came towards Daniel and the wagon.

'You know this man? Did you come here together in this wagon?' the man in the red tunic demanded.

Daniel simply nodded. He was tongue-tied.

'We are Customs men. You have been caught in the act dealing in smuggled goods. You are coming with us. Either you are in with this man or you are his associate. I have enough here to ensure you hang.'

Daniel screamed out in panic.

'I know nothing of this man's business. All I am here to do is to help drive the wagon and to sell Mr Corbett's produce in the market. I know nothing of smuggling.'

'Who is this Mr Corbett?' demanded the lead Customs man.

Then Tomkins, in a trembling voice, all colour draining from his face, said:

'Look, all I have done is carry a little bit of tea. This man has had nothing to do with this. He is an innocent abroad and has recently been employed by Mr Corbett at the Bull Inn in Limpsfield to help bring his potatoes and other things he grows to market. Leave him alone for pity's sake, he has done nothing wrong! All I have done is to carry a little tea. You can't have me hung for that surely?'

Pointing to Daniel and then to the potato sacks the Customs man demanded:

'Let's see what's in these sacks, then. Tip out those two and that one on the wagon.'

Daniel did as he was told, with the result that soon there were potatoes all over the ground. Nothing else. A crowd had formed and was enjoying the spectacle.

The Customs man took out his notepad and pencil.

'So you are from Limpsfield and you work for the proprietor of the Bull Inn down there. Give me your name.'

Daniel obliged.

'Be warned my men will be watching you. You are lucky that this wretch spoke up for you. It will be the magistrate that decides his fate.'

So saying, he turned on his heel and Tomkins was led away, held firmly between the other two officers.

At first Daniel was at a loss what to do. Then, gathering his wits, he collected up all the scattered potatoes, put them into the empty sacks and began to sell them. Eventually, and much later than on other trips, all the produce was sold.

In the distance Daniel could see black clouds coming in from the south-west. On impulse, a still shocked Daniel decided to head back to Tooting rather than set out on the road to Limpsfield, which could not be reached that day anyway.

126

He had tended to stay clear of the people at the Duke of Devonshire if he could, preferring to leave any dealings to Tomkins. This time he had no choice. On this occasion he deemed it prudent to take a room. His living might well be dependent on maintaining the connection in Tooting.

Daniel explained the events of the day to a man called Holmes. He also told him how Tomkins would 'lose' one of his sacks somewhere in Tooting. Holmes did not appear to be particularly interested or concerned, but he did raise an eyebrow at the mention of Tooting and the disappearing sack.

Chapter 7

Daniel set out for Limpsfield at the first sign of daylight. As he rode along he rehearsed what he would tell Mr Corbett. With a degree more concern he wondered how he would tell Ann Page about Tomkins' fate.

Corbett must have been listening out for the return of his cart and, especially, for his money. He strode out into the yard as Daniel climbed down and started to unhitch the team and to give the horses their much-needed grooming and food and water.

'Where's Tomkins?' he demanded.

'Would you mind, sir, if I tend to the horses at the same time as explaining to you what happened? These animals have pulled hard all day and deserve good treatment. There is quite a lot to tell,' he added.

By now Daniel was well rehearsed. He explained Tomkins' attitude to 'his personal business' to activities and behaviours in Tooting and at the Market Porter, right up to Tomkins being led away by the Customs men. He also explained why he felt he should return to Tooting rather than attempt a late journey back to Limpsfield, particularly as he was carrying Corbett's money.

As the story unfolded Corbett reached for something to sit upon.

'My money, my money. Where is it?'

'It's all here, Mr Corbett. Safe and sound,' said Daniel as he handed him a pouch from inside his shirt.

Corbett started to count the money.

'What is this? Please explain.'

'Explain what, sir?' asked Daniel. 'I can assure you that it is all there, every penny. I even paid for a room in Tooting out of my own pocket.'

'No doubt, no doubt,' said Corbett anxiously. 'But this is more than I ever received from Tomkins. Was he robbing me as well as smuggling?'

'I can't answer that, sir, but the prices I got at the market were similar to those we got on previous occasions,' said Daniel.

'You have done well, lad. You have done very well and I am impressed. It seems that Thomas Pickering has indeed done me a favour after all by sending you to me. Your first concern was for the horses and that is commendable. I will see that you are not out of pocket for Tooting. I hope Tomkins gets his just deserts both for what he has done but even more so for him swindling me. It is getting late. Come to the kitchen as soon as you have finished with the horses and let's find you something to eat. Then you must get back to see that lad of yours.'

It had been a quiet night and Ann Page had already gone back to her room. Daniel would have to tell her about what happened to Tomkins in the morning. As he sat at the table eating some re-heated broth and some bread he was sorry that she was not there.

Chapter 8

Ann's duties started early as indeed should Daniel's now that Tomkins was gone. Daniel knocked on the Pages' door and it was Ann who opened it. She had a quizzical look on her face.

'Good morning, Ann,' he said nervously. 'I need to have a word with you about Fred.'

'I was expecting you both back yesterday. What happened?' asked Ann.

'Look. I know that you and Fred had an understanding. He told me so. You need to prepare yourself for a shock. There is no easy way of explaining this to you but Fred has been taken by the Customs men for smuggling. Seems that he has been up to it for years passing on smuggled bricks of tea and they caught him at it in Southwark. They were going to take me as well, but Fred spoke up for me. The outlook looks very bleak for him. I am sorry to say that you will not be seeing him again.'

'Thank the Lord you are safe, Dan!' she said. 'Well, I can't say I'm surprised about Fred. He was never my cup of tea.'

She giggled.

'Ann! This is serious. Fred is likely to hang for what he has done.'

'Oh dear! For that I am sorry, Dan. No one deserves to hang for smuggling a few bricks of tea. Fred has seriously misled you, Dan. It might be in his head that we have an understanding, but I can certainly tell you that is not the case on my part and I have never done anything to lead him on. I do not even like the man or the way that he tried to look at me. He once tried to kiss me and I had to struggle to push him away. What does Mr Corbett have to say about all of this?' she asked finally.

'Seems that Fred has been swindling him as well by all accounts. He's been creaming off some of the money from going to market. Mr Corbett does, though, seem pleased with me, so I hope this will work more in my favour.'

'Oh, I do hope so!' said Ann. 'I am so pleased that you have come back safe, Dan. You have a lovely boy as well. I hope the three of us can become the very best of friends.'

With that she squeezed his hand. Daniel did not pull away and they stood there looking at each other. Finally Daniel said:

'Come on, it's time to get working. You know just how fussy Corbett can be at times.'

Life took on a better complexion for Bill and Daniel as they started to earn more money. The situation for Bill, however, was slightly more precarious as the growing season approached the end. Corbett agreed to Daniel and Bill doing the market run together and Daniel made the point of cultivating Jack Holmes at the Duke of Devonshire in Tooting.

Daniel and Ann would often work late indoors, particularly when there were a number of travellers and when Corbett sought to impress those he considered to be gentlemen. More often than not they would walk back to their rooms together. One night Ann said as they were leaving:

'Dan, can we have a word?'

'Of course, Ann. What is it?'

'Not here,' said Ann. 'It's just starting to rain. Over there,' she said nodding towards the stable.

As soon as they were over the threshold and Ann thought they were out of sight she put her arms around Daniel's neck and kissed him full and softly on the lips. When Daniel did not pull away and started to open his lips she pressed herself against him harder and she could feel him responding. She then broke away and drawing him by the hand they went further into the semi-darkness with the only light coming from the lantern by the doorway.

It took Daniel a long time to get to sleep that night. His emotions were torn between a sense of betrayal to Sarah and how much he had enjoyed being with Ann.

It was not to be the only time when they found themselves enjoying each other towards the back of the stables. Ann and Sam had got to know each other well and Ann seemed to, at least in part, fill a gap for Sam since the loss of his mother.

Chapter 9

Looking over Corbett's field, Bill and Daniel reckoned that they would probably have only two more market runs to do. The rain had stayed away for a week now and that made it easier to dig things up or to cut off the tops of cabbages and such like. The ground could be cleared later. If they finished the bagging up and loading of the wagon today, they would set off before dawn in the morning as daylight hours were getting shorter. There should be a full moon to help them to see along the way.

The journey to market was uneventful. As usual they stabled overnight in Tooting and with the coming end of the growing season for most crops the produce was sold in good time.

Bill and Daniel set off as early as they could for home and Limpsfield. Home? Is that what that place is now? thought Daniel to himself as they climbed aboard the wagon.

They had been driving for about three hours and Daniel was just thinking about stopping to water the horses. It had been an uneasy journey home, as had the last few trips. There had been reports of hold-ups along this way and, even though the local militia had been mobilised, they were spread thinly and the costs of such private forces were borne by major land-owners mindful of the burden on their own pockets.

131

Since hearing of the reports Daniel had split the purse in the hope that should they be waylaid they might lose only part of the takings. Daniel had created a hiding place under the driving seat and it was here, once out of sight of everyone, that he split the takings between two purses.

They had just come down a dip in the road and were at the bottom before the road rose up again when two riders appeared on either side, each pointing a pistol at Daniel and Bill. Only a fool would try and take a wagon and horses up the slope with pistols pointing at them from two masked riders on horseback. Bill pulled the horses to a standstill and kept his hands in sight by continuing to hold onto the reins.

Neither of the riders said a word. They made it clear what they wanted, making threatening gestures with their pistols for them to give them whatever they had on them. Bill lifted up his shirt to show that he was not carrying anything or hiding anything of value. Daniel slowly and deliberately reached inside his shirt and pulled out a purse, offering it to the rider nearest to him. Manoeuvring his horse round, the man snatched the purse with his free hand and for no good reason clubbed Daniel on the side of the head with his pistol. Daniel slumped forward and it was only Bill's quick reaction in grabbing his arm that prevented him from falling between the wagon and the horses. The riders then made off.

Putting his hand on his brother's shoulder Bill gasped out: 'Dan, how badly are you hurt?'

'Just stunned a bit, Bill, Just stunned. Let's just get up this rise and then give the horses their water and me a few minutes to recover. My head is beginning to throb now.'

The next substantial community along their way was Croydon. It was here, for what is was worth, that they would report the hold-up to the local militia or to whoever held authority. There was no chance of recovering the lost money, but maybe a greater effort could be made to catch the culprits. There was little information Bill or Daniel had to offer, as the men were masked and had not said a word throughout the entire episode. This added delay and Daniel's headache convinced them not to press further on to Limpsfield until the morning. Greg Page and his daughter Ann would look after Sam as they normally did when Bill and Daniel went to market.

Chapter 10

It was mid morning when Bill drove the wagon into the yard at the Bull Inn. Ann had kept an ear and an eye out for their return as best as she could whilst going about her duties. When they had not returned by nightfall the day before, all sorts of terrors had run through her head.

As soon as she saw them coming, she ran across the yard, lifting her skirts as she went. Stopping momentarily when she saw the bruising and the small cut on Daniel's head, she then threw herself on him, demanding to know what had happened. Bill gave a full account by which time Corbett had also joined them.

When Bill had finished his story Daniel said: 'They didn't get all the takings, Mr Corbett. Since hearing of these robberies I have split the money and hidden half of it under the seat.'

'Well done again, lad!' said Corbett, nodding to the pair of them. 'It seems that you and Ann are better acquainted than I thought. How long has this been going on, I wonder? We'll speak of this later no doubt. There is lots of work to be done around here, so let's be having you.'

He turned and went inside. Bill crossed over to unhitch the horses and to take care of them, leaving Ann still hanging on to Daniel's neck and in tears. Gently pushing her away Daniel looked into her face.

'It's all right, love,' he said. 'Just a bump on the head and some money missing.'

'You could have been killed,' sobbed Ann. 'I could have lost you and Sam without a father and no father for our baby either.'

'Our baby?' breathed Daniel. 'How could that happen? Well, of course I know how it happened, but how can you be sure?'

'I must be three months gone now. At first I thought I must just be late but then I started to be sick in the morning. There is no doubt, Dan, I am well and truly pregnant. Don't be angry with me, Dan, but you and me will have to marry. I may not be the wife you want and maybe never will be, but Sarah is long gone now and I will try and make you happy and take care of Sam and you both as well as our baby.'

Dan was at a loss for words. All he could say was:

'Look, we can't talk now. Let's save it for later.'

He had some serious thinking to do and the need to search his feelings. He liked Ann. He liked her a lot but marry her? What would Sarah think?

Daniel had no one else to talk things through with but his younger brother Bill. Not now, though, he thought. He should first go and look in on Sam, who he hoped to be with Greg Page.

Daniel did his best to avoid Ann for the remainder of the day and that was made easier as he was not serving that evening, there being few travellers of note staying for the night. Daniel and Bill were back in their room as dusk fell and Sam was soon ready to go to sleep.

Daniel seized his opportunity.

'Bill, what am I going to do about Ann, with her being with child?' he asked urgently. 'I do like the girl very much indeed but I still feel for Sarah. Sarah thought she was pregnant and we decided to marry but in the end she was not. What if the same happens again but this time with Ann?'

Bill pondered for a moment.

'Dan,' he said finally, 'I told you some time ago that you need to reconcile your feelings. You will always love Sarah but Sam needs a mother and you need someone yourself and Ann is a fair catch. It is you that got her into trouble and you have to take responsibility for that. Has her father spoken to you yet?' asked Bill.

'No, I have not seen Greg and I do not know what Ann has told him. I know I have responsibilities for what has happened but how do I explain this to Sarah when, as I hope, we see each other in heaven?'

'I'm sure Sarah will be fine about it all Dan. Do what is right by the girl and do you and Sam a good service by agreeing to marry the girl. If you leave it too long and Corbett notices her belly swelling up I am sure he will dismiss her and possibly Greg as well. Do you want your mistress and her baby falling on the Poor Law? You know they will interrogate her and it will all come out in the end that you are the father.'

'I'll have to sleep on it and maybe talk to Ann in the morning,' said Daniel.

Some little while later there was a knock on the door and when Daniel answered the knock there was Ann. Bill got up immediately

'I think I forgot to do something in the stable,' he murmured, as he sidled gently past Ann.

Even from the poor light of the candle that Ann was carrying Daniel could see that her eyes were puffy. She must have been crying for quite some time.

'Come in,' said Daniel, closing the door after her.

'Dan, why have you been avoiding me since this morning? Am I that bad that you can no longer stand my company? There was a time when you were happy to lie with me and you were so tender. Am I of no use to you any more? Is that it?'

Daniel could see that she was close again to tears.

'Don't go on so,' he said. 'This is not easy for me and you talking so makes things even harder. I just need to come to terms with the change in circumstances. I am ever so fond of you, Ann but I still love my wife and I was wrong to take advantage of you, but what is done is done.'

'Then love me in a different way to Sarah,' said Ann. 'I cannot replace your wife and I don't want to. I want you to love me as I love you for myself and for yourself. If you can't do that, Dan, then I will go away from here and take whatever comes, but you are breaking my heart, Daniel Weller, and I don't want your pity.'

Daniel melted. He could not let anything bad happen to this girl. After all he was very fond of her. He drew her close to him and started to stroke her hair.

'It will be all right, Ann,' he said gently. 'We'll take this journey together. You, me and Sam and the little one inside you.'

Corbett was displeased and made it clear that he would not carry a passenger when he was told of their plans to wed. By the time the banns had been read and they were married at the church of St Peter, there was a visible bulge in Ann's shape.

At the wedding ceremony the rector explained:

'What I need now is for you the groom and the bride to make your marks here and then you', nodding to Greg Page, 'to make your mark here and then when I sign this certificate that means you are married both in the eyes of God and according to the laws of England.'

He dipped the quill in ink and handed it to Daniel. Daniel then signed his name in full in a properly formed and very neat script. This caused the rector to raise an eyebrow.

'You have a neat hand, Mr Weller. This is a credit to you.'

Ann and Greg then made their marks and with the rector's signature they were married and set for an adventure together.

They had the joy of a healthy baby boy they called Michael just a few months later and he was soon baptised in the church of St Peter, just round the corner from the Bull Inn on a fine June late one Saturday afternoon.

Chapter 11

The effects of the ongoing war with France and Napoleon Bonaparte were felt by all. Food prices were again high and so was unemployment. There was a real fear and dread, stoked up by the press of those days that 'Boney' was set to invade England, or as it had been known from 1707, 'The United Kingdom of Great Britain, and that included the whole of Ireland'.

There was not enough work with Corbett for Bill and Dan and his family of Ann, Sam and now little Michael to live on. They decided to chance their luck elsewhere, moving from place to place whilst at the same time the family continued to increase. Whilst they were at Beddington, a settlement upon the old Roman road called Stane Street that runs from where the Romans built a crossing over the Thames near Southwark then south-east through Dorking and onward to Chichester, they had another son, William Charles.

There was then an occasion of national triumph and the victory of the English fleet over France that brought to the end the threat of any Napoleon-led invasion of England, but at a high cost. At his moment of greatest triumph on 21 October 1805 Admiral Lord Nelson, national hero and victor of the Battles of Copenhagen and the Nile, was killed in action at the Battle of Trafalgar.

Chapter 12

One evening Daniel turned to Bill after they had finished a rather meagre supper.

'Bill, I am minded to renew our acquaintance with Tooting and call in at the Duke of Devonshire tavern. They may remember us from the trips I did with Tomkins and with you, and they might have some notion of where we can find more regular and better-paid work. We might even find someone to give our Sam here an apprenticeship. What do you think?'

Bill replied thoughtfully.

'I don't know Tooting that well but surely the bigger the place the better chance that there be opportunities for work. What have we got to lose? I see no future for us here and what with the price of bread it is hard enough to feed ourselves let alone find enough for a roof over our heads. We may be on a major road to Chichester and London but it seems that the world passes by without giving this place a glance.'

'Well, then it's settled,' said Ann, joining in. 'Tooting it is. I have had my fill of tiny little places.'

'Don't get too carried away, my dear. Tooting is not that big but I have an inkling that one day it might be. We have to give notice to quit this room. So let's do that and move on as soon as we can. If in the meantime we pick up a bit of work here or there all the better,' said Daniel.

They were to leave for Tooting that Sunday. The church could do without them until the following Sunday.

Chapter 13

Daniel was indeed remembered at the Duke of Devonshire as Jack Holmes was still in charge, but in those few years since

Daniel had seen him last there was the first sign of greying at the side of his temples.

'Good to see you again, Mr Holmes,' said Daniel. 'I hope I find you and Mrs Holmes well.'

'As well as can be expected in these hard times,' answered Holmes. 'As well as can be expected. But what brings you here after such a time. I have heard nothing from Corbett for quite some time now. Does he take his wagons elsewhere these days?'

'Ah, Mr Corbett seems to have given up taking his produce to Southwark. Maybe the risk of losing his takings to robbers again has something to do with it. All I know is that there was no promise of a regular income and making enough to feed the family if we stayed in Limpsfield so we decided to try our luck elsewhere. Our situation is not good, Mr Holmes, and I wondered if you have any intelligence as to where we may find some work.'

Holmes frowned.

'If you look hard enough you may find something, and I can at least introduce you to some that may be able to offer you something if not straight away then maybe in a few weeks time. You have a family, you say? Just how many is that may I ask?'

'Well, you know me and my brother Bill, of course, but there is my lad Sam who is coming up ten now and I am hoping to find him an apprenticeship or something. Then there is my wife Ann and our two younger sons.'

'That is quite some responsibility, quite some responsibility,' said Holmes. 'You have a lad of ten you say?'

Daniel nodded.

'Well,' said Holmes, 'I am no charity you know, no charity. What I see around me saddens me. I see men and women not afraid of hard work struggling to find enough money to buy food and keep body and soul together. Let me have a look at your lad Sam and let me see if he has that touch with horses.

139

If he does, then what say you that I take him on as an apprentice? I will feed him and he can sleep at the back of the stable, just as you used to at first. I knew you was there, oh yes I knew you was there. Nothing much escapes Jack Holmes you know. That will at least be one less mouth for you to feed. That is the best that I can do for now but if I hear of need of a man to drive a wagon or a cart I will let you know. Now how does that sound?'

'That sounds very fair and reasonable, Mr Holmes. Thank you. You never let on you saw me sleeping in the stable in those early trips. Well, I never!' said Daniel.

Sam did indeed show Holmes that he had the touch with horses.

'It's in the blood,' Daniel told Holmes. 'In the blood for generations,' as he caught himself involuntarily mimicking Holmes' habit of repetition.

With Sam safe at the Duke of Devonshire and learning at first hand the craft of tending horses, Daniel and Bill picked up labouring work where they could. It remained a struggle, particularly at first, to find enough for lodgings and food. However, things were an improvement on where they found themselves when they were with Corbett and what they left behind in Beddington.

They had been in Tooting just over a year when David became the newest member of the family.

Part V

The Start of an Improving Situation

Chapter 1

Sam had been staying at the Duke of Devonshire for just under six years. He had grown into a striking and strong-looking young man, having a fine crop of hair that in a way reminded Daniel of his own father. He had proved his worth to Jack Holmes and had repaid his kindness with hard work and respect. He had even earned the right to a reduced wage, reduced in the main as he continued to take his meals at the Devonshire and to sleep in the stables. Sam saved every penny he could to pass on to the family.

Daniel too took driving jobs as and when he could, and had let it be known that he could wait at table but it seemed being that bit closer to London people that could afford to take on servants looked for qualities that rustic Daniel did not possess. Besides, Daniel had sold his livery some time back just to find money to put food in their mouths.

Daniel and Bill moved around farther afield to find work. First to Lambeth and then settling at Chelsea Common, where they rented a small house a little bigger than absolutely necessary but with the deliberate intention of letting a room out. At Chelsea Common they spent most of their working time helping to tend market gardens ideally placed for selling into London.

Both Daniel and Ann now felt more established and secure and considered themselves to be far more fortunate than some that they saw around them. Daniel heard horror stories of the squalor, poverty, crime and disease in London itself. He remained grateful to Thomas Pickering for his sound advice. If he had not met Ann, he wondered, would he still be that lonely and grieving widower? His love for Sarah was still there, of course, but he loved Ann as well just in a different way and for the person that she was not for being a replacement or substitute for Sarah. They were happy together, but the memory of and the loss of their infant children Rebecca and David was to remain, although it was the type of loss many families suffered.

Chapter 2

'Bill, Bill,' cried Ann, 'thank heavens you have called round! Dan's not here and my lodgers have gone and left without paying a penny rent and, what's more, they've stolen from us.'

'When was this?' asked Bill.

'Why, just an hour ago. I had not seen them since yesterday and I unlocked the door to their room and their things were gone and so were mine. He said, the German, that he was going home to get some money and would settle with me then. That's ten weeks with no rent. Oh Bill, this is a disaster!'

'Leave things with me Ann,' Bill said quickly. 'I know where the ships for Germany dock. I'll find him and set the Runners on him. We'll have them arrested before Dan gets home, don't you worry. Now what's missing?'

'As far as I can tell, a counterpane, a pair of sheets and a tea-caddy,' Ann told him.

It is a fair stretch from Chelsea Common to the docks from where Bill knew that ships for Northern Europe departed. He was himself waiting to get some work, so took it upon himself to grab a few things before making his way to the docks in search of the German and his woman. He had seen them on several occasions so he would have no problem in picking them out from the crowd. All the following day and part of the next Bill prowled the docks and, having identified which ships were sailing for Germany, and when, he kept a close watch for them.

Around midday he was waiting on the quay, watching who was boarding or disembarking from the ship *Denmark Hill* when then he saw his two quarries about to embark. The ship was set to sail on the late afternoon tide. He had no time to lose. He quickly hailed a cab and gave directions to the Queen's Square Office of the Runners, or the 'Principal Officers' as they preferred to be called.

Entering the office he was able to explain the situation to one of the officers and was taken in one of their vehicles to where the *Denmark Hill* was berthed. Arriving at the dock, Bill pointed out the German standing on the deck watching the preparations for sailing. There was no sign of the woman.

The officer went to board the ship and after a brief exchange with a member of the crew approached the miscreant lodger. A few moments later the two of them disembarked and the lodger was locked in the back of the vehicle to be taken away.

'Right,' said the officer. 'He denies that he intended to do wrong and had promised to pay the missing rent. The woman is not with him at the moment but we will track her down and then it's off to court with them. Give me details of where you and your brother live and you will be served a summons to attend Court.'

'Where will that be?' asked Bill.

'The Old Bailey,' he was told.

Just over one month later on 10 May in the year of Our Lord 1815 Dan, Ann and Bill found themselves at the Old Bailey for a case to be heard by the Mr Common Serjeant, the Deputy to the Recorder of London, the most senior judge at the Bailey. The three of them were overawed by the occasion. At last, late in the morning their case was called.

The Common Serjeant read out the details:

'I have before me a charge against David Duett and Anne Carroll late lodgers of Mr and Mrs Daniel Weller of Chelsea Common that they did feloniously steal on 11th April last one counterpane value 8 shillings, two sheets value 4 shillings and a tea-caddy value 3 shillings, these being the goods of Mr

Daniel Weller at his lodging house. Daniel Weller, come forward and identify yourself to the court.'

Daniel did as he was told.

'I live at Chelsea Common, in the parish of St. Luke's Chelsea. I rent a house. The two prisoners at the bar took lodging of me, a ready-furnished room, as man and wife. My wife let the lodgings to them.'

'In that case,' said Mr Common Serjeant, 'Mrs Weller, give your account to the Court.'

And so she did.

'The prisoners arrived on the 6th of February, and took the first-floor front room, ready furnished. The man said he was a Serjeant Major in the German Legion. They were to pay me four shillings and sixpence a week for these lodgings. They lodged with me ten weeks, they never paid me any lodging rent. They left the lodging on the 11th of April. They gave no notice. I did not know they were going away that day. I asked him for some money. He said, he had no money and the he should go home to Germany for forty pounds. On the 11th of April, I was gone out awashing; I was at home at seven o'clock in the morning, to breakfast. She came to me, and asked me to lend her a seal. I did not lend it her. They both went on the 11th of April, and never returned; they left the door locked. I opened the door on the next day, and missed the things, a pair of sheets, a counterpane, and a tea-caddy; they had these things with the lodgings. I later saw the counterpane at Queen Square office; the two prisoners were in custody then. The sheets and tea-caddy have never been found. The woman prisoner took the lodgings herself.'

Glancing down at his notes, the Common Serjeant then looked up and said:

'There is also a William Weller who has something to relate in relation to this case.'

Bill stepped forward:

'I traced the two prisoners. I found them on board the ship

146

Denmark Hill. I found them on 14th April and they were due to leave England. I went to the Queens Square offices and explained the circumstances and had them arrested. As I passed a shop near to the quay whilst making my way home, I thought I recognised a counterpane that was on show.'

'There is one other I want to hear from,' said the Common Serjeant. 'John Hawkins, you also know something of this matter.'

'I am John Hawkins, sir, and I know the two prisoners. They came to my house with others at the same time as there were other soldiers going aboard the *Denmark Hill.* The female prisoner asked me to purchase the counterpane. I gave her five shillings for it as it was in a dirty state. Mrs Weller later came by the shop and claimed the counterpane so I took it to the Queens Square offices.'

At this point the arresting officer stood up without being invited.

'I am the person that took both the prisoners into custody,' he announced, 'and I confirm that the said counterpane has been with me as well.'

'Prisoners, what do you have to say?' demanded the Common Serjeant.

Duett spoke first in a strong accent and in not very good English.

'A German woman came on board and bought this counterpane. The next day I wrote a letter to Mr Weller telling him that I would come back and settle with him. I went to his house but there was nobody there.'

Anne Carroll then said: 'This man knows nothing about it. I did it all myself.'

Without further ado the Common Serjeant rapped with his gavel and announced:

'In the case against David Duett judgement is respited. In the case against Anne Duett I fine you the sum of one shilling and you are discharged.'

The Weller party were then ushered from the courtroom and the arresting officer followed. Bill turned to him.

'Judgement respited? What on earth does that mean? What about the unpaid rent?'

The Officer replied blandly:

'"Respited" means that the Common Serjeant has suspended his sentence and your best hope is that he does return from Germany and keeps his word.'

Ann waited until everyone was out of earshot.

'Well, if that is justice then it's not for the likes of us. Now I suppose I have to walk all the way to Queen's Square to get my counterpane back.'

Bill said:

'Well, I hope I never see the inside of this place again!'

He was wrong on that account.

The German never did return to pay his owing rent but then things with Napoleon Bonaparte were coming to a head.

Chapter 3

Chelsea Common was a mixture of buildings, comprising housing of diverse sorts and nature, but there was also the Royal Military Asylum and the York Hospital. The open land being used for growing things, and cattle and horses were left to graze on the heathland.

Daniel and Bill worked mainly in the market gardens or the nurseries to the west and to the north, these grounds being bisected by the Common and by the Chelsea Common Field where local residents, including Daniel and Bill, had strips of land they could use to grow their own produce. At least enclosure had not taken this right of common use away in this small part of England. Next to the Common was a paddock where horses for drawing cabs and carts and wagons were kept.

What intrigued Daniel and Bill was the provision of the cricket ground, not that they had much time to appreciate what was going on during games there. What little they had seen was beyond their comprehension.

The houses around Sloane Square and in Sloane Street and Cadogan Terrace were grand in style. The properties in Smith Street, where Daniel and Ann lived, were modest in comparison but by far the best place they had ever lived in before.

When the news of Wellington's victory over Napoleon at Waterloo arrived, celebrations were quickly organised on the cricket ground. Such fun and celebration was had! After all these years Napoleon and France had finally been dealt with.

No one at that time gave a thought to what would happen to all those soldiers and sailors when they returned home from war. The effects were to be terrifying. For so long food prices had been high and this had hit the poor badly, but now with free trade with Europe and the rest of the world being restored food prices were set to fall. As a consequence, landowners, who had benefited from the previously high prices, started to lay off their workers to maintain their profits. With all those men returning from war mass unemployment was inevitable.

The Government's response was not to look after the men who had fought for their country, but instead to look after the landowners and their profits. The Corn Laws (established in the first place to protect landed interests) were further amended by the House of Commons. This followed intense pressure from landowners and farmers and the amended Corn Laws had the effect of banning imports of foreign corn unless the price of domestic corn rose above 80 shillings a quarter (8 bushels). The price of bread then rose significantly. Those of the poor and labouring classes who were lucky enough to have work in industrial towns went on strike for higher wages so that they could afford to buy bread they needed to survive. There were also food riots that were brutally put down, with a significant number of deaths and maiming inflicted by various militia.

In the countryside things were even worse. Not only was there insufficient work to support the population, but the harvest in 1816 was extremely poor. More and more people were forced to leave the countryside to look for work and for somewhere to live in the filthy and already overcrowded slums of the towns and cities.

The Poor Law relief system, for so long the last defence against abject poverty and starvation, came under considerable strain.

Daniel considered himself fortunate that there was work for him at the nursery and in the market gardens of Chelsea Common with its enormous market of London to satisfy.

Chapter 4

It was Sunday, the Sunday before Christmas. Sam had called in on his parents but he had brought someone along with him. On entering, he kissed his step-mother on both cheeks, and father and son embraced, each slapping the other heartily on the back. It was late, and the children, Michael and William, were already in bed. Sam's brother, strictly speaking his half-brother, the two-week Richard was in his basket also sound asleep.

'Well, son, introduce us to your young lady,' said Ann.

'Ann, father, this is Sarah, Sarah Smith. We both live down on the Square in Richmond. As you may have guessed, we are wanting to marry,' answered Sam.

'Another Sarah is it?' said Daniel. 'Sam's mother was named Sarah, you know.'

Sarah nodded eagerly to show that she understood.

'Well, sit down, Sam and you, Sarah,' said Ann. 'We have a lot of catching up to do.'

'First things first,' said Sam. 'We have been to see Sarah's parents and they have given their consent to us marrying as Sarah is eighteen. Even though I am now of full age we would like to have your blessing as well and, father, we would like you to be one of our witnesses. Although we live and work now down in Richmond we would both like to have the wedding here at St Luke's in Chelsea. It's the place we go to ever since we came here to Chelsea.'

'Your mother and I were very young when we married, son,' replied Daniel, 'but we were very much in love. Do you two love each other so much that you cannot abide being apart? And, forgive me for asking, is there any need for you to get married quickly?'

'The only reason why we should get married soon', answered Sam 'is so that we can be together and live together as man and wife.'

'Well, that's good enough cause for me,' said Daniel.

'For me too,' said Ann.

Holding Sarah's hand tightly Sam went on:

'Then we shall go to St Luke's and ask for the banns to be read as soon as we can. Now let's catch up. It seems like ages since we had a good old natter. I really like it down in Richmond. I am learning so much. Sometimes I am a coachman and I drive gentlemen and their ladies into London, particularly in the evenings. Sometimes they have me working inside which is how Sarah and me got to get to know each other.

'You know I told you that we used to see Lord Nelson when he was home from sea visiting Lady Hamilton down at Herring Court, well it seems that her Ladyship is now moving

151

out. Maybe it's the smell from the pond in the Square that she disapproves of. I cannot understand why people put all their rubbish in there. I am told that not so long ago the water was fresh. Not now, though. No, what is more likely is that her Ladyship has heard about plans to build an hotel and does not care for all the disruption that will cause and that her privacy will be invaded. She is still in mourning you know.

'Any news from Uncle Bill, by the way?'

'Your Uncle was here just two weeks ago,' answered Ann. 'He too is getting married.'

'And about time too!' cried Daniel. 'We are taking baby Richard to be baptised at St Luke's in two weeks' time. Do you think you can both make it? Now then, mother ...'

Daniel turned to his wife and patted her on the backside.

'... do you think we can have something to eat tonight or are you going to starve us to death?'

Chapter 5

Some twelve years later

Daniel was at Ann's bedside. He had been keeping vigil for some days now. Up until a few days ago he had been feeling content with his lot.

His eldest sons, Michael and William, from his marriage to Ann, had moved away from home and were employed as paper-stainers, workers who printed wallpaper. Not perhaps a glamorous job, but Daniel was pleased that they were not tied to the land. He was sick of it and wished he was back with his horses. Their younger son Richard was now thirteen and would soon be looking for work.

Michael had been blessed and cursed with mixed fortunes.

He had married and lost his little girl before her second birthday but was then blessed with another daughter, only then for his wife Ann to fall ill and to die. Michael had nevertheless picked himself up and, knowing that he had to look after Mary Ann Louise, had taken Harriet as his second wife.

Ann opened her eyes and turned her head towards Daniel.

'Dan dear. We did not do too badly in the end did we? Two short of thirty years together Dan. There were times when we were so hungry I could have eaten my boots but for the cold that my feet would feel.'

She coughed as she tried to laugh.

'Where are the children? It seems so long since I have seen them. Try and bring them to me before it's too late.'

'Don't talk that way, dear. In a week or so you'll be up and about as normal,' said Dan, trying hard not to show his own distress.

'I'm worn out, Dan. Just try and get me to see the children one more time. I always considered Sam as one of my own, you know. I would have liked to see him one more time as well, but that's not to be with him down in Bath.'

They made it in time, Michael and William, to see their mother. Richard went and made sure of that. Daniel knew that he would have to see out the rest of his days alone.

Chapter 6

Daniel's son William, as was his wont, called upon his father unannounced and, although William was in the habit of not knocking before entering. Daniel was nonetheless pleased to receive a visit from his son. Now that there were just him and Richard, Daniel had decided to move into smaller accommodation further down Smith Street. What had been the family home was beyond their means to maintain, and was too large anyway. He was not minded to be bothered with lodgers, particularly as Ann was no longer around to keep an eye on things.

'Hey, Father, guess what? I'm going to the Old Bailey. This time a Weller is a witness to an attempted murder. I saw him do it. I saw him stab someone. He's for the gallows I bet and good riddance!'

'Don't expect me to get excited about anything to do with so-called justice,' answered Daniel sourly. 'I've seen enough of it first hand. It seems to me that justice only serves to protect the rich and well-to-do not ordinary people. Tell me about it afterwards and then see if I am right. You'll see soon enough.'

It was the day of the trial, and William's fiancée Sarah, curious to see the English legal system at work, had a place in the gallery.

'All rise for Mr Justice Littledale,' called the Court Usher.

After he had seated himself, and the rest of the court had settled, the Judge turned to the prisoner in the dock.

'You are Isaac Pearson? You are charged that on 5th October 1831 that you did feloniously cut and maim one William Alden with intent to kill and murder him. You are in addition charged with threatening to disable or do some grievous bodily harm to the said George Miles. How do you plead?'

The prisoner answered: 'I am Isaac Pearson and I plead not guilty to all the charges against me.'

'Very well,' said Justice Littledale. 'I will hear first from ...' – he paused and looked down at his notes. 'George Miles.'

After being sworn in, George Miles gave his evidence.

'I live in Chapel-place, Brompton, with my father, who was door-keeper at the Italian opera house, but is now out of employ. I am a shop-boy or light porter. On the 5th of

October I heard a noise at number 14, Chapel-place, four
doors from my father's house. Mr Thompson keeps the
house and the prisoner lives there; he is a shoemaker. I
found a few people outside the house; they were not making
a noise. Then I heard a noise inside the door, and saw a
policeman parading up and down Chapel-place. I heard him
say if there was any noise in the street, by man, woman, or
child, he would take them in charge. The door being open, I
went in to see what was the matter. Alden followed me in.

'As soon as I went in I heard the sound of a bell inside, and
something else like someone rubbing a washboard but I am
not quite sure what. I had not been in the passage for more
than five minutes before the prisoner came out of his
parlour. I believe the noise I heard was the prisoner
attempting to serenade his marriage. I was standing directly
opposite the parlour door when the prisoner came out, and
he tried to knife me on my right side. He failed. He then ran
from me, and went towards Alden. I did not see the prisoner
stab him, but I heard Alden cry out.

'I had nothing in my hand when he came out, but when I
first went in I had an empty quart pot, and knocked it against
the wall two or three times, but I decided to lay it down, and
did so.'

The witness was then cross-examined by Mr Phillips
appearing for the defence.

Question: 'Did you know the prisoner?'

Answer: 'Only by sight. I never spoke to him. I went into his
passage, seeing the neighbours there. I know the people
were tormenting him night after night, but I had nothing to
do with it. I made a noise with the quart pot: I knocked it
against the opposite wall.'

Question: 'Had he not previously been irritated by a gang of
boys in this manner?'

Answer: 'He had been irritated the night previous – I did
not intend to make a noise when I went, but seeing other

people do so, I did so for my own amusement. They were all grown people there – some of them were tormenting him; six or eight people were there. I heard the policeman say if anybody made a noise outside he would take them, but if there was a noise inside he could not prevent it.'

At this point Justice Littledale intervened.

'Did not the policeman tell them if they went inside they might make as much noise as they liked?'

Answer. 'It was something to that effect: he did say so – I believe the prisoner had been married the day previous; he had given the persons no provocation.'

The judge then announced: 'I will now hear from William Alden.'

William Alden then gave his account.

'I live in Chapel-place, with my father – I am a compositor. On the 5th of October I was going to bed, about half-past ten o'clock; my father was at the door, and called me down. I saw a few people assembled outside number 14, where the prisoner lives; he had been married the day before. I went and mixed with them. The policeman said the first that made a noise outside should be taken to the watch-house, but if there was any noise inside he could not prevent it, they might make what noise they liked.

'I went in; six or eight people were there. I had a tea-board, and there was a person with a bell. Miles had a pewter pot – they were all making a noise; the bell was put into my hand and I began ringing it. This continued for three or four minutes. I then saw Pearson open his room door, and come out; he stabbed Miles in his right side, then came, and stabbed me in the left side with a knife. I have seen the knife since – it went through my coat and waistcoat. I was taken to Dr Anderson's, in Brompton Road. He dressed the wound, and I was then taken to St. George's Hospital.

'He stabbed us the instant he came out – he had no malice towards me.'

Mr Pearson for the defence then cross-examined Alden.

Question: 'You were ringing the bell three or four minutes?'

Answer: 'Yes – it was a little hand-bell. I heard no kettles. Weller and Driver were beating the tea tray with their fists. The policeman said we might go in and make what noise we liked and we made as much noise as we could, and that no doubt irritated him very much.'

Justice Littledale then called for William Weller to give his account.

'I am William Charles Weller and I live in Chapel-place, and am a paper-stainer. I went to the house to see Thompson, the landlord, but was not one of this party. I saw Miles and Alden there – the noise continued four or five minutes. The prisoner came out of his room with a knife in his hand. I saw him stab them both. I caught hold of Alden, unbuttoned his clothes, and put my hand on the wound. I took him to Dr. Anderson's, and then to the hospital.

'It was a pointed shoemaker's knife. The doctor said the wound was an inch and a half deep. The prisoner might have been irritated. I have heard the boys in the street making a noise but he has insulted people as they passed his window. When children have made a noise he has come out with a strap, and hurt a boy very much once which I believe started it all. This time there were grown-up people there.'

Mr Pearson then cross-examined William Weller.

Question: 'Who were the grown-up people?'

Answer: 'I knew Miles and Alden, but not the others. Mr and Mrs Driver were there – one of them had a tea-board. The prisoner lived in the front parlour of that lodging-house.'

Mr Justice Littledale called for the constable to give his account.

'I am James Appleby, a policeman. I was on duty in Chapel-place. I heard a noise, and went to quiet them. When I got to number 14, it was over. Five or six people were standing in the street – some at their own doors, and some looking out of the window. I enquired what the noise was about, and understood there had been a wedding. I stood there a moment or two and some person came out of number 10 or 11 with something in his hand, and hit it. I went to tell them the very first who made a noise in the street I would take them to the watch-house.

'I saw Miles and Alden go into number 14. A female said, "If the Policeman won't let us do it in the street, we can go inside". The landlord was standing in the doorway of his apartment, and I believe I said the landlord was master of his own house. I believe I said they might go to their own apartments and make a noise. I was standing a little distance from the door, and heard somebody say Alden was stabbed.'

Mr Pearson then cross-examined the policeman.

Question: 'Did you not know the persons did not live in that house?'

Answer: 'Yes, if I told them to go in, and make as much noise as they liked, it is more than I recollect. I was on duty in the street, and should think the landlord master of his own house. If he had called me to prevent it, I should.'

Mr Justice Littledale then decided he had heard enough. He declared Isaac Pearson not guilty and the case was dismissed.

With Sarah hanging on his arm as they walked away from the Old Bailey homeward bound, William turned to her to say:

'Damn it! I hate it when father is always right. Maybe we should not have provoked Pearson so just after his wedding, but he should not have come at anyone with a knife, let alone stab them.'

Chapter 7

Richard had moved out and had married his lovely Charlotte and now lived in Lambeth. Daniel was surprised to find himself wondering how things were back on the Weald. Why, for years he had yearned to get away from the place and now he wanted to go home!

He had turned sixty years of age, and while quite grey he still had an unkempt mop of full hair. He now had an even more leathery and weather-beaten face, and he certainly took far less care over his appearance than he used to when Ann was alive. Quite frankly he could by his appearance be taken at times to be an undesirable. Yet he still felt fit and he still felt strong. He was well able to put in a hard day's work. He decided it was time to leave. Not perhaps for Rusper or for Newdigate but somewhere else on the Weald where the land was better and there should be more work. His children had their own lives to lead and their own families to look after.

So, he took himself off there and managed to find irregular work, first on Coulsdon Common near Croydon. Eventually he was to fall upon the Croydon Union Workhouse for support. He passed away in the Workhouse Infirmary in 1851 at the grand old age of 77.

As for Daniel's youngest son Richard, he was to break with all that went before him. He, Charlotte and the infant William departed Lambeth for Stepney where he found work as a dock labourer; but that's another story and life as a dock worker was hard and harsh.

Part VI
Life in Bath

Chapter 1

A key part of this journey concerns stagecoaching, where Sam, or Daniel the Younger, if we stick to his baptised name, is the first professional and full-time coachman in the family. So, a little about coachmen and coaching, and in particular along the route between London and Bath and Bristol.

Coachmen of the time we are talking about here were at the top of their profession. In days gone by little heed was paid to the horses, and their life span could be as short as three years. Early coachmen knew nothing of the art of coaching, and often the same poor brutes would be driven down rutted roads with the whip from sunrise to sundown. In a short story by Charles Dickens following an accident with a coach in which four horses died the driver comments, 'They were but horses.' It is said that the Spanish had a proverb: 'England is heaven for women but a hell for horses.'

Coachmen eventually evolved to take a more professional approach, partly as the result of pressure from the stage-coach owners. That is not to say that all came up to scratch. For example, some drivers drove their coaches and passengers at dangerously high speeds risking accidents, or they took further risks on bends, and the coach driver would be taken to court by injured passengers pursuing damages. At the other end of the scale, there is a tale about a coach-man on a West Country route who was reluctant to turn a passenger away even if the coach was already overloaded with passengers and goods. As a result of this, he was definitely a slow coach.

The good coachman was held in high regard by those that supported him be that stable lad, groom or ostler, and many coachmen made their way up this ladder. In cold weather the coachman would be of extra large proportions given the number of garments and coats that he wore, with the top coat being one that reached to the floor. He would have his strapped-on hat and mufflers and scarf to cover his face from the worst of the wind and the weather.

The main road linking Bristol, Bath and London was the Bath Road. The distance from London to Bath was 108 miles and from London to Bristol 123 miles. This was one of the most used and popular stagecoach routes in the seventeenth and eighteenth centuries, and when regular services commenced it took just two days for passengers to travel between Bath and the capital. Then, thanks to road improvements and better coaching design, including spring suspension, it became possible to do the journey to Bath in just eighteen hours. The road improvements mainly came about because of the introduction of turnpikes and the charging of a levy or toll to use parts of the road, thus providing a revenue stream to ensure the upkeep of the road. With the exception of the night mail coaches of W. Chaplin & Co. that made by far the quickest time, the fastest stages made the journey at an average speed, including stops, of eight and a half miles per hour. They were called 'stagecoaches' as the journey was undertaken in stages.

By 1836 the night stage from London to Bath took as little as eleven and a half hours. Teams of horses were changed every 15 miles. It is thought that there were as many as 150,000 horses used on stage coaches around the country and this explains why coaching and the support services were such a major industry. Some estimates suggest that up to 20 per cent of the working population supported the industry in one way or another during the heyday of coaching in the sixty years leading up to the time when the railways became established over long distances. That winter of 1836 was exceptionally harsh with a heavy blanket of snow covering most of the country. The postal coaches tried their best to get through, but many ran into difficulties getting stuck in the deep snow or finding their way blocked by drifts. For a number of weeks passenger coach services did not run or found their journeys cut short.

Chapter 2

We have some catching up to do regarding what happened to Sam and Sarah from the time when they got married as planned at St Luke's in Chelsea back in the summer of 1816. They had not quite been truthful when they had told Sam's parents about their plans to marry, since Sarah was already two months pregnant with their first son, John.

Sam had finished work for the day down in Richmond. They were both living and working in Richmond when they first met, but obviously Sarah no longer worked as they had started a family.

It had been a long day. Sam's first duties involved him undertaking his valeting for Mr Barnes, including setting out the clothes and footwear that he would have cleaned and polished the previous evening. Sam would more often than not then perform other personal tasks for his employer.

Sam then had to tend to his duties in the stable yard, ensuring the horses were well groomed, their feed and water bins topped up, the tackle polished and shining and Mr Barnes' personal coach prepared and made ready for the evening should he feel the need to go out. Indeed, Sam had taken his Master and Mistress for an engagement that very evening. He knew when he got up that that morning that it would be late when he finally got to see his bed. Indeed it was, and later than he had expected or wanted. Tomorrow looked set to be another long day.

Sarah had waited up for her husband. Their two young children John and Charlotte had settled down several hours previously and Sarah was in need of some company.

'You look tired my love,' she said as Sam pulled off his coat and hung it on the hook behind the door.

'It comes with the job, my dear,' Sam replied. 'Mr Barnes is a hard task master, expecting me to valet, tend the horses and stables and to be his coachman all, it feels, at the same time. Other families would employ more than just one person to do all these things.

'The one compensation about nights like tonight is that it does give me a chance to read whilst I am waiting for the Master to be taken home. Why there is the *Monthly Magazine* with stories being serialised by a new writer and I have the chance to read the newspapers as well.

'Whilst reading the newspapers tonight it occurred to me that we could do better than stay here in Richmond with Mr Barnes. Everyone seems to say, and maybe they are right, that people should not get ideas above their station, but that does not mean that we should not seek to improve ourselves and our situation. There are now new staging companies establishing themselves and they want to compete for the traffic and revenues for carrying passengers and goods between London, Bath and Bristol and places along the way. They are advertising for vacancies for coachmen, and I am thinking of applying so as to get my foot inside the door so to speak and maybe once established and known we could aim after that to run a company stables. The more I think of it, the more I am attracted to aiming for Bath. Why, apart from the carrying of people to and from London there must be opportunities for business in and around Bath for those that have not arrived in their own carriages. What do you think, Sarah? Should we take the gamble? Should I quit Mr Barnes if I can get a position with one of these new companies?'

'It is late, Sam dear,' Sarah said quietly. 'You know I will support you in whatever you think is best for us and the family. I must say that I see little prospect of things changing if you stay with Mr Barnes. Why don't you sleep on it, not straight away, mind you. I have other plans. Then in the morning, if you think the same way, see if you still want to get an interview when you can next take some time off. If anyone has any sense they will see that you are better than any ordinary man.'

They embraced and kissed and then went to bed. When Sam awoke the following morning his mind was clear. He would indeed try and find a new position.

Chapter 3

Sam eventually enquired as to whether there were any openings for a coachman with two new and one established stagecoach operators. If he was to gamble he was going for broke. He made it known that he had experience with maintaining a stable as well as being a competent coachman and would be looking for an opportunity to prove to his employer that he had an eye for business and would look for opportunities to make money through expanding their enterprise. He also made it known that he was able to read and write and knew his arithmetic.

The established operator was less than impressed with Sam's ambition. Both the new operators showed an interest in Sam but in the end it was Robert Grey, one of the smaller operators, who seemed to show the most interest in Sam and his ambitions. Sam was pleased that they had, as he worked out in his own mind that being smaller than their competitors they would have to be more ambitious and perhaps more open to new ideas. Sam was starting to form ideas about how to serve the environs of Bath or the Bath to Bristol runs as a separate business than the through stagecoach services and he had yet to see Bath.

He was promised by his new employer that they would find

him accommodation in Bath ready for him and his family to move into. Sam gave in his notice to Mr Barnes, who was outraged that he should quit and leave such a good and considerate employer in difficulties. Under the circumstances he was told not to expect a reference. This pleased Sam all the more as it further convinced him that he was making the right decision.

Chapter 4

Some years later

It was coming up to seven o'clock in the morning and there was a great deal of activity around Le Belle Sauvage on Ludgate Hill. There was the customary throng of long-distance coaches preparing to get under way. Sam was waiting for his passengers to board his coach when he saw a familiar face coming straight towards him. With a beaming smile and an extended hand Sam took a step forward to greet the new arrival.

'Why bless my soul, sir! If it isn't Mr Dickens. I would recognize you anywhere from your illustrations appearing in the *Monthly Magazine*. What an honour, Mr Dickens sir, to have you riding inside my coach! I so much enjoyed your serialisation of 'Sketches by Boz' and 'A Dinner at Poplar Walk' and I read that you are about to start on the new tale of *The Pickwick Papers*. I look forward to the opportunity to read more of your works. Am I taking you to Bath, sir, for the Season, or are you headed for Bristol?'

'What a fine greeting!' said Charles Dickens, graciously accepting the hand extended to him. 'The weather seems to be set fair so I have purchased an outside ticket for the journey to Bath. I like to observe what is going on around me and how people conduct themselves, which I find I cannot do quite the same from inside the cabin. I would consider it a privilege to be able to ride up there in the front with you. It is going to be a long day and perhaps if you have a mind to we can have some conversation along the way?'

Sam beamed.

'I am doubly honoured, Mr Dickens,' he cried, 'that you should wish to ride with me and to hold conversation. I suggest though that you find a way to secure your hat or place it under the seat otherwise you and it are likely to part company. A gentleman passenger of mine once failed to do so and his hat was blown off into a pond. He was not amused.'

The two men laughed heartily.

'Now if you would excuse me, sir,' said Sam, 'I must get ready to be away promptly. We are proud of our reputation for good time keeping. In the meantime if you will be good enough to take your seat then I will ensure all our fellow passengers and their luggage are safely aboard. Mrs Weller, my late dear wife, sir, would have been so proud to know that I have driven with Mr Charles Dickens and with him sitting next to me, to boot. Now is your luggage safely stowed on board or can you still see it hereabouts?'

'That is my luggage there that those fellows are about to load,' replied Charles Dickens. 'I shall climb aboard now. I do not want to be the one responsible for delaying our departure.'

Once under way, and on time, Charles Dickens did not at once engage in conversation with Sam. He did not wish to distract the driver as he negotiated the four-horse team and coach out from the boundary of the City of London along the Strand and then through the expanding area to the south of what is known as the 'West End'. It was Sam who decided to take the initiative, wishing to take every advantage of the opportunity afforded by this fortunate encounter.

'Excuse me for asking, Mr Dickens, but is this journey connected with your proposed serialisations of *The Pickwick Papers* or some other writing or are you intending to mix with society once in Bath?'

'I am indeed in need of fresh ideas on how to take *The Pickwick Papers* forward and to bring characters into the tale,' replied Dickens. I am hoping that a change from London and this journey will help me achieve this. That is the most important aspect of this adventure. Mixing with people of so-called "society" is not exactly something that I go looking for or enjoy. Perhaps you will be my inspiration now that the road is almost clear and we are well away from London. Would it be impertinent for me to ask you something about yourself? I do find it helps me with my writing to be able to talk with and to listen to people and hear about their experiences. This after all is what the Pickwickians are all about; travelling to parts of England by coach and coming back together as the Pickwick Club and telling each other about their adventures.'

'No, sir, that will suit me fine,' said Sam. 'We will soon be pulling up at the Roe Buck Inn at Turnham Green where we will have our first change of horses. Our stop will be no more than two or three minutes and then we will be under way again. I would be honoured to tell you about myself, though you may find yourself fast asleep by the time we get to our next stop.'

As the coach pulled up in front of the Roebuck, a voice called out: 'Good morning, Sam. Nice day for a drive.'

It was one of two stable lads waiting to unhitch the team and replace them with a team of fresh horses. The change was affected in less than two minutes and the coach and its passengers were soon back on their way.

'Well, Mr Dickens. What would you like to hear?' asked Sam.

'If it is not too intrusive,' replied Dickens, 'I should like to hear how it is you came to be a coachman and anything about yourself that you would care to share with me. I gather from what you said earlier about your dear late wife that you have suffered a recent and sad loss. May I offer my condolences? With your consent, and as best I can with all this bouncing around, may I take some notes?'

'Certainly,' Sam said, 'and thank you for your words of condolence. My wife has been gone for some six months now. My eldest John is working with me as a coachman and it is he who would normally be doing this run as I am now the company's stable keeper in Bath and my five youngest are still at home and in need of looking after.

'Previously, I was employed for a rather exacting gentlemen that expected me to valet for him, maintain his stables and horses and frequently drive his carriage for him, and that with them often returning late at night, particularly during late spring throughout the summer and into the autumn.

'In the mornings my gentleman would expect to see his clothes for the day laid out all neatly pressed and brushed. His shoes were to be polished as well. Each morning I would lather up his shaving soap for him and some mornings prepare his bath. As my gentleman was bathing I would come downstairs and ensure his newspaper was pressed and laid out for him on the breakfast table. All this was to be done before he came down for breakfast at 8:20 exactly.

'Whilst he was taking breakfast I would gather up his clothes from the previous day and inspect them, sending what needed to be washed to the laundry and setting aside other garments that might be in need of attention whether that be cleaning or repair. At any time my gentleman might give me new instructions to undertake errands or tasks for him prior to his return home from his business in the evenings or in time for luncheon on Saturday.

'I then had to organise my day, ensuring that the horses

and tackle were tended to. On days when it was raining I was required to drive my employer to his office or to collect him from there in the evenings if bad weather was expected. At other times he would walk to the office, and that allowed me a little more time to undertake my duties.

'Then, as I said, some evenings I was required to be their coachman. It was following one such evening returning late at home that I said to my dear late wife that I see no prospects with my current employer and I asked her whether or not we should take the gamble and that I should look for a position as a coachman with one of the new stagecoach companies. The days are equally long but better paid and at least during the times between my doing these runs I would have the chance to see more of my wife and our children. Now things are different of course. My father, Daniel Weller, was prepared to take an even bigger gamble to try and better his lot. He struggled to provide for us but his perseverance won through.

'Horses have been in our blood for generations, Mr Dickens. Whilst I was happy to valet, it was beyond me to do all those things without assistance and that is what my former employer demanded of me. Being with horses is my first choice. Why, I once said to Mrs Weller that, if we should be fortunate enough to find ourselves down in Bath, then I might look to being more than just a coachman. We know our station dictates what our ambitions should be, but that does not mean that we should not strive to improve on that position whilst remaining within the normal and expected boundaries.'

'That is an interesting and vivid picture,' Dickens broke in. 'Tell me, are there any particular anecdotes or examples that you would care to share with me – where as a valet you may have come to your employer's rescue or saved him from embarrassment?'

Sam was silent for a few seconds and then in a more serious tone replied, 'I am sorry, Mr Dickens sir. That would be indiscreet of me. Even if my former employer is unknown to you, there are things that should remain a secret between my gentleman and me.'

'Of course, of course,' replied Dickens quickly. 'It was insensitive of me to ask.'

Sam nodded.

'That's all right, sir. No harm done.'

The coach continued to stop every fifteen miles or so to change teams and there was a longer pause of about half an hour when they reached the White Hart at Hungerford. Hungerford was a major staging point on the Bath Road and in terms of time was some seven and three-quarter hours from London, four and three-quarter hours from Bath and six and a half hours from Bristol. Both inside and outside passengers looked forward to this brief respite from their trial of endurance.

All along the way Sam and Dickens fell into conversations sometimes punctuated by periods of silence. It was after all a long journey. The conversation became more and more relaxed and Sam was comfortable telling Dickens about his father's encounter with Tomkins and the Revenue men, the experiences of the trials at the Old Bailey and the hand-me-down account of how one of the family ended up going to India with the East India Company. Strangely, in Sam's view, Dickens was most interested in what Sam could tell him about the difficult times his father had before becoming established at Chelsea Common and about what Sam could tell him about what he knew of life on the Weald after enclosure and the loss of the iron making, which obviously Sam had no first-hand knowledge of anyway.

Arriving at their destination in Bath, Sam prepared to leave. He was not to continue with the coach to Bristol. He had been away from the stable for too long as it was and had only done this run owing to sickness and no replacement being available.

Before they left the coach Dickens buttonholed Sam.

'I am most obliged to you, Sam Weller. Your good company has made a tiresome journey all the more interesting and worthwhile. Would you have any objection if I were to draw upon your anecdotes when I continue with my writing?' he asked.

'Mr Dickens,' said Sam warmly, 'if there is anything that I have told you that is of the slightest of interest to you then please feel free to do so. For me this adventure from London has been something I will carry with me for the rest of my days.'

'I don't know when we may meet each other again but no doubt we will. Bath is a special place and if it is not my good fortune to have you drive me again during this visit or upon my return to London then maybe there will be other occasions when I come back to Bath,' said Dickens who then extended his hand before going his own way.

Sam was so excited, but now there was no Sarah at home with whom he could share his news. A crushing sadness came over him once again. It seemed ever so cruel that his wife and the mother of their children should be taken away from them before she was to reach forty years of age.

During his infrequent visits to his local hostelry Sam would recount this story so often that most of his friends were soon tired of hearing about it. In any case some of them had yet to learn about who this Charles Dickens was!

Some four weeks later Sam received a package at the stables in Catherine Mews. Inside was a brief note signed 'With the compliments of Charles Dickens' and a copy of the Monthly Magazine. When Sam had the opportunity he opened up the magazine and turned to the next instalment of The Pickwick Papers. On this occasion he was amazed to find that Dickens had included a character who was a 'gentleman's, gentleman'. His name was Sam Weller. Sam was too embarrassed to write to Dickens but he was immensely proud to see his name in print.

Chapter 5

'Charlotte,' said Sam one day, 'it is time for you to find work. You are coming up to fourteen now and need to start to make your own way in life. Out in Widecombe Parish they still have their hiring fairs, or the Mop Fair as I have heard some folk call it. There is one coming up the Saturday before Easter Sunday. Has anyone told you what these affairs are like?'

'No, father,' replied Charlotte.

'Well, these hiring fairs happen only once a year. They are held at the same time as the normal weekly market but the occasion makes for something special and people tend to make a holiday out of it. There will be all sorts there. There will be girls like you looking to work for the first time and there will be other girls and women from parlour maids to cooks looking for new employment. You are a handsome lass, girl, with a good figure and a good complexion. This should work to your advantage over some of those others that might look like lazy puddings.

'The boys and men will be there too. There'll be shepherds and there'll be grooms and want-to-be coachmen. The girls and the women stand apart from the boys and the men, so it is usual for ladies looking for servants to walk down the line, for you will all be standing in a row, to see if they find someone they think will suit their requirements. As any lady approaches you, curtsey with your head slightly down. If they should stop in front of you, put your hands together.

'If they address you, ever so slightly lower your head so that you are looking at their midriff. You know your manners, girl, so I have no worries on that score, but only answer their questions and do not presume to say more than what is sufficient to give a satisfactory answer. Is that clear?'

'Yes, father, I'll try my best,' answered Charlotte.

'And Richard,' continued Sam, 'next year will be your turn. So pay attention to what is going on.

Charlotte was indeed hired by an elderly couple who did nothing for themselves and Charlotte was to help them both run the house and wait upon them for their every need. They were kind in their way and being elderly went to bed early. So Charlotte was spared the fourteen- or fifteen-hour days that some servants worked. She was, though, subjected to the so-called 'penny test'. Employers would test the honesty of their staff by leaving pennies behind a plate or even under a carpet to see if the penny was returned or pocketed. If it wasn't returned, they would be dismissed on the spot.

The following year Richard was also engaged as a general servant and groom. Like his sister Charlotte he too was a presentable youth and looked the part when it came to someone who would not be workshy.

Chapter 6

Sam now took over the driving from his son John, or other drivers, when they arrived in Bath from London and would take the coach and passengers on to Bristol himself. Sam would then drive back from Bristol the same day in the return coach.

When John was driving, he could then come back to Catherine Cottage, put his feet up and keep an eye on things. If John was not around, Sam would still take the coach to Bristol and back and he was happy with the fact that his son Richard, now coming up to fourteen years of age, was able to look out for his younger brothers and sisters. The journey between Bath and Bristol could be comfortably achieved within two hours. Sam would have just under two hours before making the return trip to Bath and he fell into the habit of taking himself away to the Cock and Bull Inn just round the corner from the Old Crown that was the terminus for his coach. Sam preferred to take himself away and to sit quietly in the corner with an ample and appetising meal and a glass of beer and time to read the newspapers, or occasionally the *Monthly Magazine* which John would bring him from London.

Over the months he had become to get to know the widowed daughter of the proprietor John Todd quite well. Ann would always come and serve him his food or his glass of beer. Sam tried to guess her age but he was not quite sure. She was in any case a handsome-looking woman. Why was he trying to guess her age, he thought to himself? At forty he was not exactly in the spring of youth himself.

Chapter 7

Sam had for some time been giving serious consideration to the question of how to secure the future for himself and for his family in Bath. It was clear to see that the days of long-distance coach travel from London were coming to an end. The railways would see to that and building works were already under way, supervised by Isambard Kingdom Brunel.

With the consent of his company, who were also well aware of the implications of the coming of the railway, Sam had planned for what he called 'transfer services' to serve communities and towns beyond the environs around Bath once the railway service opened up. His intention was that his sons at least would then have a more secure future. Memories of the terribly hard times that he had shared with his father and the family when he was young were never far from his thinking.

It was some two years since their last encounter when Sam next saw Charles Dickens. There he was, and even more famous these days, sitting up at the front of the coach with

Sam's son John driving. Dickens saw Sam and a broad smile appeared on his face. Sam returned the smile.

'Well, well. If it isn't Mr Weller Senior,' said Dickens heartily.

He climbed down from the coach and he held his hand out to shake with Sam, which was gladly reciprocated.

'No doubt you will be off to Bristol soon. I am staying in Bath for some little while this time, but I shall have occasion to go to Bristol a few times as well. Not today though, Sam. I want to find my room and rest up as I have a reading engagement this evening. People want to hear me read to them these days. Can we ride together in a few days' time? Or is the famous Sam Weller particular about the company he keeps these days?'

Dickens smiled wickedly. Sam beamed in return.

'Mr Dickens what a joy to meet you again. By all means let us pick up where we left off last time. It will be good to share a journey together again. Mind you, look out for the weather. We had good fortune last time but unless you have the correct riding gear it can be a very uncomfortable time for outside passengers when it rains,'

'Then, until we meet again one sunny day, Sam.'

With this, Dickens strode off to collect his luggage and take a 'fly' – a small single-horse, two-wheeled carriage – to wherever he was staying.

Chapter 8

Sam, as usual, had made his way to the Cock and Bull when he arrived in Bristol. He had been there the day before but when he arrived this time the premises was closed. Sam was confused and he tried staring in through the window but all he could see was an empty room and no sign of anyone inside. Sam made his way to around the back and thought that he would try and find his way in through that way. The door was open and he could see men carrying out furniture and piling this up in the rear yard alongside all sorts of goods ranging from kegs to bottles in crates and what was presumably all the contents of the kitchen.

The normally cheerful and smiling Ann Todd was standing in the corner of the yard with her head resting on her father's shoulder, weeping bitterly, her body convulsing. John Todd was standing there was his arms around her shoulder and with his eyes closed as if to shut the scene out.

Sam approached them.

'What is going on here? What are these men doing,' he asked.

Todd opened his eyes and spoke in his soft northern accent.

'We are done for, Sam Weller. They will not let us back in but say they will bring us our clothes and then that is it. They are taking us off to debtors' prison. I do not have enough to pay our creditors and they have foreclosed on us and I am a ruined. As soon as they come out with our clothes they are taking us off to prison.'

Ann raised her head from her father's shoulder. Her eyes were red from weeping. Sam was touched to the heart to see her in such distress.

'Look, I cannot do much today as I will have to take the coach back to Bath. How much do you owe or how much will it take to keep you out of prison?'

'In all, quite a lot,' said Todd. 'Maybe when everything is sold and if I can find a little more the creditors will be content. What about Ann, though? She has nowhere to go and does not deserve to be in gaol with me.'

Sam found he did not have to think about it.

'Ann, will you come back to Bath with me? I have been on my own for sometime now. Will you let me look after you?'

Ann just stood there with a bemused look upon her face. Todd started to bridle.

'Just what are you suggesting, Sam Weller!?'

Sam looked at Ann and placed his hand gently under her chin.

'What do you say Ann? Do you want to come to Bath with me? We'll do everything legal and proper. Marriage at our age is not unheard of you know and we have known each other for some time now. I do have a little money about me and certainly enough for you to to find a room for a day or two and until we can see if things can be sorted. Not the most romantic of propositions I know but a sensible course of action under the circumstances.'

Todd turned to his daughter.

'What do you say, Ann? Here is as good and as honourable offer as you will ever get and I have seen the way that you look at him. You seem to have some feeling for this good man. It will put my mind at ease if I know you will be settled. I just thank the Lord that your mother is not here to see this dilemma.'

'Yes, Sam Weller. I will be your wife and I promise that to the end of our days you will not regret it,' said Ann.

Sam looked at his watch. It would soon be time for him to be on the move. He dug into his pocket and pulled out two guineas, which he passed to Ann.

'Wait for me tomorrow at the coaching inn, Ann. You know what time I get there. I will have a word with these fellows to be certain that they do not detain you. John Todd, for now you will have to go with them. I will do what I can as soon as I can to get you out of prison. Then we have a wedding to arrange.'

Sam went to have a word with the bailiffs. It cost him a further two shillings but he secured Ann's freedom. He then went to drive back to Bath.

Chapter 9

Sam arrived the next day back in Bristol. He had brought another driver with him as he did not intend returning to Bath that night. There was far too much to do. Ann was waiting for him beside the coaching inn and out of the rain. They kissed each other on the cheeks in greeting. The first intimate contact they had ever had.

'Hello, Ann,' said Sam affectionately. 'It is good to see you. All things considered, how are you? Have you been able to find lodgings and have you seen your father yet?'

'Sam, it's more than good to see you,' she replied. 'I have been in turmoil thinking about father being in that place and I don't know what would have happened to me if you had not been there. I have a room in Nicholas Street by the church. I have not been to see father yet. I want you to be with me, I do not want to go to such a place on my own. How long have we got?' she added nervously.

'I return to Bath with the coach tomorrow,' said Sam, 'so we have some little time to try and sort things out. I suggest first that we go to St Nicholas and request that we get married under licence. We may have to stretch the truth a little if we are to get a licence through quickly so I shall say that I am living also in Nicholas Street. After that we can go and visit you father and see if there is anything we can do to get him released and then I must find my own lodgings for the night.'

'Oh, Sam!' cried Ann. 'You have it all worked out haven't you. No wonder they made you a stable keeper and not just an ordinary coachman. Come on, let's go and see about this marriage licence and then we can go and see father. As for tonight Sam Weller you are to stay with me. We have both been married before and let's pray that we will be again before this time next week. It is a long time since I have lain with a man and it is probably quite some time since you have been with a woman. Let's comfort each other tonight, it is

181

the only chance we will get until our wedding night, that is, unless you find me unattractive and then if you do I will still keep and maintain a home for you even if you do not want me.'

'If that is your way for fishing for a compliment Ann, then it is not necessary. And you know it. I am sure you have seen men's eyes following you around as you have been serving, mine included. So, let us be with each other tonight,' said Sam. 'We are old enough to know what we are doing and we need not tell your father about our intended arrangement. Now let's sort out the church and then go to your father.'

The wedding was set for a fortnight later, subject to the licence coming through. Sam and Ann went to see John Todd in gaol. All the effects from the Cock and Bull were to be reclaimed by the creditors where this was possible and other items were to be auctioned off the following day. Sam promised that he would guarantee any shortfall thereafter so that Todd could be released and his bankruptcy annulled.

Chapter 10

Two days later, as Sam was waiting in Bath for the coach from London to arrive so that he could then drive it on for Bristol, Charles Dickens walked up towards him.

'Well, Sam Weller, it seems I have picked a fine day to go to Bristol. May we remake our acquaintance along the way?'

'Why indeed, Mr Dickens sir,' cried Sam, 'and I never did thank you for the kindness of your note and for that copy of the *Monthly Magazine*. I look forward to our conversation very much. The coach should be here soon.'

He pulled out his watch.

'A man always looking at the time,' remarked Dickens. 'The ever-punctual Mr Sam Weller. As for that copy of the magazine, it is nothing. It seems that character of Sam Weller was the making of *Pickwick Papers* and the public liked to read about him. They are putting all the things together as we speak and the papers as I call them are to be published in book form. I shall send you a copy of that to. This looks like your coach. You will be busy for a while so I will leave you to do your job and we can start up again once we are under way.'

The coach was soon ready to leave and there was Sam driving and Charles Dickens sat next beside him.

Once the road ahead was clear, Dickens began the conversation.

'What adventures have befallen you since we last met, Sam Weller? I looked for you the other morning expecting you to be driving, and when I saw you were not there I made enquiries and they said you would not be doing the Bristol run until today. You looked well enough when I saw you last and you look your normal robust self today.'

'Oh, things have become complicated, Mr Dickens,' said Sam. 'In some ways things have turned out for the better but it is the circumstances leading up to it that I do not like.'

'How so?' asked Dickens in a concerned voice.

'Well, sir, for quite some time now when I leave the coach in Bristol it has been my habit to go to a place nearby and take something to eat and maybe the occasional glass of beer and sometimes I can catch up on my reading. Anyway, I have become known to the publican and to his widowed daughter. All right and proper, you understand.'

Dickens nodded sympathetically.

'Anyway, l turned up one day as usual to find the place shut and the inside empty. I didn't know what to think. Nothing had seemed strange or odd the previous day. All quite normal in fact. Anyway, such was my concern for people that I now consider to be my friends that I went round to the back to see if I could discover more.

'There were men taking everything out of the place and stacking the things in the yard. Then I saw in a corner of the yard my friend, Ann, with her head on her father's shoulder and him with his eyes closed and his arm around her. I asked him what was going on and he said that his creditors had called him bankrupt and they were to be sent to debtors' prison and all the goods that were being taken out of the place were to be auctioned off for the benefit of the creditors.

'Well, Mr Dickens, I thought I must do something to stop this from happening. Anyway, and to cut a long story short, with Ann being a widow and me a widower – although I was not intending to look for a new wife – I asked Ann to marry me. Her father seemed up for it and so we have applied for a licence and our intention is to marry in Bristol in ten days from now. I will then bring Ann back here to Bath and Catherine Cottage and that will make things all the better both for me and for the children still at home. We quite like each other so it seems a good and sensible arrangement. As for her father, we should hear today how much debt is still owed and if it is not too much for me I have said that I will guarantee the balance so that his bankruptcy can be cancelled and he can attend the wedding as a free man. That's about the size of it, Mr Dickens.'

'What a remarkable tale and what a remarkable man you are, Sam Weller!' said Dickens warmly. 'This is a tale that would surely have gone down well in the Pickwick Club. You have rescued this no doubt good woman by making her your wife and you are prepared to secure the release of her father from prison. Capital, absolutely capital! I deplore this practice of throwing people, some good people as well, into gaol just because they have fallen on hard times. They then hold them in the same deplorable conditions as thieves and murderers. I know you are a discreet man, Sam Weller, so I know that I can tell you that my dear father was once held in a debtors' prison.'

'You do surprise me with that, Mr Dickens,' said Sam. 'I now recall my father telling my about the Marshalsea debtors' prison in Southwark and how he used to see the tall outside walls when he went to market with Tomkins. Tomkins, if you recall, being the man arrested by the Customs men for selling contraband tea.'

'There is so much wrong and so many injustices in this land of ours,' said Dickens with conviction. 'I am resolved to do what I can about it. If my writings continue to be popular then perhaps I can show through my works why such a country as Great Britain should be ashamed of what we let happen within our own shores. Maybe one day I can write a story around someone who has fallen on bad times and finds themselves in a debtors' prison.'

For the remainder of the journey Dickens was content to relate to Sam his observations about the way British society conducted itself. This was a turnaround from their first encounter. On that occasion Dickens wanted to hear from Sam about his experiences. This time Dickens wanted to talk about what he perceived to be the social injustices and ills that should be put right.

Ann was waiting for Sam's coach to arrive and, when he pulled up at the coaching inn, she could see from Sam's description of him that he had been sitting with Charles Dickens. Sam introduced Ann to Dickens.

'Good day to you, madam,' Dickens said, doffing his hat politely. 'I am sorry to hear about what has happened to you and to your father, but I am glad to hear of your intended marriage. I consider Sam Weller to be a fine man and I sincerely wish you all happiness for the future.'

Then, turning to Sam, he said, 'I am returning tonight

with a different service. I intend to return to London some time next week but I am not quite sure of that. If I do have cause to come to Bath again I suspect it will be on the railway they are starting to build. Maybe we will meet again some time. Goodbye to you, Sam Weller, and to you ma'am.'

Chapter 11

John Todd was now free, with Sam having paid enough to settle the outstanding amount of money owed to the creditors. The night before the wedding the three of them had discussed what to do about Todd's future.

'What plans do you have now, John?' asked Sam.

'I am in my seventies now, Sam, too old to start up again. It is time for me to go back home to Penrith. That is where I want to spend the rest of my days. We still have family up there and I want to see the hills and the lakes again before I die. Thanks to you, Sam, and with the money I have left from what you gave me, I will now take a coastal packet from here in Bristol in the morning to a nearby port.'

'You can still come with us, father,' Ann said. 'Me and Sam have discussed this.'

'No, my dear, my mind is set on going back home,' answered Todd. 'As for you, Sam, if it weren't for this damned class society of ours I could call you a gentleman. You are by far more of a gentleman than many a so-called gentleman that I have had the misfortune to meet.'

'As Mr Dickens once said to me,' said Sam, 'I was once a gentleman's gentleman. That seems a long time ago now. I will settle for what I am. A stable keeper and an employer of men.'

Sam found his own lodgings for the night and Todd stayed

with his daughter. They met at the church in the morning. The ceremony was simple and quickly over with just the three of them and their two witnesses known by Ann and John Todd from the Cock and Bull.

After the ceremony Ann said to Sam:

'I'm curious, Sam. You signed your name as Daniel Weller. Why was that?'

Sam smiled.

'Why, my dear, Daniel is my baptised name, the same as my father's. It's the family that gave me the familiar name of Sam.'

Todd knew of a packet leaving for the north coast early in the afternoon and he was anxious to catch it. Sam and Ann would take his company's coach service back to Bath later that same afternoon. They would spend their wedding night back at Catherine Cottage. Waiting to greet them were all of Sam's children, except John who was on the London to Bath run and had his own home in Lambeth with his wife Elizabeth and Charlotte who was serving her employers, the elderly Griffiths family out at Widcombe.

Chapter 12

Some two weeks later John arrived back at Catherine Cottage having completed yet another run from London. He brought with him a small package addressed to Sam.

'This was handed me before I left for Bath,' he explained. 'I asked what it was about and the man just said that he had instructions to give it to me with the request that I pass it on to my father. He could tell me no more.'

'Well, I'd better open it and see what it is all about then,' said Sam, carefully undoing the wrapping. 'Why here is a brief note. It says "with the compliments of Charles Dickens

and congratulations on your wedding". Let's have a look
further then.'

He undid one further layer of paper.

'Why, it is a watch. It is the biggest watch I have ever seen in
my life. It must weigh a pound at least.'

He turned the watch over and read the inscription on the
back.

'*Mr Weller Senior*'.

Sam was deeply moved and, for once, at a loss for words.

Dickens and Sam never met again. The era of long-
distance stagecoaches between London and the West
Country was drawing to a close. By 1840 the Great Western
Railway train services were first running between London
Paddington and Reading and by the end of that year the line
had extended beyond Swindon. Work had started in the
other direction and by 1840 there was also a train service
between Bristol and Bath. In one sense it was the end of an
era but for Sam and the family the coming of the railways
opened up new opportunities now that he was freed from his
obligation to support long-distance stagecoach services.

The family's association with certain places that supported
the shrinking levels of stagecoach services was to be renewed,
but in a somewhat different form.

Chapter 13

A few years later

It was Christmas and the family had planned and worked
hard to make sure that they could all make it to Catherine
Cottage for what might be their last chance for a meal
together. Everything was changing and the family members
were now all scattered in different directions. Everyone was

waiting on Richard. He could not make it until his employer freed him to go. Then he had but a half-hour's walk up from the Bristol Road. The door opened and Richard entered, briskly closing the door behind him against the cold wind blowing in from the north-east.

'Richard, my lad. Welcome, welcome.'

Sam had already enjoyed the benefit of several quarts of beer during the day. He didn't mind, in truth he welcomed the fact that the business was shut up for the next couple of days.

'Warm yourself by the fire. Supper won't be long now.'

There was much hugging and cheek-kissing as Richard worked his way round the room. Ann came in from the kitchen.

'Merry Christmas, Richard. It is good that we are now altogether. Supper will be about another half hour.'

Sam picked up his mug of beer again.

'Good, enough time to tell each other what is happening. Some of you haven't seen each other or me and Ann for quite some little while now. John, let's start with you.'

'This is daft,' said John. 'Half of Bath knows I'm back and forth between Bath and London. What more do you want me to say?'

'Then tell them what you're doing here,' said Sam.

'Oh, for heavens sake! I've got a couple of days off before I go back to London, you daft bugger, and Elizabeth is spending Christmas with her parents and younger sister. If you carry on like this then it looks like I should quit London and come down here and take it all over.'

John gave a huge disarming grin.

'Enough of that. Enough of that,' said Sam. 'Now then you, Charlotte. What's your news?'

'My news, as you well know, father, is that I want away from here. Old Mrs Griffiths, God bless her, can't be going on for much longer. I'm only here for another couple of hours and then I have to get back and look after her and she does not sleep well these days. A fine Christmas this is going to be. I want to go to London. This place is dead. The old lady has promised me a reference as long as I promise to stay with her until the end. I've already written to uncle William and Charlotte in Lambeth and they said I can stay with them until I find a position.'

'Another one flying the nest, then,' said Sam. 'Just like Eliza and her farmer. How long has he been courting you, girl? I have to admire the man for his persistence and his fortitude coming here all the way from Devon every couple of weeks. Must need to have his head tested, that's all I can say. How did you manage to reel him in? Can't see you getting up at the crack of dawn to milk the cows, and that's a fact.'

'Calm yourself down, Sam Weller. I'm beginning to hear the beer talking,' snapped Ann.

'That's right,' Eliza chimed in. 'Frank Rowell is a good man and I'd rather be with him on his farm than skivvying away for some tight-fisted so-and-so. As soon as he asks me to marry him I'm going to say yes.'

'Good for you!' said Mary Ann, butting in. 'My Robert and me write to each other nearly every day and he thinks he will soon be in a position to be taking over the Packhorse and Talbot in Turnham Green and as soon as he does I hope he will ask me to marry him.'

'Stop. Stop,' demanded Sam. 'A daughter of mine working one of my old haunts!'

'Oh, shut up you old fool!' snapped Ann. 'You haven't been there for the best part of twenty years or more.'

'That's not the point,' protested Sam. 'It's the principle of the thing.'

He took another swig of beer.

Not being prepared to let things go herself, Mary Ann joined in.

'Robert is not just an innkeeper. His father is a gentleman of independent means and Robert is a victuallar.'

'Do you know what that word means, girl? It means he is an innkeeper and that he possibly knows his way around the kitchen. And don't start with them tears either,' said Sam, sounding a bit slurred.

'Well, if that's the way of things I had best tell you my news,' said Richard. 'It nearly being Christmas and all, I asked Kate last night to marry me and she said yes.'

The room erupted into whoops of joy and another round of hugging and cheek kissing. The best Sam could manage was a splutter of the mouth full of beer he was trying to get down him. This then brought on a coughing fit.

When he'd recovered enough to manage another sip, Sam turned to eighteen-year-old Edward and fourteen-year-old William.

'You two buggers had better not be getting married.'

'No fear!' they said in unison.

'Now you've got that sorted out, Daniel Weller, put that mug down and Eliza, Mary Ann, you come and help me serve up supper,' said Ann.

'Yikes!! I know when she's got the hump with me when she calls me Daniel. I'd best shut up then.'

Sam drained the remainder of the contents of his mug in one long gulp.

'And, girl,' looking across at Mary Ann, 'I didn't mean what I said. I hope your Mister Shelley does come through for you. Now stop with that wet face. It's nearly Christmas.'

Throughout the meal conversations were flying across the table. Everyone, except for the two youngest boys who felt left out of it and Sam who was busy concentrating hard on eating, was in an excited mood.

Eventually Charlotte stood up to go

'I must get back,' she said. 'It's been wonderful to be here together like this. I just wish I didn't have to leave so soon.'

191

'I'll walk you part of the way,' said Richard. 'I am expected to call on Kate and her parents anyway.'

In one sense the evening showed just how the new generation was making its own way in life. John had married Elizabeth back in London and Eliza, Mary Ann and Richard were looking to their own marriages while Charlotte was ready to leave Bath for London.

The conversation continued as they caught up with each other's news. Eliza and Mary Ann were talking amongst themselves, comparing notes on their prospective lives of a farmer's wife and the wife of an innkeeper. William was trying to be adult and take part in the conversation between his less than sober father and John.

'Why don't the Queen and Prince Albert ever come here?' asked William.

'Huh. Now there's a story,' said Sam. 'Some years ago when she was about eleven and still the princess, she came to Bath to open the Royal Victoria Park up at the front of the Royal Crescent. We were all there at the time. Your mother and me, John, Charlotte, Richard, Eliza and Mary Ann. It's not every day you get to see a princess. Well anyway the story is that during the park's opening ceremony a gust of wind blew her skirt in the air. Someone joked that she had fat legs, and people laughed. The Princess Victoria was said to be so upset by this that she vowed never to return to Bath from that day.'

'You sure that wasn't you that called her "fat legs"?' asked Ann.

'Very funny!' Sam retorted. 'A royal visit would be grand for business but I hardly see that happening now until after the railway gets here.'

Chapter 14

Old Mrs Griffiths was now confined to bed and she relied on Charlotte more and more. She refused to have a nurse attend her and the doctor advised that it would not be long now. True to her word the old lady had already written a reference for Charlotte. She had asked Charlotte a number of times what her plans were and had always ended up saying:

'You will stay with me, child, won't you? I don't want any strangers when my time is nearly up.'

Charlotte always gave the old lady the reassurance she wanted but there was no need for that any more. Once the money she was owed was settled she was off to London. Not quite yet, though, as she had a wedding to attend. Richard and Kate were in a hurry. Why, it was only three months on from when they were altogether for the Christmas gathering at Catherine Cottage and Richard broke his news.

Richard was a servant and groom down on Bristol Road where Katherine, or 'Kate' as she preferred to be called, also lived. Kate had come over from Ireland with her parents who were in need of finding work or they would starve in Ireland.

After the wedding John found Richard standing next to his bride.

'Well, you two. What are your plans now? Are you going to stay with your employer, Richard?'

'No, John. I'll be handing in my notice to quit next week. I've secured a position as a post boy guard on the post coach. Even when the railway opens up fully to London and to Bristol they will still need post coaches to get to other places. The money is better and it will help tide us over until we get away from Bath.'

'Look,' said John, 'I've been there and I've done it in London both as a bachelor and as a married man. London is not that great, you know. I can foresee a time when I will be happy to leave London and we can come and work from here.'

'Well, maybe not London itself,' said Richard. 'If Mary Ann gets a move on and marries her Mr Shelley and he gets the Packhorse and Talbot we can join them in Turnham Green.'

'Don't hold your breath too long,' said John. 'With the speed at which Robert Shelley and Mary Ann are carrying on you'll still be here when you are grandparents.'

Kate gave Richard such a look. It was clear that she wanted away from Bath as well.

Charlotte left to stay with uncle William the following week but it was almost a year later until Mary Ann married Robert Shelley, who was twenty years her senior. Still what mattered was that Mary Ann felt she had found a good catch and knew she would do no better even though it transpired that Shelley had been waiting for what they call 'dead man's shoes' and that was why there had been the long wait before they found themselves at the Packhorse and Talbot.

It took a little while after that before they considered themselves established there. Mary Ann had long since forgiven her father for what he had said. He was right. Robert Shelley was little more than an innkeeper and she an innkeeper's wife, but in her mind she had made the right choice.

Chapter 15

Even with the better money as a post boy the best that Richard and Kate could find was a shared tenement with fifteen others in Lampard's Buildings. Kate had not been able to find work and she wondered if it was because she was Irish and spoke with a strong accent, but in reality she had little to offer as she was not trained to come into service. Her father had been more lucky and he had found work briefly as a servant but then as a labourer helping to build the railways that were now being constructed to meet up with the main London to Bristol railway. It was the loss of Richard and Kate's baby daughter Eliza Mary to the measles and then a son called Richard to convulsions that finally persuaded them to leave Bath.

Richard had written, or rather his father had done so for him, to Robert and Mary Ann Shelley at the Packhorse and Talbot through the penny post. Richard and Kate were at Catherine Cottage for an evening and parting meal as they were to catch the train towards London the following morning.

'Well, another parting of the ways,' said Ann, 'and just a few months after Eliza finally gets to wed her Devonshire farmer and she is expecting already. So what next for you two?'

'Before that we want to tell you that Kate's having another baby,' announced Richard.

'My, that is good news after your loss of both little Eliza Mary and then Richard! I'm sure this time everything will turn out for the best.'

'I wonder how many times I will become a grandfather? It seems good cause to have a celebratory drink,' said Sam.

'Fine idea,' said John and Richard nodded his agreement as well. William thought it a good idea as well.

'You men!' said Ann. 'All you can think of is your beer and what goes on in between the sheets. When you've had too much of the first then you are not much good at the other. Thank heaven for small mercies! Come on, Kate dear, come and give me a hand and let these oafs get on with their beer drinking. Don't forget that Edward and his young lady are hoping to get here later if they can get away.'

The men settled themselves down for the main event of the evening.

Part VII

An Interlude in Turnham Green

Chapter 1

Mary Ann and Robert Shelley seemed determined to make up for lost time. Within the year they had their first born, a son they called Robert William.

Richard and Kate were staying with them at the Packhorse and Talbot and Richard had a position as an ostler in the stables at the close-by Roe Buck. The Roe Buck was obviously operating on a smaller scale than when his father Sam and later John knew the place, but there was still plenty of work for him to do. But was it what he really wanted?

It was midsummer and it had been a long hot day. Kate felt tired, even though she had hardly worked all day owing to the discomfort of her large belly and the oppressive heat. The baby was due within a few weeks. Where is Richard, Kate asked herself? He should be home by now. He'd better not be wasting what little money we have on gambling on those Roe Buck boxing competition fights. If he's not back soon then I'll go and get him.

After another half hour or so there was still no sign of Richard, but she decided to give him a few minutes longer.

'*Muc* [Pig]!' she said out loud, but no one was in earshot. 'I'll go find the pig myself then,' she grumbled.

Kate pulled herself out of the chair by the door leading from the kitchen to the yard and slowly and clumsily made her way towards the Roe Buck stables. If he was not there then woe betide him if she found him gambling and watching the fights in the big barn nearby.

Kate had to pass the barn before she reached the stables but the doors were closed and there seemed to be nobody about. Well, he's not at the fights then, she thought, that's something at least. Now what is he about if he is not there?

She made her way the extra hundred yards or more to the stables where Richard worked. There he was with two other men. Why is he standing like that? Why, he looks as though he is cuffed. Are those policemen? Kate got that little bit nearer and, yes, there he was, her man cuffed.

'What's going on?' said Kate furiously. 'Why have you taken my husband?

'Wife or not, this is police business and we need to know if this fellow is involved or not,' said one of the constables.

'*Leathcheann* [halfwit]!' shouted Kate. 'He's not clever enough to be up to any mischief and he knows I will brain him if he did. What's he done that you think you need to cuff him?'

'Nothing, Kate, I swear!' protested Richard.

'Not another sound out of you,' said the constable.

Then he turned to Kate again.

'We are after questioning him and making sure he does not get away. I'm Irish too, and if you call me an idiot or any other name I'll run you in as well despite your condition.

'A serious crime has been committed by someone who is very bold and very stupid and you woman have just confirmed that what we have here is someone who has little brain,' he continued.

At which point another two constables emerged from the stable on each side of a struggling youth.

'So now we have two of them!' exclaimed the constable. 'The thief and his accomplice who would no doubt help him fence the stolen goods.'

'Accomplice! What do you mean, accomplice? said Richard indignantly. This lad's only been here for a day and a piece. He's only a stable lad who mucks out and cleans up after me so how can we be in partnership over anything? You haven't even told me yet what has been done and yet you cuff me.'

'Caught him in possession so we did,' said one of the constables having hold of the still-struggling lad. 'Didn't even have the wits to hide the stuff. We found it under his mattress at the back of the stables.'

The constable held up a small pouch-like bag presumably containing what they had been searching for.

'Heavens sake, can someone tell me what is going on?' exclaimed Kate.

'And me,' added Richard.

'Very well,' said the first constable. 'About an hour ago a rather elderly and frail gentleman was on his way home across the Common, driving himself in his own carriage after dining with friends. Someone then took the opportunity to seize the reins, as the gentleman was going rather slowly, owing to the gentleman's footman having taken to his bed with some sort of ailment, so he had no one to drive him. That person brought the carriage to a stop and, armed with a knife, threatened to cut the gentleman if he did not get down and give him everything he had.'

At that point the other constable who was holding the new lad held up a knife. The first constable then continued.

'The gentleman was then relieved of his watch, a ring and whatever money he had about him. The thief, then, in a most cowardly and brutal fashion and with no regards to the gentleman's condition, struck the gentleman hard and pushed him to the ground. Whilst the gentleman was seriously dazed he remained conscious. He watched as his assailant ran to the near edge of the Common and was seen to enter into these here stables. Perhaps he thought the gentleman was unconscious, but even so it wasn't the cleverest thing to do. To commit such an act upon your own doorstep and not even to attempt to go to earth via some other route but to go straight to where you hide out. Some little while later another rider comes across the Common and goes to the gentleman's rescue, takes him to the nearby doctor's for attention and sends word to the Watchhouse to bring us here.'

'When was this?' demanded Richard.

'About an hour ago,' replied the first constable.

'Well, I was in the big barn with a lot of others watching the fights. You see it could not have been me. As for being an accomplice, as I have told you, I hardly have had time to talk to him let alone form a criminal association, which in the first place is not my nature.'

'You were at the fights, Richard Weller!' Kate broke in, her voice quivering with anger. 'I might have known. Things are tight enough as it is without you gambling away what little we have!'

The first constable turned to the boy.

'What's your name, son?'

'Tom,' the boy replied, then paused. 'Tom, Tom Jones.'

'The truth now,' growled the first constable. 'We'll get it out of you in the end and all the worse for you if you don't give us your real name now.'

'It's Tomkins. Tom Tomkins,' was the response.

'Tomkins,' said Richard. 'That's a bad name.'

'How so?' asked the constable.

'My grandfather knew a Tomkins once. Fred Tomkins. He and my grandfather used to come up from the country together and take my employer's produce to Southwark and the market at Borough. He was caught red-handed by the Customs dealing in smuggled goods and he was stealing from his employer by shorting him on the money he should have got from selling at the market.'

'Fred Tomkins was my uncle,' came the sullen admission.

The constable undid the cuffs and Richard rubbed his wrists. The four constables and the apprehended Tom Tomkins then left without further explanation.

Richard had other problems now. He had to explain himself to Kate.

Chapter 2

Kate was holding her newly born son in her arms.

'What shall we call him, Richard? Something Irish perhaps?' she said, a hopeful lift in her voice.

'Kate, we've had this before. He is English born, he lives in England so we will stick to English names. Daniel was good enough for my father and for his father and it will be good enough again. Daniel Frederick. Let's have no more argument about it.'

Richard spoke with finality. Mary Ann was also in the room and Kate could see that there was little point in pressing her case any further.

A week or so later Kate and Richard were in their room as Richard was getting ready to leave for work.

'What are we going to do now, Richard? I see the Roe Buck as offering you little opportunity. Can we not aim for something better? Can you not find a position as a coachman? We need more money with the baby and maybe with a bigger family to follow.'

'Kate, to be a coachman here in London I need to become known either to a family or to an agency that will recommend me,' said Richard impatiently. 'As yet I have yet to find my way around London's streets, so we will have to get by as best we can until my situation improves. In any event, I think we should also move closer to London itself,' he added.

'And how are we going to do that?' asked Kate. 'Why, you are just about the only one in your family that did not learn to read. You can't even print your own name. At least I had an excuse as no one expects a girl like me to get learning.'

'All I have ever wanted to be is a coachman,' said Richard. 'I didn't take easy to learning how to read and it don't bother horses none when they can't read. We can ask Robert if he can look in the papers for rooms to rent.'

Chapter 3

Mary Ann and Robert Shelley were sitting in front of the fire after supper one Sunday evening. John had brought his cab up from Lambeth with his wife Elizabeth.

Robert raised his voice to drown out the various conversations in progress.

'Mary Ann, why don't you try and arrange a family reunion for the Great Exhibition. Why it's almost upon our doorstep just down in Kensington. I hear that tickets can be had for as little as one shilling. Why there could be you and me, Richard and Kate, Charlotte and George Eydmann, you John and Elizabeth. Why not try and bring your father up from Bath with William and Edward? It will not take long by train and they can take rooms here for the night. You have uncles hereabouts as well, don't you?

'We could all meet here for some fortification and then go and see the Exhibition together. It will be a truly wonderful experience. The whole world will be able to see what a great and powerful country this is. What do you say, everyone?'

'Well I'm all for it!' cried Mary Ann enthusiastically.

'Then we shall do it,' said Robert. 'I shall write to Catherine Cottage and as for everyone else, we will no doubt see them over the next month or so. You know, when my father used to entertain for dinner it was sometimes the custom for each dinner guest to come up with an anecdote, with a little wrapped prize going to the one who tells the best story. What do you think?'

'If I hear about father and his blessed watch and Mr Dickens one more time, I think I shall leave for Australia,' said John. 'We will be lucky to escape the story-telling as it is without giving him a further excuse.'

'All that said, Ann is not that strong these days,' said Mary Ann. 'I don't think father will be inclined to leave her and come up to London or even to prise himself away from the

York Mews Tap. He is as strong as an ox but have a mind to her being ten years his senior, and she has had to look after him all these years. By all means Robert write to father but in a way to let him know that we expect it will be difficult for him and Ann to make the journey. Maybe we could say that we will take the train to them and visit them some day. In any case, maybe William or Edward can make the trip.'

'Well, maybe it's about time me and Elizabeth uprooted ourselves and went to Bath. I must admit I am beginning to feel I've had my fill of this place for some time now,' said John. 'It worries me also that the business is going to pot and he is sitting on a little gold mine there, or should be if it weren't for his increased interest in the York Mews Tap.'

Part VIII

Richard and Kate in London

Chapter 1

Richard left the Roe Buck one night to see Robert and ask for his help in finding accommodation and maybe also a new position. He had told Kate to expect him home late and the reason for his lateness.

He found Robert seated at the kitchen table.

'Good evening, Robert. If you are not too busy can you spare a moment?

'Come in, Richard,' answered Robert, 'come in and sit yourself down. I've just made myself some tea. Would you care for a cup?'

'Most welcome. I'd love a cuppa,' Robert replied. 'Robert, I wonder if you could help us? I think it is time to get away from the Roe Buck. The best I'm ever going to be there is an ostler and it's no secret that being a coachman is what I really want to be. I find myself in a sort of horse and cart situation if you like ...'

He paused and smiled at his little joke.

'... we need somewhere else to live but then I need to find new employment to be able to afford to move somewhere else. What do you reckon is the best way of going about things?'

'Well now,' said Robert. 'That's an interesting puzzle. Finding a situation can be tricky, particularly if you are not known in London. So much depends upon personal recommendations. It's the same in some ways nowadays as it was when your grandfather was back on the Weald.

'We have none of those hiring fairs like what you and Charlotte went to when you were living in Bath. There are the agencies, of course, but some of these are run by rogues, including some who have been dismissed by their previous employer for wrongdoing.

'There are those agencies at the top end such as Mrs Hunt and Masseys that cannot be faulted and rely upon their high reputation. It will not be easy to get them to take you on, though. Of the rest, many will take anything as much as a shilling in the pound commission out of a placement's first year's wages and that's not the end of it. Everything is done on a verbal basis and what the agency tells you and what your employer requires of you can be quite different things. Then, if you don't like it and you leave employment for elsewhere through the agency, they will charge you another fee and there is no guarantee that you will not find yourself in an equally bad situation.

'Then there is the employer. Those that run the big houses and the real gentry are the best, but it can be difficult to find work there. At the other end there are mean and tight-fisted employers who will work you fifteen or sixteen hours a day and even then try and find ways of making deductions from your wages.

'Now it always helps if you have a good character reference. Have you got such a thing?'

'No, I haven't,' replied Richard. 'I suppose someone could write for me and ask for something from my employer when I was a servant in Bath but that is a little while back now as I became a post boy between leaving service there in Bath and coming here. Do you think we should write to the post in Bath? Maybe they will give me a reference.'

Robert thought for a moment.

'Being a post boy shows you were trusted and courageous, I suppose, but perhaps as landlord of the Packhorse and Talbot I could give you a character reference and say that I have known you for some years and I dare say the Roe Buck could oblige as well. Still, the best thing is if myself or my father knows of anyone who may be looking to take someone on. Once we have that problem sorted then perhaps we can look for new lodgings for you at some place that is convenient and within your means. Now, I am going to have one myself before I retire. Would you like a beer before you go?'

'Perhaps another time, Robert. I had better get back to Kate. Goodnight and thank you, brother-in-law.'

'Goodnight Robert. Save that beer for Sunday then and it's all off to the Great Exhibition.'

Chapter 2

It took a little longer than Richard had hoped but Robert came up trumps. Using his own and his father's connections he had found for Richard a potential employer of good repute in Westminster. The gentleman's family had their own coach and mews and Richard would be expected to work as a footman both inside and out.

The family already had a coachman, but in Robert's view Richard should take this opportunity if he wished away from the Roe Buck. It was now all up to Richard. If his prospective employer accepted him upon interview, then Robert had identified accommodation that he could take in nearby Hanover Place where he and Kate could rent a room in a tenement building. Robert considered that from the description in *The Times* that the accommodation he had in mind should meet the needs of Richard, young Dan and the now again pregnant Kate.

Richard was to present himself to his prospective new master – well, actually the mistress as she was responsible for staff appointments – the following Monday morning at 10 o'clock sharp. Richard would have to make his peace with the Roe Buck for being absent for half a day.

Richard arrived for his interview and presented himself at the entrance to the kitchen just as a nearby clock started to chime the hour. He was first seen by the butler before being taken upstairs.

'You come recommended by Mr John Shelley, and his son

is your brother-in-law, I see,' he said, holding what was obviously a letter in his hand. 'My name is Mr Thomas and if Madam finds you acceptable you will be answerable to me in all things. Now tell me what experience you have.'

'Well, Mr Thomas,' Richard began. 'I started in service when I was thirteen with a family in Bath. My duties there were varied. I did some work inside and was taught how to wait at table, but in the main I worked in the stables and with the horses. My father runs a stable yard in Bath and both my father and my eldest brother have driven the Bath to Bristol stagecoach. Horses and coaching are in the family blood, so to speak.

'With the coming of the railway my wife and me decided to come to London. My brother-in-law runs the Packhorse and Talbot out at Turnham Green so that seemed a good place to start and most recently I have been an ostler at the Roe Buck.

'What I am looking for, Mr Thomas, is the opportunity to become known here in London and work for a good family and my hope is that I will eventually rise to my position as a coachman.'

'That sounds credible,' said Mr Thomas. 'You are married, then, and do you have children?'

'Yes, Mr Thomas. We have a young son and another baby is on the way. If taken on, I am hopeful of finding rooms nearby. My brother-in-law has proposed somewhere in Hanover Place.'

'That may appeal to Madam, you being a family man and with commitments,' said Thomas. 'The Master, Mr Chesterton, and Madam entertain frequently. The Master has many interests both in business and in politics and Madam is a second cousin to late Prime Minister Sir Robert Peel. You will owe a duty not to listen to or hear any conversations going on and to be absolutely discreet. It will be as if you did not exist. You will wait table when required and act as a hall porter receiving guests and delivering messages to the

Master or to Madam. You will ride as footman on the coach and you will assist Mr Rogers the coachman in whatever way he decides. You will be provided with your uniform and livery. Now are there any questions before I take you to see Madam?'

'No, thank you, Mr Thomas,' answered Richard.

'Very well, let us go upstairs. You will only talk to Madam if she addresses you directly. Madam is in the morning room.'

Mr Thomas knocked on the door before entering the morning room and closed the door behind him leaving Richard standing in the hallway. After a few minutes the door was opened again and Mr Thomas signalled Richard to enter.

'Weller, Madam,' he announced.

Richard entered the room and bowed his head before standing bolt upright looking into space. He had quickly taken in all around him. The morning room was lavishly furnished, the like of which he had never seen before. The bright sunlight coming through the window showed off the pastel shades of the furnishings and drapery.

Madam was a tall, elegant and extremely attractive lady.

'So, he comes well recommended then, Thomas, and by Mr Shelley no less? she said. 'He has passed your examination, Thomas?'

'Yes, Madam,' replied Mr Thomas.

Madam continued, 'He has a wife and child, you say, and with another on the way. A man with responsibilities should make for a reliable man. Are you content with not having a living-in footman?'

'Weller is proposing accommodation nearby Madam. I do not forsee any difficulties on this account.'

'Very well, Thomas, then given his height, a tall footman makes all the difference you know, he can start on £18 a year and I will review the situation after six months, given that he is living out.'

Then, addressing Richard directly for the first time.

'I will expect you and your wife to attend church every Sunday.'

'Yes, Madam. Thank you, Madam,' he answered.

Thomas beckoned him to go and followed Richard out into the hallway. Without a further word, Richard followed him back down below stairs. Once there, Mr Thomas told him:

'You will start tomorrow, Richard, or the following day if you need a little more time to move your family and yourself into new accommodation. Below stairs we are all on first-name terms with the exception of myself, of course, and Mrs Thomas the cook. Mrs Thomas and myself have no connection. It is just a coincidence that we share the same name. I will leave it to Mr Rogers and yourself to agree if you wish to be on informal terms. Now I will introduce you to the rest of the staff and give you a note so that you can go and collect a suitable uniform.'

In between leaving his new employer's house and going to collect his uniform Richard went to look at the room in Hanover Place. The rent was a little more than he was hoping to pay but needs must, he said to himself. Richard was delighted to find that his employer was generous enough not to make him pay for his own uniform by means of a deduction from his wages. This was the most common practice even for the lowest skivvy maid and tweeny maid-of-all-work.

Having arranged for his new uniform to be delivered to the house after some small alterations, Richard then made his way back to Turnham Green. Kate was delighted with the news. Robert lent them a horse and a cart to take themselves and their few possessions to Hanover Place. Having unloaded and installed Kate in their new accommodation, Robert drove all the way back to Turnham Green. He then walked to Hammersmith where he was able to catch one of the new horse-drawn omnibuses to Westminster. It was gone eleven o'clock before he saw his bed. It had been a long and eventful day. Tomorrow, with it being his first day he did not have to report for work until seven o'clock.

Chapter 3

The first two months with the Chesterton family were like nothing Richard had experienced before. The Master and Mistress received all sorts of guests, mostly people that Richard had not heard of, but he was assured by Mr Thomas that they were important and included government ministers. Richard had no interest in politicians, let alone what they stood for or believed in. After all he could not read the newspapers and this was not the sort of topic that people of his class and position included in their conversations.

Richard had never eaten so well in his life. Mrs Thomas was an excellent cook and it was certainly not a rare event when those downstairs ate pretty much the same as those upstairs. Richard was even beginning to feel that his uniform was getting tight and pinching him in places. Mr Thomas had to warn Richard not to eat too much and to take more exercise as any new uniform would be paid for out of his wages.

Miss Caroline, their daughter, was, like her mother, tall and elegant. Why was it the rich and the nobs always have the good looks, was a question that often occurred to Richard? Even their teeth were different and they always looked so fresh. He repeated this to Kate when they were home together one Sunday afternoon and she was nursing their new arrival, Jessie. Kate called him stupid and told him that he was talking about his betters as if he was judging the condition of the horses.

The staff were aware that the Master and the Mistress had

planned to entertain and to celebrate, rather peculiarly, the fifteenth anniversary of Queen's accession to the throne this coming June.

In Richard's eyes Mr Thomas was a clever and well-read man, and this was the opinion of everyone below stairs. He had explained it all to everyone during luncheon one day when the Master was at his business and when the Mistress and Miss Caroline had decided to walk to visit friends nearby.

'Her Majesty will have been Queen for fifteen years this coming 20th of June. Did you know that she was only eighteen when her uncle King William IV, King of Hanover and the King of the United Kingdom, died at the age of sixty-four? Mind you people liked the old King. He had served in the Navy and some liked to call him the "Sailor King", but there was another side to him. For many, many years he had a mistress the actress known as Mrs Jordan and they had, I think it was, nine children. Most of these children were given titles and the daughters in particular were part of the royal court, so everything was out in the open. When he died the King, after just seven years on the throne, had no surviving children from his marriage to the Queen. So, what happened was the British title of his kingship then fell to his niece Victoria, now our Queen, whilst the Hanoverian or German title of his kingship had to pass to a male successor as it was not possible for a woman or a girl to assume the title under their laws of succession.

'Now, to the point in hand. Within the next few days Madam will set out her plans for the celebration. This will no doubt be a lavish affair but I am sure, Mrs Thomas, that you will be able to rise to the occasion.'

'I cannot for the life of me understand why they would want to put on a do for such an occasion,' said Mrs Thomas plaintively. 'I have never heard of this before. I will need help here in the kitchen if Madam is planning for large numbers. I can't cope if its just going to be Alice here and me.'

'It is not our place to question the Master's and the Mistress's motives, Mrs Thomas,' replied Mr Thomas sternly. 'We will do as we are instructed and have no further discussion on the point. On the other hand, I'm sure Madam will let you take someone on to help out in the kitchen if you see the need.'

'Could my Kate help out?' asked Richard. 'I'm sure we can find someone to look after young Dan, and the baby sleeps in her basket all the time so she will be no bother. It would save having to look elsewhere, Mrs Thomas, and that little extra bit of money won't go amiss.'

'I can't say that I am happy about the idea of having a baby below stairs. What say you, Mrs Thomas?' asked Mr Thomas.

'I'll work her hard, Richard. There'll be all the preparing to do and the cleaning and putting away. She'll be expected to do as much as Alice here, baby or no baby,' said Mrs Thomas.

'You need have no fear on that account,' Richard assured her.

A few days later Mrs Chesterton summoned Mr Thomas and Mrs Thomas to the morning room to let them know of her plans for the evening celebrations. It was indeed to be a grand event and Mr Thomas was instructed to hire in some more footmen to attend and to assist in waiting at table. It was to be a very special event and a very important one for the Master. Mr and Mrs Thomas were left in no doubt that a great deal was to be expected both from them and from the rest of the staff. Mrs Thomas was instructed to plan a menu for forty persons and present it for Mrs Chesterton's approval.

Mrs Chesterton also had a further announcement

'Mr Chesterton, myself and Miss Caroline will be leaving for the country two days after we entertain. I expect to be away no more than two weeks so we will not miss too much of the Season. We shall all be dining out the evening before our departure. I will say no more on the matter for now but you have my permission to hold your own staff evening downstairs then.

'We will need the services of Rogers to drive us out and back but the footman can stay behind with the rest of you on this one occasion. Weller may bring his wife and the others any followers they may have but I leave it to you, Thomas, to ensure that any undesirables will not be admitted downstairs. Everything of value will be kept safe and the doors to upstairs will be firmly locked.

'Now, as for the journey itself, we can only take two servants with us. Reynolds will have to act as lady's maid both to myself and Miss Caroline, and Weller will be required as footman but also to act as Mr Chesterton's valet. I hope that Weller is up to the task. This is an opportunity for him.

'As for the rest of you, make the most of your celebration because, whilst we are away, I expect a deep spring clean of the entire house, including the back stairs and the servants' quarters.'

'I'm sure Reynolds and Weller will cope admirably,' replied Mr Thomas. 'May I ask, Madam, where you are intending to go so that I can make travel arrangements?'

'To Bath, Thomas. We are going to stay with friends near Bath,' was the reply.

'I am sure Weller will be delighted, Madam. His father runs a stable out of Bath. If I might be so bold to suggest, Madam, that should you and the Master need use of a carriage during your stay, that you may want to bear this in mind.'

'Thank you, Thomas. We might just do that if it is too great an imposition or inconvenient for our hosts to use their carriage. Now that is all. Thank you.'

Chapter 4

It was the day of the celebration evening. Preparations had been going on for days before but Mr Thomas ensured that the family would not be inconvenienced or notice all the work that was being put in. It was after all general practice, even within enlightened households and with employers such as the Chestertons, for all cleaning and making good of rooms to be done out of sight of the family. In fact, apart from the lady's maids, butlers and principal footman, the staff were not expected to be seen at all.

Mrs Thomas had placed her various orders with the grocer, the butcher and the poulterer and had started some of her baking before the big day. Kate and Alice the kitchen maid had their work cut out keeping up with Mrs Thomas' demands. Two additional footmen had been brought in from one of the more reputable agencies that handled such short-term engagements. Mr Thomas had also seen to the need for additional table placements that somewhat exceeded the normal capacity of the house.

Mr Thomas was very thorough. Several times he went through with Richard the order of serving the wines in relation to the courses being served and making sure that he was satisfied with Richard's ability to serve at the table. Mr Thomas remarked dryly that his wine cellar, to which only he and the Master had a key, would have to be restocked. The Master had also insisted upon a number of cases of champagne being ordered in as the current stocks were not enough and it was all to be held back until towards the end of the evening when there would be what the Master called 'a very special announcement'.

It being a fine summer's evening the French windows were open, leading out onto the terrace and the small but adequate town garden. Richard's first duty that evening would be to take the gentlemen's hats, gloves and cloaks if they were wearing them. Reynolds, Mrs Chesterton's lady's maid, would look after the ladies' things. Mr and Mrs Chesterton stood in the hall ready to greet each new arrival.

Reception drinks were being offered by the two temporary footmen in the drawing room with Mr Thomas ensuring that everything was running smoothly and that all the guests' needs were being catered for.

Downstairs, Kate was to tell Richard afterwards how close it had seemed that things would not be ready in the order required, but that somehow Mrs Thomas had seen it all through so that no one upstairs would never have guessed just what a close-run thing it had been.

The guests arrived. They were served their reception drinks and then at the allotted time were invited to move through to the dining room. The courses came out one after the other. With Mr Thomas again keeping an eagle eye on proceedings, the various wines were also offered to correspond with the course being served. To Richard's comparatively inexperienced eye things seemed to be going smoothly.

When Mr Chesterton could see that the last of his guests had finished the final dessert course he rose to his feet. Not for him the vulgarity of tapping a spoon against the side of a glass or of clearing his throat loudly. He stood there quietly, but with that innate presence that some seem to possess. Having one hand slightly raised he waited for the guests to suspend their conversation. It was also the cue for Richard, the two other footmen and Mr Thomas to move back into the drawing room and to start setting out glasses of champagne on trays.

After ten minutes or so Richard and others could hear the sound of clapping coming from the other side of the now closed doors to the dining room. A short while later Mr Thomas, as if obeying some unheard signal, went to open the doors to the dining room. The diners began to move out across the hallway and into the drawing room where the doors were still open to the warm evening air.

As the guests filed into the drawing room, most took a glass of champagne offered on one of the trays. When one tray was emptied there was another filled with glasses to replace it. Last to come back into the drawing room were Miss Caroline, followed by Mr and Mrs Chesterton. Picking up their own glasses as they came into the room everyone turned to face them and then a voice said loudly.

'A toast, a toast to Sir Wilfred and Lady Chesterton.'

It was very late before the last of the evening's guests departed. When Richard finally went below stairs again, Mrs Thomas had gone to her bed, exhausted. Kate too had taken the baby home. The exciting news would have to keep until the morning.

Chapter 5

There was a drizzle in the air as they prepared to set out from Westminster on the first leg of their journey to Bath. Rogers, with Richard riding beside him, drove the family and the considerable amount of luggage to Paddington Station. Sarah Reynolds, as the lady's maid, was given the unusual privilege of riding inside. Richard's first task was to see the family to their carriage and to see that they were comfortable and everything for the journey was to their satisfaction.

Richard then returned to the carriage to supervise the loading of the luggage on board the train. Finally he took himself, Sarah Reynolds and the hamper for the journey and his own personal effects to a second-class carriage.

En route to Bath every time the train came to a scheduled stop it was Richard's job to race down the platform to the first-class carriage where the family were located and ask Sir

Wilfred and Lady Chesterton if there was anything they required. Richard would be able to offer to make tea for them and there were pastries in the hamper back in his compartment. Richard was not the only servant performing this task but he was fortunate that, out of consideration, whenever asked, the response was:

'No thank you, Weller. We are quite comfortable and in need of nothing.'

It was in between stops that Richard and Sarah had their first really long conversation. Apart from at mealtimes, their paths rarely crossed when they were back in Westminster.

'How did you come to serve the family, Sarah?' asked Richard.

'I started as the nursery maid when Miss Caroline had a nanny. They had another child you know. Master Robert. Master Robert died before Miss Caroline was born and I never knew him. I was told that he was never a strong boy and he got the whooping-cough.'

'But how did you actually get the position in the first place? I don't even know where you come from,' said Richard.

'Well,' Sarah continued, 'it was a bit of good fortune for me. I mean, getting the position was a bit of good fortune as before that I was orphaned when my parents died of cholera out in India working for the East India Company. I was only a baby at the time so I never really knew my parents but I was taken in by the chaplain and his wife to the outpost where they were serving. They were a fairly elderly couple who had never had children of their own.

'We stayed in India until I was about nine years old and then my guardians decided to return home to England, although I don't think there was any formal arrangements. Of course, they brought me back with them. You know it's very strange now I remember it. The ship that brought us to England was the *Albion* and you'd never guess the Captain's name I saw on the top of the door opposite the gangway was Captain Charles Weller. What a coincidence!

'Anyway the Reverend Jessop had a small pension from the East India Company and he and Mrs Jessop took me with them to where they brought a small but comfortable house not far from Tamworth. This was nearby to where her Ladyship's cousin Sir Robert Peel lived. I was treated kindly and well by Mr and Mrs Jessop and I was Mrs Jessop's personal maid. Well, what with my guardian being a clergyman, even though he was retired, he was known to a number of families in the area including that of her Ladyship.

'I obviously didn't know who was who in such circles, but I do remember the occasion of Miss Peel, as she was then, becoming engaged to Mr Chesterton. It was quite an occasion when they wed by all accounts, and when they were married they came to live in London.

'Well it was some years later when dear old Mrs Jessop passed away. Without my knowing at the time my guardian had decided that he did not want me in the house any more and he wrote to a number of people, including her Ladyship, asking if they had a vacancy in the household. It was my good fortune that Mrs Chesterton, as she was then, replied saying that she had a vacancy as a nursery maid. So I was off to London.'

'So how did you get to be a lady's maid then?' asked Richard.

'There again I was lucky. Well, we are all lucky really as the Master and the Mistress are such kind and considerate employers. When I started at Westminster all my job was to get up at 6:30 and clean and light the nursery fire, make the nanny's early morning tea and bring up her breakfast from the kitchen, do all the usual cleaning and washing and the changing of the baby. Unless it was raining, I would then be able to get out of the house and take Miss Caroline out for a walk in the pram. There was always lots of mending to do and I have always been good at that.

'In those days I was on £11 a year and Nanny Smith had me running around all over the place tending to her needs as well as those of Miss Caroline but I still consider myself lucky to be with such a good family.

'I had been with the family about four years and during that time had only spoken to the Mistress about half a dozen times such as at Christmas or at staff parties that were arranged and held for us. Anyway, one day Nanny Smith received a letter from home saying that her mother had suffered from some affliction that had left her incapable of looking after herself. Downstairs we were all shocked when Nanny Smith decided to quit the family and go and look after her mother.

'What I did not know at the time, but this is something Miss Caroline told me later, was that Miss Caroline had told her Ladyship that she had not liked Nanny Smith one little bit and that she had liked me. Evidently she had begged her Ladyship to let me be her nanny and her Ladyship agreed a trial basis at first but then my position was made permanent. I did ask Mr Thomas if it would be possible for one of the parlour maids to come and clean and light the fire in the morning and to clean the nursery and if so that I would not need a nursery maid. Maybe this helped me to get the position permanently.

'Anyway, as Miss Caroline grew up and no longer needed a nanny but needed a personal maid, it seemed the natural thing for me to take this on. Miss Caroline and me still have an understanding of each other and I am very fond of her and I like to think she is of me.'

'How long have you been with the family then?' asked Richard.

'Coming on some fifteen years now, I would guess,' answered Sarah.

'What happens when Miss Caroline gets married some day?'

'Well, that will be up to her and her husband, I suppose. I may not fit in with what they want and some husbands I have heard do not like their ladies to be too close to their servants,' answered Sarah.

'You have no plans yourself for marriage then, Sarah?'

'Where would I have the time?'

'What about that Mr Perkins you brought to the staff Jubilee celebration? Is he not your follower?' asked Richard.

'We have walked out together on three occasions now. It depends on whether or not Miss Caroline still needs me after she is married. We'll just have to wait and see and I will have to wait and see just how interested Mr Perkins really is,' answered Sarah.

'The train seems to be slowing for a stop. I best get up there and see if everything is needed by the family,' said Richard.

When the train arrived at Bath Station, Richard alighted taking the effects that he had carried aboard with him. Sarah did likewise. Sir Wilfred and Lady Chesterton and Miss Caroline also alighted and waited on the platform whilst Richard saw to the unloading of the luggage and making sure that everything was accounted for. He then went in search of the carriage that was expected to collect the family and take them to where they were staying. Richard hoped that he might have known the coachman from his own time in Bath but this wasn't so.

Although he was acting as Sir Wilfred's valet for the duration of their stay in Bath, Richard found that he was isolated from the other ranking servants in the Grand House set in its own estate outside Bath in which they were they were staying. It seemed a different world to the one he knew at Westminster.

There was an even bigger division between the servants. Those such as the house steward and the butler were served by their own footman in their own dining room. Then there

ANDY P WELLER

was the likes of the ladies' maids, the under-butler, the valets and the coachmen and the footmen who were served by the hall boys. As for the outside staff such as the grooms, gardener's assistants and yard boys, they were in a different category altogether. In his time there Richard never got to see the governess who was responsible for teaching the children. She was neither a servant nor part of the family and took her meals in isolation in her own quarters.

Richard felt out of his depth in these surroundings. He had come as Sir Wilfred's, albeit temporary, valet but, whereas His Lordship's valet and the under-butler wore ordinary clothes in the form of suits, Richard felt self-conscious in his footman's livery. He would be far happier, he thought to himself, when he achieved his ambition of being a coachman. Sarah also felt an inferior person in these circumstances and looked forward to the return to Westminster and what she was accustomed to.

Chapter 6

Richard did not know exactly what to expect or what he would see during his time at the Great House. He thought it might be like London with the Master and Mistress paying many visits for evening entertainment or His Lordship hosting large and spectacular occasions. Not at all. Everything was on a much smaller scale than Richard had imagined.

Some evenings Sir Wilfred and His Lordship would be driven alone by His Lordship's coachman without a footman in attendance, returning late at night. On other occasions a few coaches would arrive at the Great House with gentlemen unaccompanied by their ladies. There seemed also a conspiracy of silence about the house, although Richard had little experience on which to base this conclusion. However,

Sir Wilfred spoke as little as possible when Richard was attending him. Just sufficient to give out his instructions. This added to Richard's confusion and unease and was not helped by Richard for perhaps the first time in his life finding that there were parts of the day when he had to look for something to do. Sarah thought he was lucky as she was rushed off her feet attending to Lady Chesterton and Miss Caroline and their wardrobes.

Around mid morning one day a message came down to Richard that he was to drive Lady Chesterton and Miss Caroline into Bath. One of His Lordship's open carriages would be placed at their disposal. This was to break all protocol as the best that Richard would normally expect would be to attend as a footman. His instructions were to drive the ladies around Bath but that they would not be disembarking. It was as if they were being taken out for the day but without the opportunity to converse with anyone.

It was Saturday morning and Richard was attending Sir Wilfred in his bedroom. It the first time Sir Wilfred had spoken at any length to Richard.

'Weller, I am told you have family here in Bath.'

'Yes, sir.'

'I am sure you would want to see them before we return to Westminster. For various reasons we will be returning earlier than was planned. You and Reynolds must prepare for our departure on Monday. I must be back in London by Monday evening.'

'Yes, of course, sir.'

'Now with regards to visiting your family, I can spare you on Sunday afternoon. We shall all be dining here on Sunday evening over a private dinner with His Lordship, so you must lay out my clothes beforehand. I trust that will give you enough time to pay a visit to your family.'

'Yes, and thank you, sir, for your kind consideration,' answered Richard.

Richard managed to get word to Catherine Cottage and that Sunday just after noon Richard's younger brother William was waiting a discreet distance away from the estate with a spare mount for Richard.

'Good to see you, brother,' said William.

'And good to see you, William. How are things at home?' asked Richard.

'Things fare very badly, Richard. You know from when we didn't come the Great Exhibition last year that Ann is in poor health. She is now fading fast, Richard, and although we have had the doctor to her he says there is not much that can be done for her now. It is now a matter of time only. She has passed her sixty-fifth birthday and seems to have no fight left in her. Father is taking it hard. Any doubts we had about their feeling for each other are unfounded. Over the past year he has been spending too much time down at the York Mews Tap but not now though, he is very attentive to her.'

During their ride William questioned Richard about London life, about himself and Kate and Mary Ann and Robert Shelley and about Charlotte and George Eydmann and of course John and Elizabeth.

When they finally arrived at Catherine Cottage, he said, 'Look, Richard, I need to be about my work but I will be back later and we can ride back before it is dark. Edward is working also, otherwise the business will go to pot. You'll find father and Ann inside.'

Sam stood to greet his son as he entered.

'Welcome, lad. I heard the horses in the yard and guessed it was you two.'

'How is Ann?' enquired Richard.

'Sleeping for now, son. Sleeping for now.'

'I'm awake Sam,' came a weak voice. 'Who have we here?'

'It's Richard, Ann. My Master is visiting in Bath so I thought I'd come and see you both.'

'That's nice, son. I wish the others were not so far away. I would like to see them one more time.'

Ann soon drifted off back to sleep again and Sam and Richard talked quietly catching up on each other. Later they heard William leading the horses into the yard from the mews opposite. It was time for Richard to leave and return to the Grand House.

The return to London and Westminster was uneventful. A few days later it was announced that there was to be a General Election and Mr Thomas was able to tell the staff that Sir Wilfred would be standing as a prospective candidate for the newly named Conservative Party in the constituency of Westminster.

Whilst not having the slightest interest in politics, Richard slowly began to piece together the course of events around the family's visit to Bath. That in itself followed on from the rather odd reason for holding a dinner to celebrate the Queen's fifteenth anniversary of accession and his Master announcing that he was to be knighted by the Queen.

The Conservative Party did win the election but Sir Wilfred did not himself get elected, as a Whig and a Radical were returned instead. Out of loyalty to his employer, Richard was sorry that Sir Wilfred was not elected to parliament. In a strange way that would have reflected on them below stairs as well. That said, Richard had no understanding at all of the issues involved and he did not have the right to vote. Even if he could vote he still had the problem of not being able to read or write.

Chapter 7

It was some two or three weeks since Richard had returned from Bath. Richard was called into Mr Thomas' pantry one morning after Sir Wilfred had left the house to go about his business. Richard was both puzzled and worried. This had never happened before. Have I done something wrong, he asked himself?

'Come in, Richard.'

Mr Thomas closed the door so no one could hear them. He took a piece of paper from his jacket.

'A note has been delivered for you from your brother-in-law. I have not opened it yet. Would you like me to do so and read the contents to you?'

'Yes, please, Mr Thomas.'

'Very well.'

Thomas opened the envelope and began to read.

'"Dear Richard, We received news this morning from Bath of the passing away of Ann. She died peacefully in her sleep on Sunday evening and the funeral and burial are to take place tomorrow. Mary Ann is taking the train to Bath tonight so at least someone from London will be able to be there. I am sorry for your loss. Regards Robert."

'My sympathies, Richard. Was Ann a sister or something?'

'Ann was my father's second wife and, yes, I suppose she did feel like a big sister,' answered Richard.

'Well, I'm sorry for that, Richard, but as she is not your blood relative I really don't think that we can spare for you to be away for two days without any notice.'

'Of course, Mr Thomas. I understand. I can barely afford the train fare and the loss of wages anyway. At least it is my good fortune that I was able to see her once more during the family's stay in Bath.'

'On another matter, Richard. You have requested a leave of absence of two hours this coming Saturday morning. Is this something that should concern me?'

'I have some personal matters to attend to, Mr Thomas, that is all,' replied Richard.

Saturday morning arrived. Having taken his leave of Mr

Thomas before departing, he returned to their room in Hanover Place and changed out of his uniform before going out. He walked the comparatively short distance to Belgrave [now known as Belgravia]. He needed to get back to his horses. He was not cut out to be an inside man. There was a large stable in Belgrave that was used by a number of households to keep and maintain their carriages and horses. Through his contacts Richard was aware of a vacancy coming up soon for a stableman, but a little more than just a stableman owing to the size of the establishment and the important households that used its facilities. Within the mews was accommodation perhaps more suited to the needs of Richard, Dan and baby Jessie and the newly expecting Kate.

Subject to a good reference from Sir Wilfred and Lady Chesterton, the job was Richard's to take up when the current incumbent should leave, as he was considered to be getting to be too old for the job. Richard was glad to be leaving his uniform behind and getting back to wearing proper working clothes.

Chapter 8

The next several years were full of mixed blessings. Richard was happy in his work as a stableman and he felt secure in his situation.

The children Dan, Jessie and Sidney, or 'Sid', since his name had been shortened, were thriving. Dan was now receiving schooling and seemed to be enjoying this. Kate too was in reasonable health and good spirits. After two miscarriages following the birth of Sid, she gave birth to their third son John.

Being a stableman was fine, but it was not the top of the tree in a profession that Richard yearned for: that of being a proper coachman. Richard would soon be forty years of age and that was not necessarily a bad age for a coachman. As had happened when he moved from being a footman in the Chesterton household to become a stableman, Richard's chance came with the expected retirement of another coachman. The coachman's fraternity was not a brotherly one but the network was a good source of information. Richard now had behind him, including he reckoned what was due from his current employer, that all-important requirement of good references. The accommodation in St George's Place was now somewhat cramped for a family of six.

As a domestic coachman Richard could now say that he had completed his 'apprenticeship'. With his elevation to the ranks of coachman came the welcome increase in wages and the opportunity to take bigger accommodation in a tenement in North Kensington near to where his new employer resided.

Not long after Richard's elevation the country was plunged into mourning following the death of Prince Albert, a man who had earned the respect and admiration of the British people.

Chapter 9

'What of the children Kate? Have we done right by them?' asked Richard. 'Have I done right with you over these years? You know you used to cuss at me and you were right fearsome when that Irish temper of your showed itself.'

'You have been a good husband and a good provider Richard Weller,' Kate assured him. 'You were brash yourself in those younger days back in Bath. There you were when I first met you just a servant in a small household and yet you had already set your sights on bettering yourself. I didn't know it at first but now I think it is what your grandfather and then your father and your brother John had done that made you so determined.

'It was not long before you caught my eye and me yours it was soon clear to me. At first I thought you were just after what you could get. Why during our kissing sessions you were always trying to run your hand up underneath my skirts. Shame on you, Richard Weller! I would not let you but you still wanted to follow me and to court me. Some lads would have moved on but no not you. You continued to try and then we came to grow together.'

'But I did get to where I wanted in the end, didn't I,' said Richard.

'Yes you did,' answered Kate. 'It was the day you came to me all proud like because you had got a job as an ostler. You were so excited and eager that for the first time I let you have your way and throughout our marriage you have never changed in that respect. I was expecting trouble with my father when we said we wanted to get married. It was never easy to read him. Whether he thought I was carrying a child or whether he was just glad to know that someone would take me off his hands or a bit of both I will never know. You were turned twenty-four and me two years younger. Lots of folk had started on their family by the time we got wed.

'Looking back now on what we have here and those early days in Bath makes me shiver. It was bad enough losing Mary Eliza at two to the measles and then when we lost tiny Richard I didn't know how to carry on. We weren't the only ones to lose our babies, I know. Even so, I thought is this what life is all about? Having babies and losing them or trying to raise them in that place? Then you decided to become a post boy and risk the dangers of hold-ups or being shot just to bring a few more pennies in. I loved you for that.

'Then you decided on another change and we were off to the Packhorse with Mary Ann and Robert. Dear Robert. He was such a good man and a wonderful provider to your sister and to their family. I miss him and Mary Ann must miss him something terrible.

'Then we had Dan. Good solid, dependable hard-working Dan and he too seems to have found his match in Charlotte. They are like us those two and Dan is just like his father in so many ways.'

'Except he don't deal with horses and is content to serve inside,' Richard interrupted.

'True, Richard, but he has set his sights high just like you. I see the same drive in him as you had.

'Then dear Robert helped us and he found for you a new position and you could leave the Roe Buck and we went to Westminster and the Chesterton family. The there was all that funny business about celebrating the Queen and him getting knighted and you going down to Bath. You then get that stableman job in Belgrave and, not content with that, you still want to be that coachman you set your sights on as a boy. Here you are now twenty years a coachman.'

Richard then burst into a fit of coughing. Kate helped him to lean forward in his bed where he was propped up on his bolster and pillow. She placed a bowl in front of him to catch what he was coughing up. This went on for some minutes before subsiding and then Kate took the bowl away from him and helped him to fall back again onto his pillow.

'You are tired now, my love. Why don't you rest a while?' said Kate gently.

'No, carry on,' pleaded Richard, 'Remind me again of our children.'

'Very well,' she murmured, 'I'll continue if you like. Our Jess had told us that on her next Sunday afternoon off that she wanted to bring her young man round for tea. You remember that, Richard?'

He nodded.

'Well it was getting to be some half hour or so after they

were expected and you were getting yourself in all of a state wondering where she could have got to. You were no doubt remembering what you and your hands used to be like when we were first going out. You were standing there looking out of the window to see if there was any sign of our Jess. Any minute I expected you to pull on your coat and go looking for her. Granted she is a beauty, Richard, but you really should have trusted your own daughter not to do anything improper. Then you stand bolt upright, not moving a muscle. I can still see it now. You standing there as stiff as a board, and young Lizzie pulling on your arm asking what the matter is and you unable to answer.

'A minute later there comes a knock on the door and there is our Jess and standing behind her in all his uniform is a tall policeman. Jeez! You were as white as a sheet as if you'd seen your own ghost. The Jess comes inside and pulls him in by the arm and announces him as her young follower, Police Constable James Rendall.

'Lord knows what was going through your mind, Richard Weller! As if our daughter had the nature or the capacity to get herself into trouble with the law. All you could say was "A policeman? You are going out with a policeman?", as if that wasn't obvious by the uniform he was wearing!

'The rest, as they say, is history. They marry, having asked you to be one of the witnesses, and now Jess has given you three grandchildren and with another one on the way with the promise that if it is a boy they will baptise him Richard Weller Rendall. Now what do you think of that?'

Richard starts to cough again and Kate goes to sit him up more upright but he waves her away and the coughing subsides.

'Tell me more,' he implores her.

'Well, there is not much more to tell. Sid is with the Great Western Railway as a porter and him and Charlotte must be at it almost every night. Including the twins, seven children in just under ten years with time enough for plenty more.

'John will be home from work later and that just leaves Lizzie all wrapped up in her religion.

'Would you like some broth? I can soon warm some up for you.'

Richard shakes his head and closes his eyes to sleep.

Chapter 10

Richard did not pull through the following winter. The years had caught up with him and being exposed to all sorts of weather he succumbed to pneumonia at the age of 58.

A few months after Richard's death Jessie and her policeman had a son and kept their promise to name the boy after him. They went on to have seven children and the family relocated to Torquay.

Sidney and Charlotte continued to reproduce and had eleven children.

John carried on as a railway porter and stayed with his mother until the end. He then found accommodation with his sister Lizzie until her life changed. John remained unmarried and left this world at the age of just 32.

Lizzie Alice's life took a very different course. She stayed at home with her mother until the end, then moved out with brother John. Having first taken a job as an assistant in an oriental shop, Lizzie took up a position running the Morton temperance boarding house for young ladies in Hammersmith. She ended her days as a spinster of fifty-one in Paddington.

As for Kate, she received little income apart from what her children John and Lizzie brought home. For a few pennies a week she became a 'pew opener' at a nearby church. For dusting pews, rearranging hymn books and the like and opening those reserved family pews with doors, she looked forward to the generosity of those in the congregation to give her what they thought fit.

Part IX

Daniel and Charlotte: The Last of Their Kind

Chapter 1

Daniel Frederick, son of Richard and Kate, had established himself as a domestic servant in Chester Place just a little to the north of Hyde Park. A recent addition to the household is Charlotte Rebecca Roe, a housemaid. It is a Sunday afternoon and they have contrived to take a walk in Hyde Park together.

'So how came you to this place, Charlotte?' asked Dan.

'I resorted to an agency,' she replied. 'I tried making my own way in service but it was an unhappy affair.'

'Please tell,' Dan asked.

'Very well. My family come from south of the river. Lambeth to be exact, but we later moved out to Brixton which is where I was born. My father is a coachman and my mother used to be a dressmaker. I am the second youngest of ten children. Well, as you can imagine things were so cramped in our house there was barely room enough for us to find somewhere to sleep. It was when I was eleven I was sent into service by my parents as a kitchen maid at a big house out on Streatham Hill.

'I can remember to this day walking up to the big house trying to find a way round to the rear and the servants' entrance. The house was as big as I had ever seen and had its own big gardens all nicely laid out and the grass trimmed short. When I found the right door I knocked and there was this figure in front of me when the door opened all dressed up fine as footmen do. Well silly me, and not knowing any better, I curtseyed to him. It's funny to look back at it now but I was terrified. I felt like dropping my little box with all my things in and running back home. Anyway, I didn't and some of the other servants seemed quite kind to me but others would ignore me and at first I was terrified of the cook.

'That afternoon was taken up with them showing me what I was to do. I was under the strictest of instructions never to enter the upstairs, unless it was to light the fires in the morning. I was never to be seen by the Master or the Mistress and I was to use the back stairs to my room in the attic that I shared with Fran one of the housemaids and with Alice the tweeny. Alice and me we became good friends and she helped me a lot.

'So there I was in this big house. I was to get up at half past four in the mornings in summer and four o'clock in the winter. They had me black-leading the grate and the range, scrubbing the stone floors in the kitchen and the scullery, cleaning all the pots and the pans and preparing any vegetables the cook needed. I thought I was just going to be the kitchen maid but they also had me cleaning all the servants' hall, servants' quarters and the bedrooms as well as the backstairs and waiting at table on the servants themselves before I could have anything to eat. Some nights I did not finish until nearly nine at night and I was that tired I almost crawled into my bed only to get up again at the same time the following morning. They would give me a half day off each week and this I spent in bed asleep as I was too tired to do anything. For all this they gave me ten shillings a month and if it wasn't for me mother making me aprons they would take the cost of the aprons out of my wages.

'You know, I only saw the Master and Mistress to speak to twice in those two years and that was at Christmas when on both occasions they gave me a pair of mittens.

'Well, I stuck at this until I was thirteen, by which time I had more than enough. I could have gone back home and there was a bit more room as my two eldest brothers had moved out and my next eldest brother had been hit and run over by a cart and he died. Poor Charlie was only twenty-five. Anyway, in the end I decided against going back home and I heard that there was a lady down the hill that was looking for a housemaid and I took myself off to see if she would have me.

'Mr Carlisle was a pharmacist and he worked out of a shop in Victoria. Mrs Carlisle – well, she was a right one and her daughter Louise. I don't know who was the worse, the mother or the daughter. Anyway they had a cook, a really nice woman, Mrs Swift, who lived out and would leave every evening around seven o'clock soon after Mr Carlisle and the family had finished their supper. What they wanted was a general servant who would also be their parlour maid. I went to the interview and she agreed to take me on but she said that because I had so little experience and was so young they would take me on but only on reduced wages and that any breakages or shortages would be paid for out of my wages. You know, Dan, at the interview when she asked me my name and I said it was Charlotte she would have none of that as she thought the name was, as she put it, "too pretentious". I didn't even know what the word meant but she said I was to be called Mary and have a name like any other maid.

'Well, I expected to do all the cleaning and the like but they would never lift a finger to do anything themselves. That young monkey Louise was just the same. They'd ring the bell if the fire needed making up or the curtains drawn and if the doorbell went they would never dream of answering it. That is what maids were for. I am used to long days and working hard but what I disliked the most was when the child would ring and tell me to put her things away for her or to do this or do that.

'I would be sent to do the shopping two or three times a week and Madam would have me standing there as she went through each of the bills and checked the amount she had been charged. I was never to handle money of course because Madam had an account at every shop and from what I can gather she was always making them wait for payment.

'The worst of it was when she had someone round for tea. She would then ring the bell even more and then criticise me in front of her guests saying that I was lazy and why did she

always have to ring twice. Well, after six months I decided
that I had enough of that and I walked out on her without
giving notice. She was outraged and said that she would
never give me a reference. Do you know what I said, Dan?'

'No, go on, tell me'

'I said,' and she started to giggle, 'I said, "that's all right
Madam as I won't be giving you one either",' and they both
burst out laughing.

'Anyway,' Charlotte continued, 'having taken my name back
I thought I'd try my luck with another family. I ended up with
another family in a similar situation. The Master was another
shopkeeper and they had a son. At first things went quite well
and the money was better. Just like at the previous place they
had put a bed in the attic space and there was no fire up there.
It was so cold in the winter that I would stay in the kitchen as
long as I could before needing to get some sleep.

'The son was just that little bit younger than me and he was
a day boy at a nearby boarding school so I did not see much
of him during school times. Anyway, it was coming up to my
second summer there and the son was not going to school.
Up until then we had got on nicely and if anything he
seemed a little shy and uncomfortable around me. As we
were coming into that summer I noticed a change about
him. I could see sometimes the way that his eyes used to
follow me around the room in that way that makes a girl
uneasy. At first I did not think much of it though he was
coming up to that awkward age that boys have. I should know
with all them brothers I grew up with.

'Anyway, I took to making sure I turned the key in my door
at nights. Then one day, when the Master was at his business
and Madam was visiting a friend or doing something equally
important, he found me in the front parlour clearing things
away. I smiled at him as he came into the room and turned
and carried on with what I was doing. The next thing I know
he has his hands around my waist and was rubbing his face in

my hair. Well, it was such a shock at first I just froze but he was not going to let go. So I rubbed the heel of my boot down his shin and he soon let go and I gave him such a slap. I said to him don't you ever dare try and touch me again. He threatened to tell his mother that I had hit him but of course he never did.

'It was getting towards the end of his summer holidays when again he found me on my own but this time he came at me from the front and with one hand was trying to pull up my skirt. Well I started screaming and was trying to push him away. This was enough to bring the cook running up from the kitchen and, thank heavens, she could see what was going on. Well, that night I was before the Master and the Mistress and they accused me for having their boy on and encouraging him. They dismissed me on the spot and told me to leave the house at once but said they would pay me the money that I am owed to avoid any scandal and that I was never to come near the house again. So I quickly packed my things and left and went straight back home to my parents.'

'The trouble with these people,' said Dan 'is that they don't have any breeding. They think they are it because they have a nice house and a garden and a good income. They have no class. Give me the real gentry any day. They know how to behave and treat their staff and we know our place and everybody is happy. So what happened next?'

'It was then that I threw my lot in with finding work through an agency. The first few times what I was promised by the agency was different from what I found when I got there. Either the money was a lot less and the job was not what I was told it would be or I found that I was having to pay commission to the agency out of my wages. Most of my positions were with these so-called 'middle-class' families.

'I then decided to do something different. I had some schooling up to when I was eleven so I decided to write, probably not too well though, to Mrs Hunt's agency having heard so much good about them. They wrote back to say that they would be willing to interview me and so things turned out well. My first placement was with a genteel family and my time there was a happy one. The family then decided to move away from London so I found myself back with Mrs Hunt's agency and that is how I came to Chester Place.

'Now, how about you, Dan? she asked. 'How did you get to be here?'

'Oh, mine is not much of a story, Charlotte. Horses and coaching have been in my family from a long way back. All my father ever wanted to do was to be a coachman. He was in service before that being a footman and sometimes a valet but that was not for him.

'My brother Sid has continued with the coachman line but I have decided to go into service the other way. I have been fortunate with my positions and I have learnt much but still have a lot more to learn if I want to be a butler. Anyway, enough of this talking about being in service. I think we have enough time to take a stroll around the Serpentine before it is time to walk back. Maybe the next Sunday we can have together we can really push the boat out and take ourselves on to the water and tea afterwards?'

'Yes, Dan. That would be very nice. Very nice indeed.' She tucked her arm into his.

Chapter 2

'How many times do you think we have walked around this lake, Charlotte?'

'More times than I would like to count, Dan, but that does not matter. You know I just like being with you.'

'Well, in that case perhaps you should start thinking who you would like to invite to our wedding.'

'Daniel Weller! Do I take that as a proposal?'

'That's about the gist of it. What do you say? Oh, and there is one other thing. I have been told that there is likely to be a position as a butler opening up for me fairly soon now. So it's no ordinary servant you'd be marrying. What do you say?'

'What do you expect me to say! Of course I will and the sooner the better I don't think I can wait much longer to be able to wake up in the mornings with you beside me.'

'That's settled that then. I'd best make the arrangements,' said Dan.

'You could have been a bit more romantic, Daniel Weller, but that'll do.'

It was a cold and raw March day when they married at St James' church in nearby Sussex Gardens. Charlotte asked her younger sister Eliza to be her bridesmaid.

A few months later Dan was offered through Mrs Hunt's agency a position as a butler in nearby Chapel Street in Marylebone. His world was complete. Dan had reached his goal of being a butler and he was wedded to his Charlotte who worked alongside him at Chapel Street as a housemaid. All that was needed now was to start a family, he thought. It took two years but then Alfie was born and they set up a new home together in Star Street where number 41 was in use as a boarding house for servants.

Chapter 3

The next few years were Dan's 'steady years'. He found regular employment as a butler. While Charlotte was slow to conceive, some seven years after Alfie was born Sidney arrived and then two years after that their last child Frederick Edgar also arrived on the scene.

Then when life was looking set fair for Dan, Charlotte and

the family, England, Europe and then the United States were hit by the Depression of 1893, triggered, amongst other things, by the collapse in Britain of Baring Brothers bank. Agency work for butlers and for other domestic servants became more limited as a consequence of the economic downturn. Dan and Charlotte were forced to leave the comparative comfort of Star Street for the basic and overcrowded tenements of Woodchester Street in Paddington, the very worst housing and accommodation in that part of London.

Part X

At Home with the Christie Family

Chapter 1

William Christie, known as Bill the chimney sweep, was on the point of entering from the street the two-storey tenement in Woodchester Street. His family of eight were amongst the sixteen people sharing No. 54 Woodchester Street, a street considered by the authorities to have the worst housing conditions in the parish.

He could hear the screams of a child and he bounded up the single flight of stairs to the first-floor, two-roomed accommodation they rented. The door was ajar and he pushed it open into what served as the living room, where they had their meals and scullery where they cooked and washed and laundered when it was raining. It was also where the the four eldest of the six girls slept at night.

He saw his young daughter Cate sitting on the floor· and screaming her head off, rocking herself side to side as she tried to support the lower part of her right arm with the other but as she did so she screamed even more.

His wife Mary Ann was standing there looking her usual austere self in her high-necked, dark-brown dress. She had, though, an ashen look on her face and the large wooden paddle that she used to stir the washing was held loosely in her hand. The three youngest girls were standing stock-still at the other end of the room by the door into the room that served as a bedroom for the parents and the two youngest girls, including nine-year old Cate.

'What in God's name is going on here?' demanded Bill.

He moved towards his daughter but did not want to touch here as he had yet to change his clothes and to clean off the grime and soot from his day's work. He bent down and looking up to his wife said:

'I asked you, woman, what is going on here? What has happened to the child? Have you hit her? Answer me, damn it!'

251

His wife pulled herself up to her full height and took on that stern look she normally displayed.

'She brought it upon herself,' she said defiantly. 'I told her to wash up and they are still traces of food on the plates. She needs to learn to do as she is told and to do it properly.'

Looking at her with anger in his eyes Bill said:

'And so you whacked her on the arm with that there paddle, did you, woman? I've a mind to take my hand to you. With that temper of yours you are too free with your hands.'

'Cate, just give me a minute, just give me a minute to get out of these things and to have a quick wash and then I will take you to the hospital myself.

'If I find this child's arm is broken, woman, you had better get those rosary beads of yours working overtime. It's time you received what you are too quick to dish out.'

Changed and with the worst of the grime and soot washed from his hands and face, Bill tried to make a crude sling to support Cate's arm. Cate had stopped screaming but there was still sobbing interspersed with groans of pain and 'it hurts, it hurts'.

Gently Bill picked up his daughter, keeping the injured arm as far as possible away from his body. Mary Ann stood by the window staring fixedly down on to the accumulation of rubbish in the small back yard below where she would hang out their washing,

Bill carried his daughter to St Mary's hospital, ten-year old Alice preferring to go with them rather than remain there with her mother. Poor Cate's arm was broken. The neighbours were to hear the consequences of Bill's earlier threat. No one intervened in such scenes even though they lived on top of each other. It was the way of things and short of murder no one would ever summon the police. The police would probably have loved to get their hands on a good number of the people that lived round these parts and for all sorts of reasons.

Chapter 2

Mary Ann was born Mary Ann Carter, the daughter of Samuel Carter who had once been a potato dealer in Cork. The consequences of the potato famine caused him to bring the family to England where he set up in his old trade.

Mary Ann had brought with her the traditions of her faith and, although Bill loved each and every one of his six daughters, he now wondered what had caused him to want to marry such a woman. Why, he had even converted to become a Catholic so they could get married in her church, and he had made a promise that the children would be raised in the Catholic faith.

Bill was by no means religious and hardly ever attended Mass despite pressure from the priest to get him to do so. Nevertheless, and true to his word, he did not intervene when the girls were not too willingly taken to Mass by their mother.

The family of Daniel Weller and Charlotte had moved into Woodchester Street when Dan could no longer find work in service. Fred Weller had therefore known and played with Cate since Cate was about five years old, even though Fred was some two years older than her. For a number of years they were just two out of a group of children that used to play around together but for the past year or so they had tended to seek out each other's company rather than that of any of the other children.

Fred had heard about Cate and her broken arm. Cate had not come out onto the street for a few days but Fred was terrified of Mrs Christie and would not dare to go and ask after her. He found that he missed his special friend. It was over a week before Cate finally came out onto the street. Her arm was all strapped up. There was to be no running or chasing about whilst the arm mended itself so they would sit down on the edge of the pavement and just talk.

They were being watched. Mary Ann Christie did not like the idea of her daughter becoming so friendly with a boy obviously older than her. What was more, that family had obviously fallen on hard times. Mary Ann never saw the Wellers go to church and they were definitely not Catholics.

It was time that she laid down the law and that husband of hers needed to be reminded of his promise to bring the girls up in the right way. Her husband had overruled her when their eldest daughter, also named Mary Anne and at nineteen under the age of consent, had been granted permission by her father to marry someone who was not a Catholic. She was not going to see this happen with her other daughters. She had her priest and God to answer to. For now she would bide her time but she would find a means for getting her own way.

Chapter 3

There had always been a degree of sickness in the family. The dampness of the rooms and the way they and all the others all lived together made certain of that. Even though they had now left Woodchester Street for Brindley Street, just a few minutes' walk away, the conditions were hardly any better.

Mary Ann had not been feeling well for some time. They could not afford to pay for the doctor to visit, and in any case, Mary Ann thought she could see this latest bout off as she had done before. She wasn't even fifty until next year so she had plenty of time left, she reasoned.

As the weeks dragged by and the cold and damp of autumn came on, Mary Ann resigned herself to the fact that she was seriously, even dangerously ill. A doctor was finally called but his conclusions were not very helpful and certainly gave no hope of an improvement. Mary Ann knew she was fading fast and that she must now act to preserve that promise made in church over fifteen years ago.

'William Christie, you made promises when we married. You made a promise to the church and to God. You made a promise to yourself and you made a promise to me that our children will be brought up in the Catholic faith. You broke that promise once when you gave permission to our eldest daughter to marry outside the faith. I can tell that I have not got much longer but I want a promise out of you before I go. I want your solemn word that you will not do anything to allow our daughters to marry other than to Catholics. Will you make that promise to me?'

Bill Christie agreed. Although the gloss had worn off their marriage quite sometime ago she was his wife and the mother of his children after all.

'I want my priest,' said Mary Ann. 'If I am to leave this world then bring my priest to me.'

The priest came within the hour. Mary Ann slipped away the following day.

Part XI

The Last Servant

Chapter 1

Charlotte had been awake all night. It was impossible to sleep even if she wanted to with Dan coughing and the wheezing and with the rattling of his breathing. The money would have to be found somewhere within the family. They must try and get a doctor to attend. It was early January and it had been a harsh winter so far. Fred and Cate were in the rooms upstairs. Fred would have to go and ask for the doctor to come in the hope that he would, even though they did not belong to a friendly society or were on the doctor's panel. Charlotte went up the stone stairs and knocked on the door. It was not yet six o'clock but she knew that Fred would be getting ready to leave for work. Fred answered the door.

'Fred, go for the doctor. Your father has got worse during the night. We will have to find the money from somewhere,' Charlotte urged. 'Tell the doctor he has chest pains and is finding it hard to breathe and he is shaking so. Tell him to come as quick as he can.'

Fred left and came back half an hour later rubbing his hands and chilled to the bone.

'Mum, Doctor Wilson is attending a birth. I was asked if Dad is a panel patient and I had so say no, but I said that we would pay for his visit as my father is so bad. A message has been left for the doctor at his surgery for him to come as soon as he can. I was told in the meantime to keep him warm.'

'Keep him warm! Keep him warm in this hole of a place! Just how do we do that? It's icy cold outside and not much better in here and there is hardly any heat coming out of that coal fire. You better get yourself off to work. Let's hope they don't dock you too much money for being late. We can ill afford to lose a single penny. I've already told Sid to get himself off to work. There's nothing the two of you can do anyway. I'll just have to wait for the doctor.'

259

Fred left for work.

It was midday before the doctor turned up only to demand two shillings before he would examine Dan. His examination was quick and he turned to Charlotte.

'There is nothing that I can do. His heart is in poor condition and he has pneumonia. My best recommendation is to take him to the Workhouse Infirmary where at least he will be warm and dry. This hovel is a disgrace. It is a disgrace that people should have to live in these conditions.'

'It's the best we can manage, Doctor' said Charlotte. 'He was once at the top of his station being a butler and then there were the hard times and people did not want a butler of his age. He briefly had a job as a street cleaner with the Corporation but then they thought him too old and his health was failing. The children help where they can but my husband still needed to resort to being a crossing-sweeper and relying upon good ladies and gentlemen who would give him a penny or two if he swept the road free of horse dung when they wanted to cross over. He would be out in all weather looking for a penny here and a penny there.'

The doctor stared at her in disbelief.

'Good God! Charles Dickens wrote about crossing-sweepers some forty or fifty years ago, and here we are in 1909 and people still scrape a living in such a manner. I will send the infirmary cart for him. He at least deserves to die in more comfort and dignity than this.'

Dan was to die soon afterwards at the age of sixty. Charlotte survived her husband by ten years and died in Paddington close to where her children lived.

Charlotte was hit by a second loss just two months after Dan died. In March of the same year her son, Sidney, who was a conductor for the Metropolitan railway, died from pneumonia. He was aged only twenty-six and had been married for just two months.

Of her remaining children Alfie became a bootmaker and had his own family, while Fred went to work in the stables at the Great Western Railway.

Part XII

Fred and Cate in Paddington

Chapter 1

Fred had gone to work in the stables for the Great Western Railway. He would in but a few years time be able to drive the passenger goods wagons and bring home something closer to a man's wage. Cate had gone to work at the nearby McVitie biscuit factory.

Fred and Cate had long left those childhood days behind as they had left those times behind when they were becoming more and more aware of each other. In the rough and tumble of these streets in Paddington not everyone followed the accepted rules of social behaviour. Fred and Cate had become unmarried lovers. It was the spring of 1903 in Edwardian England and Cate was an eighteen-year-old young woman, unmarried and expecting Fred's child.

Fred and Cate were independent-minded people. Many of the conventions of Edwardian England were not for them. At first marriage was either not a priority for them or circumstances got in their way. However, when Cate reached the age of consent, which in those days was twenty-one, they did marry.

Had Cate's mother's attitude put in Cate a spirit of rebellion? Had Cate's strict upbringing caused her perhaps to react in an opposite manner to the way her mother would have wanted? Had Bill Christie withheld his parental consent because of a promise to his late wife? Was it Fred Weller who was the rebel and the one not anxious to marry and to legitimise their firstborn?

Whatever the truth was, they did marry some twenty months after William 'Christie' Weller was born. Then followed a son and then two daughters followed by another daughter, who was later brought up by another family as Fred and Cate did not have the room, only for them then to have another daughter they called Violet but who tragically died in infancy.

When the First World War broke out Fred wanted to join up and fight for his country. He was most upset when the enlisting officers turned down his application owing to the importance of his occupation on the railways and the fact that he had a large family to support.

Fred and Cate then went on to have seven more boys, one of whom they called Eric who also tragically died in infancy.

After the war the Great Western Railway began to withdraw its horse-drawn vehicles and replace them with lorries. When Fred became a lorry driver, the long association between working Weller folk and the horse came to an end.

Appendix

The Chronicles of John (a coachman's journey)

'One more perhaps for my aching bones,' John says to himself at he refills his mug from the soon to be empty beer jug. After taking a couple of gulps he replaces the mug on the table beside him. He reaches forward to toss some more wood onto the fire and then settles back into his chair and stares into the flames of the fire.

John can hear the wind causing the door behind him to rattle in its frame. 'That's fine,' he thinks to himself. 'There'll be nobody to bother coming round tonight.' The combined effects of the warmth from the fire and the patterns in the flames, the now empty beer jug and the lateness of the hour cause John's mind to wonder and for his eyelids to start to feel heavy.

* * *

How strange that this image should come back to me now, thinks John! Why it must be all of seventy or more years ago.

John is looking up at his mother as she picks up baby Charlotte and the three of them get ready to leave to go to church. Almost every week it seems that his mother Sarah would say something like, 'Your father will meet us outside the church just as soon as he can.' John remembers grasping at his mother's skirts from her Sunday best that have that funny flowery type of smell that he likes, and that he now knows as the scent of lavender. The same scent that came from the chest where his mother used to keep her best clothes and linen. That seems such a long time ago now and his mother's voice he remembers as being so much softer and more gentle than when he is older.

John has vague memories of the rooms where they lived on the edge of what was then Chelsea Common. Almost every Sunday, especially during the Spring, Summer or Autumn, they would follow the same ritual of taking breakfast some considerable time after father had already left for work. They would wash, and baby Charlotte was always bathed before they went to church and then when dressed they would walk along the side of Sloane Square to the church with its yellow stone and the tower that seemed to reach right up until it nearly touched the sky. Why is it, John thought to himself, when I went back years later everything seemed so much smaller and more ordinary? St Luke's, yes that was it, St Luke's. Now was it there that Richard was baptised when he would not stop screaming the place down? No, no of course not, we were down in Bath when that happened.

Then it all changed. I was so excited when I was told that we were going on a long coach journey. This was to be aboard a coach unlike any coach I had seen before. I remember we were waiting for it to arrive at the coaching inn that father later told me was the Roe Buck. There was such a coming and going the likes of which I had never seen before. It was like some magical world that you could only dream of. There was the small carriages with a single horse and coaches drawn by two horses that I knew from Chelsea Common and they were familiar to me. What I had not seen before were the stage coaches. They were magnificent. Some coaches were all bright colours such as yellow and red. Some were not but then to see them being pulled along by four horses and with those big men holding on to the reins, that made my eyes nearly pop out of my head.

Lying around us on the ground was all our baggage and things. Mother had little Charlotte in her arms and father had put me on his shoulders so I could see more of what was going on. I think that I thought that every coach that came along was ours and I hoped it was especially if it was one of the painted ones.

Then, when the coach for us pulls up, father sets me down. Mother and Charlotte are to go in the cabin, but father lets me ride on the outside with him. The thrill of it as father passed me up to a stranger already on board before climbing up himself. Then the coachman is barking out his orders to get underway and for people to hurry themselves along. I can picture him now. A giant of a man with a ruddy round face and the biggest set of side whiskers I had ever seen. Was it then that I decided that was the life for me or did that come a little later? Was it the fact that father was to become a stage-coachman that decided things for me? I can't rightly remember now which it was or even if it was a mixture of the two.

Then we are off and at such a speed. There is me wedged in between father and the man who helped lift me on board. With the feel of the wind blowing in my face it was not long before we came into open country and with the exception of the coaches passing us coming the other way there were few people about.

I must have said to father about my wanting to become a coachman as I can remember him now saying to me something along the lines of:

'Don't think it is always like this, John. The weather can be foul with driving wind and rain and bitter cold and sometimes snow in the winter. The roads can be dangerous and sometimes a coach will come off the road. The hours are long and it is hard work. Sometimes you feel as though the horses are trying to pull your arms out of their sockets.

'Then, that all said and done, when you are like that man

269

up front you are in charge. This is your coach and it is your responsibility to get everyone there and if you have any pride in your work and in your own ability you will want to get your passengers there safe and in one piece. Some are not too fussy, mind you, and they are a disgrace to the profession. They will take risks that endanger the passengers as well as themselves and care not a hoot about the horses.'

At first I was alert and all attention for this wonderful experience and adventure. Yet despite the bumps and the lurching of the coach and the many short stops along the way as they changed the horses, I must have fallen asleep on more than one occasion. I remember how tired I was when we did reach Bath. I was something between being four or five years old.

*　　*　　*

Poor little Emily. I hope that those that caused her grief had their own comeuppance later in life. Life can be hard and cruel but she had more than her fair share of adversity in her far too short life.

I can see her now, sitting on the wall on her own whilst the other children played and had their fun. Emily with her poor withered and gammy leg would have loved to have joined in but she couldn't. It right tugged on the old heartstrings to see her sitting there like that trying to join in the laughter when something funny happened and not feeling sorry for herself. Even when they started to call her by cruel names she still tried to show that they had not hurt her.

Just like the others, well apart from those that called her names, I ignored her at first. I ignored her right up until the time that I turned my ankle and could not run and chase around with the others. It was only then that I went to sit down beside her and got to know her. Then when my ankle no longer troubled me I still would spend time with her. It was from then that I started to stick up for her. If they called her names I would tell them to shut up and take it back. At first they did stop bad naming her, or at least they did when I was around. Then one day George Riggs thought he could get to both of us and he came out with something exceptionally nasty aimed at Emily. That was it. I snapped. I still feel good now for picking up that piece of wood and whacking that bugger so hard. That was the first time I ever saw Emily cry.

What dear good friends we became after that. Emily did not have much in the way of family. She had a brother that she never knew that well as she was still young when he died of the consumption and her mother went the same way too just a few days later. So, there was just poor little Emily and her father. She said that I was the only true friend she ever had. As we grew up together we grew closer together. Often Emily would come round to the stables when I started to work from a boy with my first aim of getting to know horses as a stable lad and then becoming a groom. I remember mother in particular, and Charlotte as well, were good to her.

Then one day after a bitterly cold night when the snow had turned into ice Emily's father appeared at the cottage. I was at the stables at the time. I had not seen Emily for a few days. I thought that she was just being sensible and not risking a fall with that bad leg of hers. When I got back home mother explained to me that Emily had gone across the yard to bring in some wood for the fire and that she had slipped and smashed that leg of hers in several places. Within the day she was gone.

I missed her so much and I swore that if ever I was to have a daughter she would be named after Emily.

I kept that promise you know Emily. My youngest was called Emily Elizabeth, Elizabeth taken from my first wife's name.

*   *   *

I remember now father saying to me:

'If you want to get on and if you really want to become a coachman then you have to push yourself and work hard. Grooms are two-a-penny and stuck away as you are here in the stables in Bath nobody will get to notice you.'

'What do you suggest then, father? Where should I go next?'

'Go back to London for a while, lad. You are now in your twenties and if you remain here you will just stay as a groom. If you go to London then you can aim to become an ostler at one of the coaching inns and then, if you are fortunate and you show willing, you will get noticed and then you may be given the chance to be a coachman. If this is what you want and you are prepared to do it then I can have a word at the company to see if they can find a position for you.'

So that was it, I was on my way back to London. If only I had known I would have stayed where I was for a while longer. How was I to know that my dear mother would be lost to us within six months of my departure? Oh, she could be tough at times, but then she had seven children that she had brought up. She never lost that habit of smelling of lavender whenever she put on her best clothes. Every time I smell that scent it reminds me of her.

I had never seen London. I remembered, just about, the area around Chelsea Common and although father tried to tell me what to expect I could not imagine anything more than the place being like Bath but bigger. Oh, sure, there are rough bits of Bath and people did what they could to stay out of the workhouse even when it was difficult to find work, but this did nothing to prepare me for what I found when I got to London. Father, God bless him, had set me up with somewhere to stay not too far from where all the coaches arrived and left on Ludgate Hill. Go to Crown Court he said without knowing just how many Crown Courts there are. Even years later, between the two of us we never did work out which one I was expected at.

When I got off the coach in Ludgate Hill I tried to ask directions in the hope of finding my lodgings only to be asked:

'And which Crown Court would that be then? There'll be the one in Cheapside, the one up by Holborn and the one off the Strand.'

Well, I tried Cheapside first and it was starting to get dark by then. I took one look at the place and decided not to even go into the Court itself. It must be one of the others I determined. So, I came back upon myself and was in two minds to try either Holborn or the Strand first. I set on the Crown Court off of the Strand. At least it was along the route I had taken in the coach up to Ludgate Hill. It was to be one of the best decisions I ever took. When I reached my destination there was no sign of anyone being in charge of the place. I was told that a fellow called Tomkins was meant to be in charge but at this time of night he would be in one of the pubs nearby. All I could do was sit on the doorstep hoping that it would not be too late when he returned. Of course, I did not know at the time, and I still don't quite rightly know now, if he was from that same lot as Fred Tomkins, who was arrested by the Customs men when he was with my grandfather in Southwark and his nephew Tom Tomkins who was to be arrested some years later in Turnham Green for holding up a gentleman in his carriage and for hiding what he stole at the Roe Buck where my brother Richard was to work.

I must have started to doze off on the stairway when I heard a yelp from a woman who nearly fell over me. She was right scared and thought I was at best up to no good or was set on causing her harm. She showed some courage and nerve by letting me explain why I was there and that I was waiting on Tomkins to see if this is where I was expected as a new lodger.

She had the wit about her to at least volunteer that the room next to hers was unoccupied and so that could be where I was to have my room. After that we sort of fell into conversation and to try and put her at her ease I explained what I was about and why I found myself here in Crown Court, whether that be the right one or not. She at least found some humour in that little problem.

I then asked about her situation.

'In short I too have come to London for work. I come from Wells. I may have even travelled up on one of your company's coaches. I have been here some three years now working as a domestic in one of the inns nearby. I have just finished and I am about all in. I am up again by six so I will leave you to it in the hope that Mr Tomkins is not completely insensible by the time he gets back.'

'What's your name?' I asked.

'Elizabeth Pedwell. And yours?'

'John Weller, and if this is where I am to stay I am sure to see you again.'

Little was I to know, that despite her being a spinster some seven or eight years older than me, that within six months we were to become first lovers and then marry. I took up my position as an ostler at one of the coaching inns and we decided to take new lodgings in Lambeth where I could walk across Waterloo Bridge up to Ludgate Hill and Elizabeth could do the same to get to her work.

John smiles to himself as the memories come flooding back. Marriage suited us in those early days, didn't it Lizzie? We sure made up for lost time. Such a shame that we did not have children of our own. I think you would have been a wonderful mother as indeed you were a wonderful wife. Remember when I came home that night with the news that I was to be offered the chance to be a coachman? I don't know who was more excited you or me. We neither of us slept much that night. If we weren't talking then we were at other things.

Sweet Lizzie. We remained in Lambeth for some sixteen years until you were taken away from me. Together for sixteen years yet half that time we were apart with me doing those coaching runs. I stayed faithful to you, Lizzie. Not to say that I was not tempted, but I did stay faithful to you. Those last few days were painful to us both and for different reasons. It was a blessing in a way when you did pass on.

With you gone, Lizzie, I went to join father and the others down in Bath.

* * *

Father and the others down in Bath. Well, in Bath I was when I was not driving the stage back and forth still to London! Father was right. It was hard work but I was my own man – well, until the railways came at any rate. I just didn't have the time to make friends most of the time. The change of horses was so quick and I had no time at all for social conversation. Even with the longer stop it was just a question of something to eat, a few jugs of beer and then we were on our way again.

As for my passengers – well, there was the odd lady who would turn any man's head but they were not for the likes of me or me for them. There was, of course, Mr Charles Dickens and that blessed watch that he later sent to father. Useless great lump of a thing! It does not even tell the time any more. It's been sitting in that desk over there for years now. Maybe it will be of interest to someone some day.

John starts to have another conversation with himself. Well, Ann my dear, What a funny couple we made! I wonder if you would have taken up with me and married me if you had known that I was really fourteen years your senior? I like to think you would have done, but you were right cross with me when you found out. I even lied about my age when we

275

got married. I was that determined to have you and to have a family and children of my own.

Twenty-three years we had together and four children. That's six years now since you went. As for the children, Ann, I wonder if you have been watching them? If you have then you can tell me where Albert went. Why on earth did that boy marry? Just disappeared within weeks of him and Ellen getting married. Not a word from him ever since. Just walked out on Ellen before the marriage was consummated. Poor woman was at her wits' end. Still, now she is happy with someone else but what a to-do to get that marriage dissolved! She even had to have proof that she had never lain with a man.

Mary Ann? Well, she's twenty-six or twenty-seven now and still shows no sign of settling down. Mind you, sweet in nature as she is she does not have much going for her looks-wise and is not the brightest of things.

Edward? Now, he's turned out good. Did he give us such a fright! We thought he would succumb to the consumption, we did. Cost a small fortune to send him down to Coombe Martin in the hope that the fresh sea air would be the better for him, and praise be it was. Married to Alice now and just a week or so ago they had baby Winifred. A stableman he is now. Keeping with the family tradition.

Then there is Emily. Went to Surrey somewhere at the age of fifteen to enter into service and now back here in Bath to keep an eye on her old Dad. Has her mind set on being a cook that one and, knowing her, she will do it. You know what we are like when us Wellers set our minds on things.

Now, what was it that they say about us down at the York Mews Tap? Coming on to some fifty years that first father and later me have been helping to relieve them of their beer. Most of the old crew have gone now, of course, and it's much easier for me to have a jug of ale filled and sent to me here when the weather is bad like tonight. Still, it's nice to get down there when I can.

276

*   *   *

John opens his eyes with a start. There is a person in the room.

'Hello, how did you get in? I thought the door was bolted.'

'It's fine, John, I let myself in.'

'But I feel as though I should know you but I don't remember us meeting before.'

'Well, John, people say that about me.'

'Who are you?'

'I have many names. If you like, John, you can call me Mr Smith. How are you feeling, John?'

'Oh, a bit tired. Maybe it's the fire and the beer but I do feel tired. I want to go back to sleep.'

'That's fine, John. You have lived a good and full life. Have you been dreaming, John?'

'How did you know? Yes I have, as if it is from my child-hood recalling all that I have been doing in my life. The people and things I have been dreaming of seem so real to me now.'

'That is good, John. You have done well with your time. Are you ready for one last journey? I have a coach waiting for you and all those people you have been thinking of who love you and who you have loved are looking forward to seeing you again. Would you like to see them all again, John?'

'What about my children and grandchildren? They will miss me.'

'Yes, they will, John but everyone has their time. Here is my hand, John. Come with me.'

'I feel so warm and comfortable and my poor old bones don't ache any more.'

'That's right, John, just come with me.'

'Is that lavender I can smell?'

Author's Notes

i

The original Newdigate Free School building fell into disrepair and was knocked down and re-erected in 1838. In relation to the times, this charitable school was a credit to its benefactors.

ii

An exchange of letters appears in *The Times* in September 1919 in which a Catholic Canon, William Smith of St Mary's, Little Crosby, Liverpool refers to a watch having come into his possession with an inscription 'Mr Weller Senior'. The Canon writes saying that the watch was passed on to him by one George Parker from Uppingham and that he was an Oxford man. Mr Parker heard of the watch from a lady who had told Mr Parker that she had often seen Charles Dickens riding on the box seat next to Mr Weller senior on the Bath to Bristol coach. It is from here that there is speculation about the similarity between Mr Weller Senior the coachman and livery stable keeper (at one time employing seven persons) based in Catherine Cottage in Bath. Catherine Cottage appears to have been substantially rebuilt and now serves as a doctor's surgery. Across the road from the cottage is a mews still with the original layout of stables. These may possibly have been the same stables that Sam, John, William and Edward worked from.

The watch is double-cased and made by Edward Manley and is of hallmarked silver and has a serial number (17,304) that puts its year of manufacture at around 1830. It is no ordinary watch, being almost a pound in weight and it is speculated that it may be some kind of window-display piece. Another correspondent tells the story of the Weller family being particularly well known in Bath in the coaching fraternity and that they frequented the snuggery of the York Mews Tap in Bath and that he proposed to the widow running the establishment, but the marriage soon went wrong as Daniel Weller was up to his ears in debt and did well to keep out of debtor's prison. After all these years, where the truth lies it is not possible to tell.

However, the widow Mary Neybours was living in Bristol and not Bath at the time of the marriage. She was around fifty years old and her father John Todd must have been well into his seventies. On the certificate of marriage John Todd's occupation is shown as publican. Daniel cannot be traced in the 1841 census that took place about six years after Daniel married his second wife, the widow Ann. However, in the 1851 census Daniel is installed at Catherine Cottage with his wife Ann and they have a living-in servant.

Daniel's son John is mentioned by the second correspondent and reference is made to him going back to London as a coachman and then returning to Bath (all of which can be proved by documentation). John is referred to by the correspondent as being an instructive and an amusing man, popular with his class and excellent at repartee. He was evidently a well-known character in Bath until his death in 1893 at the age of 76.

The Pickwick Papers was published in 1836 and Daniel went on to marry Ann Todd in 1837. This would suggest that 'Sam' was known to Charles Dickens before *The Pickwick Papers* was published and became reacquainted with him when he was reportedly seen riding with 'Sam' Weller on the Bristol to

Bath coach. For a man as eminent as Charles Dickens to go to the trouble of having the watch inscribed suggests that they had developed some kind of friendship if indeed the watch did originate as a gift from Charles Dickens.

In *The Pickwick Papers* 'Sam Weller' is a gentleman's gentleman rather than a coachman, but perhaps Mr Dickens had had related to him Sam's experiences as a gentleman's gentleman when he was employed as a valet in Richmond before embarking upon his new life in Bath.

Charles Dickens, sometime later, did indeed write a book featuring Little Doritt and the debtor's prison at Marshalsea near Borough market in Southwark, and in fact Dickens' father was himself imprisoned at Marshalsea.

Cashing in on the name, there is now a modern town pub in Bath called 'Sam Weller's'.

John Weller, the eldest son of 'Sam' Daniel Weller, did come to Bath and was evidently quite a character.

iii

Census returns and birth registrations show that Mary Ann and Robert Shelley did run the Packhorse and Talbot and that Richard and Kate's son Daniel Frederick was born nearby.

iv

Daniel Frederick was a butler and did indeed work almost to the end as a crossing-sweeper. The death certificate records that he died as a result of a combination of syncope disease of the heart and pneumonia.

V

In the 1920s, when Katherine suffered from poor health owing to the housing conditions in Paddington, the family was relocated near to Burnt Oak in north- west London.

The surviving ten children all in their own way became successful with occupations for the sons ranging from factory manager at Ford, a respected confectioner, a company representative, an engineer, a merchant seaman and later an electrician, a skilled sheet-metal worker and a professional working for a multinational company. The daughters of Fred and Katherine mainly played the roles of housewives and mothers raising and supporting their families, but one of the daughters, who had no children of her own, is known to have assisted in the making of the wedding dress for Wallis Simpson who married the Duke of Windsor, later King Edward VIII.

Unlike so many families, they were spared the ordeal of losing someone during the First World War. The sons were too young and Fred Weller did indeed want to enlist but was turned down by the recruiters owing to his occupation as a lorry driver for the Great Western Railway and because he had a wife and four children to support. The story handed down to the author is that he was bitterly disappointed at not being accepted to answer the call to serve his country.

Remembered here though is Sidney William Weller, not mentioned in this story. He is the son of Sidney (Sid), who features in Part VI of the journey and he was the grandson of Richard and Katherine, the great-great-grandparents of the author. Sidney William was killed on the Somme on 28 September 1916 whilst serving with The Queen's (Royal West Surrey) Regiment. He left behind his wife Florence and their children Sidney Charles, Donald Fred, Florence Rachael, Arthur, Albert and Violet.

The author recalls two anecdotes passed on by his late

father from when the family was at Burnt Oak. Often my father and his brother Sam would be sent late on Saturday to the butcher's shop to bring home meat at a reduced price. Butchers in those days did not have freezers and so they would try and sell meat at reduced prices rather than face the risk of the meat going off over the remainder of the weekend.

My father also told me about an occasion when nuns called at the house in Langham Road. When my grandfather Fred opened the door he said something along the lines of 'Can I help you ladies?' They announced that they were collecting money to help the poor and needy to which my grandfather is said to have responded to the effect that any aid would be welcome here. He was polite but allegedly this experience did not exactly help to raise his opinion of the Catholic Church.

vi

During the Second World War some of Fred and Cate's children did see action. One joined the Merchant Navy, another served with the British Army in India as part of the Medical Corps and another served in the Royal Navy and was awarded the Distinguished Conduct Medal for staying with the radio as his ship was sinking. Those that did not serve in the forces or with the Merchant Navy played their own part with the war effort back home in England.

vii

The grandchildren of Fred and Catherine were largely to become professionals and business people as well as an academic and even a reasonably successful civil servant with a fancy to try at being an author.

The Journey of Ascent from a hard and difficult life on the High Weald, overcoming adversity there and in a number of other places, is finally achieved but this is by no means the end of the story.

This is a journey, of perhaps not an unusual family, but which shows just what can happen by intention, accident, adventure, or the need for our people and others like the family, to become what we are in now the twenty-first century.